THE
INEVITABLE

THE
INEVITABLE

GEORGE KURIAN, BHILAI

Notion Press

Old No. 38, New No. 6
McNichols Road, Chetpet
Chennai - 600 031

First Published by Notion Press 2017
Copyright © George Kurian, Bhilai 2017
All Rights Reserved.

ISBN 978-1-947851-38-2

This book has been published with all reasonable efforts taken to make the material error-free after the consent of the author. No part of this book shall be used, reproduced in any manner whatsoever without written permission from the author, except in the case of brief quotations embodied in critical articles and reviews.

The Author of this book is solely responsible and liable for its content including but not limited to the views, representations, descriptions, statements, information, opinions and references ["Content"]. The Content of this book shall not constitute or be construed or deemed to reflect the opinion or expression of the Publisher or Editor. Neither the Publisher nor Editor endorse or approve the Content of this book or guarantee the reliability, accuracy or completeness of the Content published herein and do not make any representations or warranties of any kind, express or implied, including but not limited to the implied warranties of merchantability, fitness for a particular purpose. The Publisher and Editor shall not be liable whatsoever for any errors, omissions, whether such errors or omissions result from negligence, accident, or any other cause or claims for loss or damages of any kind, including without limitation, indirect or consequential loss or damage arising out of use, inability to use, or about the reliability, accuracy or sufficiency of the information contained in this book.

Dedicated to

My wife, Namita and son, Dilip

And he took the cup, and gave thanks, and gave it to them, saying Drink ye all of it: for this is my blood of the new testament, which is shed for many for the remission of sins.

St. Mathew 26: 27, 28

How do you tell a communist? Well, it's someone who reads Marx and Lenin. And how do you tell an anti-Communist? It's someone who understands Marx and Lenin.

— Ronald Reagan —

Preface

Modern man finds himself at loggerheads between thoughts and actions. Gone are the days of intellectual honesty. It has become next to impossible to find success in achieving goals and dreams at the end of one's destination. Many a times a person is forced to strangulate his own goodness and sweep it under the carpet. For success, one may have to just die within one's self.

No one really accepts his own Machiavellinism. There is no such thing as absolute truth but only human perceptions about right or wrong. Is that not why we have coined the phrase, "I am right and you are wrong"?

Ideas and dreams are but mirages that can cause delusions, conflicts and miseries. So, our unending arguments about right and wrong never come to an end. When the illusions are on a large scale, the damages are bound to become gigantic and manifold. Acceptance of reality and faith in self is perhaps the right path. Dreams and aspirations must be rooted firmly in reality and beliefs that are our own - not borrowed from thoughts of other thinkers, no matter how great or revered. Distorted vision can result only in delusions leading to war and destruction!

The purpose of writing this book was to share the struggles that I had to undergo before I could liberate myself from the delusions of which I had been a prisoner throughout my life. It has been a rickety journey from delusions to reality and a journey from the 'world realisation' to 'self realisation.' This was inevitable.

The lesson I learned is very simple. My illiterate mother often said, "One can never change this world as per ones designs. If you want to change, change yourself!"

Chapter 1

A Remote Village in God's Own Country

The journey of my life which began on the 1ˢᵗ of January, 1946, (my D.O.B.) in a remote village named 'Anaprampal' in 'Thalavady' taluka of the Alleppey District in Kerala, to another village named 'Urla' in the 'Durg' District of Chhattisgarh in the year 2014, cannot be defined by any other word than 'destiny.' Rationalists may contemptuously reject the idea of destiny, as I did during my youthful days, but I am unable to find a better word to explain the events in my life which were neither designed nor controlled by me.

My basic character was formed during the first sixteen years of my life in Anaprampal. These years were spent in the midst of extreme poverty, hunger, shame and humiliation. During that period, in the 1950s, unemployment was the basic problem being faced by almost every middle class family in Kerala. Barring a very few, most of the families lived in semi-starvation. Holdings of small patches of land did not yield enough to fill the belly of everyone in the famiy. The only ray of hope lay in at least one member of the family obtaining even just a matriculation degree and finding his way out of the state, be it in Madras or Bombay, and securing a job. To avoid permanent starvation and menial jobs, parents pushed their reluctant children to school, either by cajolements or thrashings, to get them to secure that all important degree.

As for me, my school days were spent not only in utter poverty but also in shame, because of it.

My home being equidistant from a Hindu temple at Thalavady, and a Catholic church at Edathua, I grew up imbibing both the Hindu as well as the Christians cultures.

Born and brought up as a Catholic Christian, I was forced to live with a dual mind from my very childhood. I was baptised in due time. However, our poverty was quite evident from the difference in the rituals and ceremonies conducted in the church for me and the children of better off families. They donned new and fine clothes, sparkling head gears and shining white shoes. I had to be content with my cheap white dress and bare legs. For me it was just a ritual. For them it was a grand celebration of a festival.

During the catechism classes conducted in the school, priests and nuns tried to inculcate Christian values in me. They talked of love and compassion for the poor and the needy, about bringing non-believers into the fold of the church to save them from going to hell and Jesus Christ being the only God and all others being fake. They warned me to keep away from the temptations of temples and the idols of Hindu Gods as they were sure to harm me through evil spirits.

But in truth, I had often been witness to the poor being treated like undisirables, not only by the church but also by the faithfuls. While some lived in luxury, others, right by their side, suffered in poverty and hunger. I had seen this not only in my own family, but also in most other families, where poorer relations were not only despised but also kept at an arm's distance. Added to this, superstition and hearsay played a major role in the day to day lives of the village people.The lasting impressions of my childhood carried the stamp of unsatiated hunger, unattended sicknesses and lack of love and empathy for the poor and suffering human beings.

Though I passed SSLC from the St. Aloysius High School, Edathua, with distinction and hundred percent marks in Mathematics, a rare feat in those days, I found my future bleak because there was absolutely no possibility of my going to a college for want of money. For me, going to a college was a fervent dream. I thought that I had a justified right to a higher education. Since my father was penniless, I begged my well off relatives to help me out to join a college. Once admitted, I was confident of winning a scholarship for continuing without paying fees. At that tender age of sixteen, I even took up courage to meet our Bishop in his palace at Changanassery to request his help for my education. All my efforts were in vain. I received only scorn, insult and rejection from every one.

All these bitter experiences not only did nothing to ausage my hurt, but led to great damage in my relationship with not only my own family, but also with the whole world. My close interaction with the clergy helped only to shake my faith in the Church as the house of God. Born and brought up in an orthodox Catholic family, I had been an ardent believer of Jesus Christ. But the Bishop and the priests I came across, were, in no small degree, instrumental in severely shattering my faith. I started doubting the very existence of God. I despised religion. I even started despising my relatives and wanted to keep away from them all.

My unique achievement in the Board Exams, published in the newspapers, made me a well known entity in my village. But that very fame turned out to be the cause my misery also. After the colleges reopened, everyone kept asking me when I was going to join college. My humiliation knew no bounds. I wanted to escape from my village and the querries I had to bear. A naval officer from our neighborhood, having come to know about my predicament, showed a genuine concern about my plight and promised to help me join the Merchant Navy, as a trainee. It was during my preparation for joining the Navy that my elder brother, already employed in the then expanding Bhilai Steel Plant, in Madhya Pradesh, asked me to go to him. He promised to help me in getting admission in a college!

Oh what bliss!

None other than the thinking human being bothers to search for a purpose for living. In most cases such purposes grow out of necessity. The only purpose of my travelling to Bhilai was to continue my education in a college. My brother had promised me support. It was not possible in my native place. On 17 July, 1961, at the age of sixteen, I reached Bhilai, chappalless, with a meager amount of Rs. 20 in my pocket. It was my first experience of a train journey. The third class bogies were so over crowded that people occupied seats even in the dirty toilets. After changes in Ernakulam, Madras and Nagpur, I was able to reach Durg Railway Station after three days.

My brother was sharing his company quarter with a friend called Mr. Rajan. I became its third occupant. Brother found it more beneficial to persuade me to seek a job in the steel plant before seeking admission in a college. He said I could continue my studies even after getting a job. Having already suffered perpetual poverty, I convinced myself to drop my dream of college going, at least for some time, in favour of a monthly salary.

In those days of expansion of the Bhilai Steel Plant from one million to four million tonnes production capacity, it was very simple to get a job in the plant. My name was quickly registered in the Bhilai Employment Exchange. Within two weeks, on 1st August, 1961, I joined the Coke Ovens department of the Bhilai Steel Plant, as a non-supervisor, earning a respectable monthly salary of Rs. 115.

In the interview, an officer who was impressed by the mark sheet of my school examination certificate repeated a question which I had once considered as very humiliating;

"Why have you not joined a college?" This time I answered without feeling demeaned, "No money sir. No money." He smiled "You are selected."

There was a constant inflow of skilled, semiskilled and unskilled workers from all nooks and corners of the country, seeking jobs in Bhilai Steel Plant. No one was turned away. The gigantic plant, while expanding itself, could accommodate one and all. While a portion of the workers got company quarters in the upcoming Steel Township, a majority had to find shelter in the labour camps at Supela, Khursipar, Boria and other pockets near and around the plant. There was shortage of living space, drinking water and sanitation; often leading to clashes among people of different communities who were living in their own clusters, side by side.

It was a period when the nostalgia for ones own traditions and culture inspired enterprising leaders of different communities to organise their own people to form various religious, cultural and social organisations. Bengalis, Malayalis, Telugus, Marathis, Biharis and U.P. walas, among others, were in the forefront of mobilising their own people in different social and cultural organisations. Though initially, each community looked at others with suspicion, aversion and contempt, all learned, as time passed, to intermingle with each other and respect each other's traditions and culture. Perhaps it was the migrated workers of our country, the Bhilaians, who initially experienced the taste and meaning of being an 'Indian Citizen.'

Through decades, Bhilai had grown and emerged into a perfect example of a mini-Bharat, inculcating the best of myriad cultures, traditions and human values.

However, for me, the initial few years in the plant and in Bhilai were filled with misery. My dream of going to college came to naught. Even as a teenager with tender health, I had been tied down to the harsh realities of working in the Coke Ovens which vomited dust and gas relentlessly, along with much older rough and tough labourers from Bihar and UP. Away from my parent's protection, my soul and spirit had been trampled over and crushed. In place of the books, classrooms and teachers I had dreamed of, I found before me heaps of coal dust, leaping flames and gases from the batteries in the company of middle aged men covered with grime and soot.

Where had my brother dumped me after promising to help me join a college? He was always present with me to receive my salary so that he could carry the money home safely. But he never once mentioned my further education. Even the BSP management, in its hurry to recruit workers, had overlooked the fact that I was only sixteen years old and not eligible for a regular appointment.

I was given the job of supervising the cleaning work around the Coke Oven Batteries which was being done by hefty and hard-muscled middle aged men who enjoyed using filthy language all the time. My senses and sensibilities were wounded deeply. I felt helpless and at a loss in the matter of communication also because I knew no language other than Malayalam, my mother tongue.

Thus, I spent my initial years in the plant feeling intimidated by my co-workers as well as superiors and in constant fear of losing my job because of my inadequacy in communication. I continued in this state for about four years. By the age of twenty, I became desperate to obtain a degree so that I could escape from the Coke Ovens - a veritable hell and look for a teaching job elsewhere. Though I expressed my urge before my brother, who was married and with a child by this time, he would not think of sparing any money for my education. He needed both of our salaries to run the home, which included me also. Ultimately, I was forced to defy my brother. For the first time in four years, I received my salary in my own hands, in my brother's absence. I just went ahead and deposited the required fees for appearing in the intermediate science examination conducted by the M.P. State Board of Education, before handing over the balance to my brother.

This independent action of defying his authority was beyond my brother's tolerence. He asked me to leave his home. And so, came to an end my delusion that I was under the protection of my only brother.

Thereafter, I was left free to fend for myself.

Chapter 2

Burden of Freedom

Life in Bhilai, in the initial years, was both difficult and disheartening too. I could expect no support from any corner, other than my job. And I was in perpetual fear of losing it. There was no one near by to console me. My poor parents, staying in my native village, needed my financial help for their own survival. Day in and day out I had to face the hostile conditions of my work place, both mentally and physically. It was like a lone warrior battling against the whole world. Still, the nostalgic memories of my childhood came in handy to revive my broken spirits.

My father, a school dropout, had inherited only a small patch of land. Even this was hypothecated to a neighbor against some loan. In the absence of a regular income other than what the land offered, my father was not in a position to guarantee regular meals for our family. We had to live hand to mouth and no reprieve from this unending scarcity seemed to be in sight. He invariably met with repeated failures even though he tried his hand in different trades, along with his farming. My mother, in her desperation, expected my elder uncle, who was quite well off, to be compassionate towards us. But, he never was. Though all my cousins were well placed in good jobs and earning considerably during my school days, they conveniently looked the other way and appeared to have forgotten our family, their nearest relations and neighbours, who were in desperate need of financial support.

My village, Anaparampal, consisted mostly of rice fields. The whole area as such, was covered with greenery; paddy fields surrounded by coconut, banana, mango, jackfruit, tamarind and other myriad varieties of trees covered the landscape. The nearby villages were crisscrossed with canals and tributaries of the river Pampa. In the rainy season, floodwater from the eastern mountain regions cascaded down roaring rivers and canals, deluging all living habitats and paddy fields, not just in my village, but the whole region, called Kuttanadu. Most people had to stay put, confined to their cots or raised platforms for weeks together, in houses inundated in knee deep water.

This was the situation during the first two decades after independence. Even numerous middle class families were forced to go to sleep on empty stomachs. Conditions were such that quite a few of my mid-day meals had had subsisted on tender coconuts, plucked from the coconut trees on our land. Hungry or not, children were not spared from going to school even during those trying days. I have been witness to many a scene of unwilling, hungry and crying children in tattered clothes being shooed off to school. Their only ambition was to somehow educate their children to qualify them to seek their fortune away from the state and away from their existing misery.

Though I had come to Bhilai with a wounded self-respect and an aggrieved mind, I had at least the hope of going to college to alleviate me from my despondency. But even this was taken away from me. The hostile situation I faced in the initial years of my employment helped only to aggravate my sense of hurt. What sustained me was my confidence in my own capability of acquiring a higher education some day and to get out of the plant to seek a lecturer's job in some college.

My joining the Government Arts and Science College, Durg, in the year 1966–67 was a great turning point in my life. It was the only Science college available in the Durg district in those days, and I was one among the very few private candidates, who passed the Intermediate Science Examination conducted by the M.P. State Education Board, enabling me to get admission directly in the B.Sc. second year.

A senior officer of my department, Mr. T. Ghoshal, a qualified engineer, appreciated my efforts to improve my qualification and promised to put me in night shifts permanently, to enable me to attend college in the day time. My determination to obtain a degree was such that 40 kms of cycling every day, to and fro to the plant in the night, and the college in the day, did not matter. However, another officer, who was my Shift-in-Charge, Mr. P. M. Mazumdar, was hell bent on blocking my path. He put me to work single handedly on machines that required to be manned by two operators, turn by turn. Because of over burden and exhaustion, sometimes I fell asleep, causing break downs, leading to stoppage of production. For such omissions on my part I received many a charge sheets which could have led to termination of my service. But the management had to concede to my demand for a departmental enquiry where I could expose the intentions of my Shift-in-Charge. That saved me from being terminated. However, the physical and mental torture continued. My zeal enabled me to manage to continue with both my job and studies simultaneously.

Because of the inhibiting harsh realities, it was not possible for me to achieve any distinction at the graduate level but the result was good enough to qualify me for admission in M.Sc. Because of my keen interest in science subjects, I opted to study Mathematics, the language of science.

During my college days I had to live in a hand to mouth situation. I could afford only two pairs of dresses which I used in the plant and the college alternately. I remained the most inconspicuous student in the college during the two years of my graduation and kept myself aloof from the glamour of college life and its activities. In appearance I was thin and dark, with sunken cheeks and poorly dressed. I always carried a famished look and remained a non-entity for my college mates, till they on their own volition, forced me to come under the lime light.

All along, I had been living with an unquenchable and turbulent mind which prodded me to seek more and more knowledge about anything and everything. I believe that my unending thirst for knowledge, which continues to this day, has perhaps shaped my destiny also.

It took some time and much pain for me to transplant myself from the rustic soil of a remote village in Kerala to the vibrant and pulsating industrial environment of Bhilai, in the then Madhya Pradesh. While slowly taking root in the soil of Chhattisgarh, I was simultaneously undergoing a mental transformation. I was deeply surprised and pained by the poverty prevalent among the local Chhattisgarhi people. I could not believe that even farmers owning many acres of cultivable land, were leading a life of utter poverty and ignorance. Unlike people of my state, they were meek and peace loving people and believed in sharing everything with their kith and kin. As a people I loved the Chhttisgarhis more than my own community. Slowly, my mindset changed to suit my new circumstances.

It was the books I had been reading that goaded me to develop a new mind set suiting to my new circumstances. Though I enjoyed reading the works of world famous and Nobel-Prize winning authors, to get an insight into the different kinds of lives of people all over the world, I craved to know the minds of their leaders also. Novels gave a kalediscope view into the real life situations of people and their thought processes. But, it was the "Discovery of India" by Jawaharlal Nehru that roused my interest in Socialism and Soviet Union and opened up my mind to Marxist literature. I went on reading books written by Karl Marx, Engels, Stalin, Lenin and Mao-Tse-Tung. They were easily available in the Soviet Books Exhibitions at the Civic Centre. I read voraciously.

I felt that Marxist philosophy was the only scientific philosophy, capable of changing the world! I treasured the quote of Karl Marx "Hitherto the role of Philosophy has been to interpret the world, however the point is how to change it." I was not only dissatisfied with the world but also felt the urgent need for a drastic change of the world order.

Being a student of science, I believed that only science could reveal the truth and act as a catalyst to bring about a change in the existing order. Marxist philosophy appeared to me as the extension of science itself because Marx used the three basic scientific tenets as the pillars of his philosophy known as "dialectical and historical materialism." They are; the unity and struggle of the opposites, quantity changing into quality and negation of the negation. These could be considered the three basic scientific truths that explain all phenomena in the material world. It stands to reason that that which is true for the whole world would be true for human beings also. So, by the time I reached M.Sc. final year in 1969–70, I had also turned out to be an ardent believer of the Marxist ideology.

But my only purpose, so far, had been to fetch a P.G. Degree and get a lecturer's job. One of my cousins, who being the treasurer of our local Catholic Church at Edathua, assured me of a Lecturer's post in the St. Aloysius College, Edathua, provided I passed M.Sc. in the second division. He thought that our family, an important constituent of the church, had claim over one teaching post in the college. So, I envisioned the end to my unending drudgery in the Coke Ovens, just around the bend.

Chapter 3

Plunge into a Violent Sea

One day on reaching the college, I witnessed an unprecedented phenomenon. About half a dozen students, with a mike tied to a cycle rickshaw, were shouting slogans against the college principal. Initially, I ignored the event as just a quirky thing. But its daily recurrence prompted me to enquire.

One Mr. Rajen Choube, working as a Laboratory Technician in the Bhilai Steel Plant, had sought admission in MA (English) classes, after having passed M.Sc. from the college. Immediately after getting admission, he confronted the principal with the demand of conduction of elections for the college Students' Union. The principal asked for his admission card, tore it into tethers and ordered him to remove his presence from the college premises forthwith.

Choube, who was the Convenor of the "Lohia Vichar Manch," and a loyal deciple of the then socialist leader and correspondent of a leading Hindi daily, Nava Bharat, Mr. Motilal Vora, decided to retaliate. Slogan shouting was his methodology.

This state of affairs continued for over a fortnight, with about half a dozen of his supporters mouthing slogans. Other students preferred to watch it as an amusement and time pass. However, after gaining a modicum of publicity, he resorted to an indefinite hunger strike in front of the college, allegedly at the behest and direction of his mentor, Mr. Vora. As anticipated, Mr. Hari Prasad Shukla, a minister hailing from Rajnandgaon, an adjacent district, visited the college the very next day. The 'socialist' leaning minister not only ordered the re-admission of Mr. Choube, but also declared that college elections would be conducted in the very near future. The principal had to eat humble pie and Rajen Choube became the college hero overnight. Mr. Vora's patronage not only hurled Choube into instant popularity as a student leader, but also vilified the principal as an autocrat and dictator.

For me, the events were of no consequence as my sole interest at that time was to acquire my post graduation degree. The only dream I had nurtured was to become a lecturer in a college. I had no qualms in toiling physically and mentally, day and night, for over five years, in the most adverse situations, to realise this humble dream. And it was likely to materialise within a year.

But fate had ordained other things for me. Some unanticipated events occurred. My dream of becoming a college lecturer got diverted into an altogether different dream. It was a dream that had perhaps existed all the time in my sub-conscious mind. It was a romantic dream - a dream that was the rage of the intellectual youths of our country in the decades of sixties and seventies. We dreamed of reconstructing the world anew, on the basis of equality and justice!

As the proverb goes, man proposes and God disposes. But let me add here that in many a case, it is God who proposes and the Devil who disposes. By saying so, I am not decrying the role of the Devil but only reiterating the fact that both the Devil and God, work hand in hand!

I wonder whether it was God or the Devil, who knocked at my door at midnight of that fateful rainy day in August 1969. It was none other than one Mr. Dhiresh Kumar Guha Neyogi, the same person who later on went on to become the world famous 'messiah of the poor,' Shankar Guha Neyogi. I knew him by name only because of his dismissal from services from my own department, over a year ago, for his alleged Naxalite activities.

I recalled him to be a labour leader, along with a handful of supporters, shouting slogans against the management. I had heard that hundreds of his supporters had blocked the police vehicle that was escorting him out of the Plant premises after his dismissal. But the resistance quickly petered out when it became known that he had been dismissed, not because of his trade union activities but because of his Naxalite connections. So long as he had been in service in my department, I had had no opportunity to meet him. And, I had neither seen nor heard anything about him after his dismissal from the plant, till that rainy night.

His sudden appearance at my door, in the middle of the night, and his self introduction, threw me off guard for a while. Tall and thin, with sunken cheeks, unruly hair and soiled clothes, he looked like a famished scare crow. I allowed him into my room after a great deal of trepidation, both, because of his Naxalite background and the possibility of my room-mate and well wisher, Mr. Ravi, reprimanding me for receiving a Naxalite in his home. It was a serious matter. In those days, any contact with a Naxalite was enough for the police to arrest a person or an employee to lose his job.

So, what was this scarecrow the harbinger of?

At the time Neyogi made his first nocturnal appearance at my residence, I was staying in Sector 7 with Mr. K. K. Ravindran Pillai (Ravi), in his company quarters. During my degree course, Ravi used to give me free coaching in the science subjects. He would accept no money as fee and I had none to give. Later on, he became a much sought after and successful tuition master known to many Bhilaians. Many students thronged to the classes he conducted in Sector 1.

When I joined post graduation classes, he offered me free accommodations in his home since he was living all alone. His family at Kerala was financially sound and was not in need of his financial support. So he had been able to spend his salary to enjoy a happy bachelor's life. Mr. Sadshivan Pillai, our next door neighbor and Mr. B. K. Nair (Ayyappa Seva Sangh) staying in the floor just below, were all our bachelor friends in those days. Ravi's culinary abilities were mouth-watering. I remember them with nostalgia even today, though years have passed. Perhaps Ravi drew happiness being in my company, acting as my guardian and supporting me in the realisation of my dream.

Neyogi explained that he had come to know about me and my views about the labour problems from his erstwhile comrades in Coke Ovens. So, he was keen on making contact with me so that we could work together for the welfare of the working class. I told him outright that I had no intention of getting involved in any plan for working for a public cause. My foremost aim was to complete my education. Despite my cool and guarded reception, Neyogi kept on talking about his party and politics till, ultimately, I could persuade him to leave. I made it a point to warn him about my room partner who might resent his presence in his home.

The very next morning Ravi confronted me. He had been awake and had heard our conversation in the adjacent room. He told me that I could not sail with my feet in two boats. I would have to choose between Neyogi and my future. He said Neyogi would lead me to my own destruction and take others along with him. Leaders of Neyogi's ilk, Naxalites in particular, would have no second thought before sacrificing the lives of their friends along with their enemies to achieve their own targets. He was very specific. I could stay with him only if I parted ways with my clandestine visitor of the previous night.

Though I told Neyogi that his repeated visits would serve no purpose, he kept on visiting me again and again. However, each time I told him to desist, in my heart of hearts, I nurtured a desire for him to come back, because I had been thinking about the pros and cons of putting my Marxist ideas into practice. I became totally free from the guilt of defying my friend, Ravi, when I was allotted my own quarters. How easily had Providence solved the problem!

In the course of his repeated visits, Neyogi narrated the story of his life after his dismissal from service; how he had, for over a year, secretly carried out his activities in Bhilai and how he was publishing a Hindi periodical, "Sphuling" to spread Naxalite ideology. He claimed to have enacted street dramas with famous theatre artists Subrato Basu and Prem Kumar Simon to support the ongoing revolution and had got arrested by the police. He ranted about how he had lately been wronged and betrayed by his own comrades and how he had been expelled from the very CPI(ML) (Naxalite) party for which he had suffered starvation, police torture and jail.

The mind is like a monkey and at times listens to no reasons. Had I been carried away by the tragic story of a lone revolutionary crusader, Neyogi?

It was at the most critical and desperate period of Neyogi's life that he had identified me as the person capable of supporting him in his future plans. Stamped as a Naxalite, disowned and vilified by his own party comrades and feared by his former co-workers, Neyogi was frantically in search of a new support-base in Bhilai. A few of his Bengali friends and sympathisers had been secretly helping him with small contributions so that he could eat at least once a day, in some shanty hotel. Nonetheless, everyone shied away from being seen in his presence, fearing serious consequences. He was forced to sleep in deserted public places at nights as none of his acquaintances were willing to shelter him in their homes.

Dejected, though not dampened in spirits, Neyogi frantically searched for a new foothold in Bhilai to pursue his political ambitions. Destiny seems to have chosen me for giving him such a foothold.

I tried to ingrain in his mind that I was interested neither in him nor his party. I was going to leave Bhilai permanently, as soon as I completed my post graduation. What, then, was the use of meeting me again and again? Such arguments did not deter him in the least. On each visit he brought some or the other Maoist publication. Once he even brought a copy of the internationally famous 'Red Book,' a hand book of Mao's quotations, compiled by Lin-Piao, Chief of the Chinese People's Liberation Army.

Regular meetings with Neyogi put me in a confused state of mind. I was torn between my 'selfish' mission of getting a masters' degree for a better job and the 'selfless' mission of fighting for the 'toiling masses.' I had never nurtured ambitions of becoming a leader because none of my predecessors in my family had ever been into politics. But Neyogi, to my mind, appeared to be a potential leader who could put 'my revolutionary ideas' into practice. As time went by, I withdrew the ban on his visits and started taking lively interest in discussing with him - the unfolding revolutionary scenario of those days in the country as well as the world.

Neyogi was a man of action, and was interested only in the CPI (ML) party, its programmes and its leadership. He was not very much interested in Marxist theories or the finer details of the Maoist philosophy. He claimed that he had met in person, Charu Mazumdar, the founder of the Naxalite movement, and had been immensely inspired by his charismatic personality. His immediate intention was to re-capture the leadership of the Bhilai party unit somehow. But he lost all hope after the news of his expulsion from the party had been published in the central party organ- The Liberation, cutting off his chances of ever going back.

I lapped up thirstily all news about the Naxalite movement as I was greatly enamoured by the supreme sacrifices made by the country's educated youth for the liberation of the people. I re-read the 5 volumes of Mao-Tse-Tung's collected works in order to understand how the Maoist thoughts and the Naxalite movement were related. But, the truth has to be told.

I was stunned to see that there was not even a distant relationship between the 'thoughts' of Charu Mazumdar and Mao-Tse-Tung!

As comparisons go, Charu Mazumdar appeared to me a puny and pathetic human being in front of Mao. The state of his mind could be gauged by the jubilant awe and glee that infused him on account of the cascading reactions of the country's youth in response to his 'revolutionary' exhortations. He was in a desperate hurry to see the revolution reach its conclusion, while he was still alive. It did not take much intelligence to trace a criminal element in his declaration that 'the test of a genuine revolutionary is to drench his hand in the blood of a class enemy.'

It was Marx who said that "Ideas, when gripped by the masses, become a material force." Mazumdar applied this formula, but to what end? Bloodshed, mayhem and unending miseries for tens of thousands of youths and their families?

Though my faith in the Marxist philosophy remained unshaken, I could not identify myself with any of the communist parties working in India including the Naxalite killers. It may be the deep impression of the message of love and sacrifice of Jesus Christ that remained with me even after I metamorphosed into an atheist which may have shielded me from falling for a political ideology that advocated even a heinous crime like murder to pave the path for human liberation. After all it was my love and compassion for the poor and toiling people and my urge to do my bit to help them out that made me accept Marxism as my philosophy. I could never justify murdering anyone stealthy for any cause, however noble it might be.

All the same, my rebellion against the world persisted and I found no better weapon to fight, than Marxism. A determination had arisen in me to fight against injustice whenever it arose before me. I wanted to kick at the perpetrators of injustice and very much relished a quote of Abraham Lincon "When you kick, Kick hard."

So whenever I got an opportunity to kick, I kicked hard.

Though my spirit was soaring my flesh remained tied up to my realities, forcing me to concentrate more and more on my studies.

Chapter 4

Surfing on Tidal Waves

It was after a gap of many years that, in Oct. 1969, elections were declared in all colleges of Madhya Pradesh. It had to be done in two stages. In the first stage Class representatives (CRs) were to be elected by students of the respective classes and in the second stage, office bearers were to be elected by the CRs. Only CRs of the PG final years were qualified to be elected as President!

College elections provided Mr. Choube and his mentor, Mr. Vora, an opportunity to teach the principal Dr. R. N. Singh a lesson. It was rumoured that the Principal had tried to humiliate Mr. Vora, when he had sought admission for P.G. for one his student candidates.

Those were the times when a good number of BSP employees had also enrolled themselves in the college to improve their academic qualifications. They took no interest in extra-curricular activities but resented being intimidated by goons of the college. The Principal gave admission to such anti-social elements in order that they might enjoy college life by lording over students as well as professors and flirting with the girls. Some criminal elements used to even extort money from students. I recalled one student, Narayan Khuller, with a criminal record, snatching away my money purse.

Anyone who dared to complain to the principal was roughed up by the goons. Even professors were not spared. Many doubted the principal's complicity with the goons. So, there existed a silent discontentment and disgruntlement among a section of students and professors against the administration of the principal. But, the principal had his confidents and supporters among the teaching staff as well as the students also.

The atmosphere was tense and the split between the opposing teams at the graduation level was marked during the elections. One group supported the principal while the other opposed him. In comparison, at the post graduate level, it was rather a tame affair. There, students were more or less guided by the suggestions of their professors. A vertical division seemed to have developed in the student community of over 2800, belonging to both the Science and the Arts sections.

The H.O.D. of Mathematics Department, Prof. Kale, had already chosen me to be the President of the Mathematics Association for the year 1969–70. So when the issue of CR came up, all my classmates supported the professor's suggestion that I should be elected CR also. No one bothered about my reluctance. I accepted it only after believing that being CR would not have any consequence on my studies.

Tempers soared as the elections of office bearers approached nearer and nearer. As the principal had his panel of contestants for the office bearers, headed by Mr. Deepak Khanna as president, ready, right from the start, Mr. Choube also had his panel, minus a president. Mr. Choube, being in the MA first year, could contest only for Vice-Presidentship. For fear of the principal, none of the CRs from PG final year classes were willing to contest for the post of president in Choube's panel. No one wanted to risk spoiling his result at the end of his academic career.

I was unaware of these circumstances, till one day, on reaching the college campus, I was suddenly encircled and stopped by over a dozen students. I could not recognise anyone from among the unruly group other than Mr. Rajen Choube who ordered me to sign some nomination papers to contest elections as president. Some among them kept on addressing me as "Saale Madrasi." I felt a little shaken and intimidated by the surprise of a Gherao by unknown people. My first thought was to escape from their custody and so I asked them to give me at least one day to decide. They allowed me to go only after drawing some fun at my expense and threatening to abduct me from my home, if I failed to appear in the college the next day, which was also the last day for submission of nomination.

After reaching my class, I told Prof. Kale about my predicament and the threat meted out to me by Choube and his supporters. He took me to the Principal's chamber and introduced me as a serious student and a perfect gentleman. He suggested that I should be put forward as Mr. Choube's candidate for president. He also said that the principal would be the gainer in the case of either of the candidates winning the election. Prof. Kale was a highly respected and knowledgeable person. In addition, he was also a firm supporter of the principal. He was sure that I would never take the side of the opponents of the principal.

Dr. Singh was convinced by Dr. Kale's logic and asked me to contest from Choube's panel. He waved off all my reservations while warning me to be careful and not to fall in line with the miscreants led by Choube.

I got a whole night to ponder over the pros and cons of becoming president of the most prestigious college of Durg District, an unimaginable and unattainable honour for a humble and poor student like me. I wondered at the irony of it being forcefully thrust on me. My only apprehension was about the effect it could make on my future plan to fetch the lecturer's job offered to me by the college of my native land.

I assured myself that nothing of untoward would happen and that surely I would be able to don the 'crown' of President during the rest of my college life and at the same time become a centre of attraction for girls and envy for boys. It would be a befitting reply to all those who had ignored and snubbed me during my presence in the college for about four years.

Next day I walked boldly to the crowd of Choube supporters waiting in the campus and asked for the nomination papers. I did not know any of them personally. They also seemed to have not been impressed by my physical appearance. Thin and lanky by structure, black in colour with sunken cheeks and dressed in cheap cotton clothes, I did not look like an appropriate material for their president. Noticing my discomfiture in their midst, some of them told me not to worry because I would be president only for the name sake. Choube would be the real president. I filed my nomination papers just like a dummy without the known support of even a single CR.

On the day of elections, the whole college campus looked like a battlefield of two warring groups. Choube, flanked by over three hundred students, including 'his' CRs led one group, while the supporters of the principle, numbering over a hundred, were led by the other presidential candidate, Mr. Deepak Khanna. Quite a few students from both the groups wielded hockey sticks and lathis. Though loud laughter and guffaws could be heard occasionally, the scene was quite tense. I had heard that some of the CRs were under threat of abduction by opposing parties and had to be kept in safe custody the previous day and night. I was surprised to see CRs being brought in for voting in autos, tempos and taxis under protection of their respective supporters. I wondered who was bearing all the expenses of this great show.

Voting ended at 4 pm and the results were declared by 5 pm. All the office bearers from Choube's panel, including myself, had been declared elected. I won with the lowest margin whereas Rajan Choube, as Vice-President, won with the largest number of votes. It was only after his election as General Secretary, that I came to know Mr. Ashok Gupta personally. The same was the case with many of the office bearers and CRs, reiterating that my role in the elections had been almost zero.

It took a few minutes for me to internalise my position as the newly elected college president. It filled me with a sort of jubilation and a sense of new found confidence. I wished to show off that I was president for the whole college and was not afraid of any of the opponents.

I detached myself from Choube's crowd and strutted into Khanna's camp with a sort of false bravado. But I was brought to my senses soon, after they started pushing me around and heckling me as a 'bloody Madraasi' and shouting that it was a shame to have a person like me as their president. They looked at me with a mixture of envy and scorn and made fun of my lack lustre stature, lack of muscles, ordinary and cheap clothes and inability to speak Hindi well. I was later rescued by Choube supporters, who told me to be careful in future and keep myself at a safe distance from Khanna supporters.

Dr. R. N. Singh could not accept the blow he had received in the college elections. It was beyond his calculations that none of his favoured candidates had been elected.

The discontentment that had been smouldering against the college administration would have died down with the culmination of the election results. The professors and students opposed to Dr. Singh would have been more than happy to have taught him a good lesson. With a little magnanimity and diplomacy on his side, the principal could have won over the students. But, would an inflated ego seeped in self importance allow it?

I was not in favour of a conflict between the principal and students as I had no personal axe to grind or ambition to name and fame. Certainly, being chosen president boosted my self esteem to a great extent. However, my priority was still my degree. But again fate was not interested in my own priorities.

A week later, the first student's union meeting was held to discuss the swearing in ceremony of the office bearers. While the members awaited the principal's arrival to start the meeting, one of the CRs, Mr. Dasrath Bharati, rushed in and started shouting abuses against the principal. He hollered that Dr. Singh had slapped him in his chamber for opposing his suggestion that the principal be made chief guest in the swearing-in ceremony. Bharthi, being a CPI member and staunch supporter of Mr. Choube, infuriated the principal by saying that a 'Chaprasi' as Chief Guest would be better.

This incident was an excuse, good enough for those opposed to the principal, to raise a hue and cry. I managed to pacify them and, on their insistence, went to the principal's chamber to seek an 'explanation' to bring the matter to a close. I hoped he might have faith in me as I was supposed to be his secret supporter.

But Dr. Singh, in his fury, was in no mood to listen to any one. He threatened to put everyone behind bars. As a last resort, I reluctantly agreed to accompany Mr. Chaube and his supporters to meet their mentor, Mr. Motilal Vora, at his Durg Roadways Office, to seek his advice. He advised us not only to lodge a police complaint against Dr. Singh, but also to attend classes from the very next day, wearing black badges as a protest.

When I reached college the next day, I was surprised to see that all students of the Art faculty of the morning hours were already wearing black badges and hundreds of them were being distributed to students of Science faculty as well. I felt admiration for Choube and his followers for managing the black badge demonstration so well without seeking my help. I was also surprised to see the eagerness and willingness of the students to wear the black badges as if they were a matter of fun and excitement. I was appeased to see the badge wearing students finally showing some recognition and acknowledgment of me as their president.

That day I saw Nav Bharat and other news papers carrying the news of the principal, Dr. R. N. Singh, assaulting a student's union representative and the union's decision to carry out a protest demonstration by wearing black badges. Mr. Choube's name was prominently mentioned as an emerging student leader. It was O.K with me but I felt a little peeved that the president's name was not mentioned any where.

The black badge demonstration appeared more like a day of festivity than one of serious issues. Many students from both the Arts and Science faculty cut classes to spend time chatting with their friends. I also intermingled and had discussions with some union leaders as well as professors. It was an opportune occasion to get introduced to a large number of students and congratulate them for showing solidarity with the Student's Union.

By evening a rumor had spread like wild fire that the college council had been in session to decide on the expulsion of the office bearers of the union. At around 5:30 pm, over 500 students who had stayed put in the campus were witness to a notice being pasted on the Notice Board. It was not hard to guess that a resolution, passed by the College Council, headed by Dr. Singh, rusticated me, Rajen Choube, Ashok Gupta, Rajkumar Naidu, Gokul Singh, J. P. N. Pandey and Subhash Thakur for five years.

It fell like a thunderbolt and beyond anyone's expectation. I, for one, saw my dreams of a PG degree and a lecturer's job collapsing like a pack of cards and being blown away by the wind. The ultimate result of four years' sweating day and night and cycling for 40 kms, everyday to the college and the steel plant, were all going to result in a big zero. Out of a sense of utter desperation and disappointment, I wept silently within myself. I felt that I had been unjustifiably and severely wronged for no great fault of mine. The principal must have known that I had had no big role in any of the recent developments in the college. I knew I was innocent and an innocent person was being crucified for the sins of others! I felt like a dead person. However, soon a path of resurrection opened up before me, thanks to my deep faith in the Marxist philosophy.

Chapter 5

Newton's Law in Action

The news of the rustication of union leaders electrified the whole student community. I and other office bearers were surrounded by reporters and hundreds of students to get our reaction. What would our next step be? Surprisingly, I heard my own high-pitched voice out-shouting everyone else's to declare, 'indefinite strike till the principal is removed.' I could not believe the transformation that had taken place in me. At that moment, I believed only in myself and cared for no one else. Who was Mr. Vora to be sought advice from! I had metamorphosed into an entirely new person – a leader perhaps! I felt like a general entrusted with an army to lead and a war to win.

From somewhere in the crowd rose a slogan, "Pracharya Hatao, College Bachao." Though poor in the Hindi language, I liked the slogan instantly. When I repeated the slogan, hundreds of the assembled students followed, setting the stage for an unprecedented students' movement in Chhattisgarh- one that stretched for over three months.

Next day, when I reached the college at around 8 am, I found a vast majority of the students of the Arts faculty, numbering over 1000, gathered at various spots in the college compound. After boycotting classes, they were engaged in heated discussion. Rajen Choube, Ashok Kumar Gupta, Raj Kumar Naidu, Gokul Singh, Subhash Thakur and other office bearers accompanied by a few girl students were seen actively participating in the strike. I was surprised to see the effect of my call for strike on the Arts students with whom I hardly had any contact. I wondered how all these strangers could put their trust in me and stake their educational career. How trusting are our people and how our leaders misuse it!

It was then that I began to realise the power of my words. Students had put their faith in me though it was only circumstances that had put the mantle of their leadership on my shoulders. I felt as if destiny had chosen me to be a sacrificial goat and I decided to make any and every sacrifice required to uphold their faith. Since my only link with my followers was that of my being their president, I decided to firmly hold on to that position with utmost courage and dignity.

By 10 in the morning, students of the Science faculty also started arriving. The campus was already dotted all over with groups of Arts students who had boycotted classes. Students from the Science section did not even bother to peep into their classes. Almost the entire student fraternity was united in the strike and it was a total success. Within a short time the sprawling grounds had filled up with over two thousand students. Being a novice in leadership, I did not anticipate the turn of events that took place at around noon. Hundreds of rifle and baton wielding policemen started dismounting from police vans!

The sight of the armed police filled me with the jitters. All my bravado vanished into thin air and my initial impulse was to run away to safety and make myself scarce from the scene.

Wonderful as it seemed, I did not espy an iota of fear in any of my supporters! Rather, the arrival of the police force seemed to have inflamed their spirit and enthusiasm. The slogan shouting rose to a crescendo, as if to welcome their presence. The students' bravado helped me to overcome my own fright and boost my morale. This jubilant atmosphere created in the campus by slogan shouting students arrested my fleeing legs and I decided to face the situation 'boldly.'

The District Administration had sent forces to the campus as per the Principal's false plea that some miscreants, incited by the union leaders, were preventing the professors from taking classes and the students from attending them. To prove his point, Dr. Singh gathered a few of his PG students and persuaded them to attend his class, after first ensuring that police forces were already in place.

The striking students objected and 'gheraoed' the principal's class, shouting slogans, thus forcing Dr. Singh to leave. In the meantime, a group of students, supporters of the principal, created a ruckus in the campus, by continuously shouting slogans and pulling and pushing the striking students. Perhaps, it had been all pre-planned. The moment Dr. Singh returned to his chamber, the police started lathi-charge from different directions, to force everyone to flee hither and thither. Within ten minutes the campus was empty.

I also ran to escape the blows from the police batons. I lost my sandals while running for my life! The police chased us out of the college campus for over a kilometer. I came to a halt when I saw a group of students who, after fleeing the scene, had assembled at a nearby housing colony. Many of the students were bleeding from head to foot from fresh injuries and many had swellings on their bodies.

They were conferring on their future course of action. My appearance in their midst was received with enthusiasm. I was cheered when I announced the loss of my sandals while running, and my determination to not wear sandals till Dr. Singh was removed from the college. While fiery speeches continued with condemnation of the principal and the police brutality on 'innocent and peaceful' students, police forces were unobtrusively surrounding our meeting place.

It was too late when it was noticed. Panic gripped the gathering as no one wanted to be caught. Instantly I took over command. I advised each one of them to remain cool and advised them to nonchalantly choose different directions to run so as to escape the police cordon.

Suddenly, like startled pigeons, there was a mad dash for freedom, in all directions.

A majority of the students succeeded in escaping. However, a few dozen were caught after giving the police a good chase. I had been the first one to be surrounded by the police as I had chosen not to run at all. What was the point in running, when there was no place to run away to? I had already embarrassed myself by having run away once. Seeing that I was playing it cool with a 'bold' face, an S.I. shouted that I might be the gang-leader. With a disarming smile, as if he was taking me for a stroll, he invited me to accompany him to the police vehicle parked nearby.

In the evening, when I was taken to the police station, I found around another 30 students, waiting to be locked up. We were put up in two, face-to-face lock ups, stinking with human excreta. Going by hearsay, we sat, waiting for the severe beatings that were bound to come. However, at around 5 pm, the T. I., Mr. Sitaram Saraf, took us by surprise. Instead of giving us a taste of the police batons, he offered us tea and hot samosas. When someone mentioned about the police beatings we had suffered, Mr. Saraf laughed it away, saying it was only a small price to pay for aspiring to be the leaders of tomorrow.

As darkness settled in, my mood once again started sinking. I thought that the arrest would certainly lead to my termination from my service. It was the only thing I had to fall back upon. The strike would most likely fizzle out and I would have made a fool of myself. What a mockery life was, I lamented.

I was woken from my despondency at about 6 pm, when a commotion was heard coming from the police station compound. Vehicles carrying rifle wielding policemen were being rushed out, as if in an emergency. A constable confided that after our arrest, around six hundred students had taken out a procession towards the police station, demanding our unconditional release. It had ended up in a clash with the police and a second lathi-charge on the same day. The news of the defiance of IPC Section 144 by a large number of students and their taking out a procession in support of their arrested collegues revived my spirits immensely.

At around 8 pm, Mr. Motilal Vora visited us. He informed us that the district administration had decided to release all of us on personal bonds. When we came out of the police station, he advised us to hold our peace and go home quietly in compliance with the prohibitory orders.

Next day the strike continued peacefully. Mr. Choube suggested that, as advised by Mr. Vora, I should call for a press conference in the evening to declare 'Durg Bandh' in order to widen our support base. I did just that and declared, 'Durg Bandh' the next day, in the presence of the local reporters. All news papers carried the news prominently.

Next day accompanied by scores of students, I set out to observe the effect of my 'Bandh Call' in the city. To my surprise and sense of shame, not one shop was found closed. The business community seemed to have ignored the call with contempt. I never had much respect for the self-loving trading class anyway. So while roaming around the city, I contemplated on a plan to teach them a lesson and make the subsequent Durg Bandh a success.

I conceived a plan for the future.

The 'indefinite' strike continued for about two weeks. The principal confined himself to his chambers. A few hundred students shouted slogans for some time in front of the principal's chamber. And this was the only sight that met the huge police force encamped as mute spectators in the college premises. As I spent nights working in the plant and days leading a strike, realisation came that the number of students coming to the college was dwindling. I would have to rejuvenate the agitation and so I called a public meeting outside the periphery of Durg city as the city itself was under the prohibitory order of Section 144.

The day before the public meeting, I discussed my secret plan and strategy with a few of my confidents. Each one would enlist 20 supporters and take them quietly to a busy spot in the middle of the city. Unobtrusively, each one was to load his pockets with two stones. They were to go on shouting slogans to attract a crowd, till a police vehicle appeared. Lastly, they were instructed to pelt the vehicles with the stones and run in different directions to evade arrest.

Durg Collector, Mr. Banerjee and S.P., Mr. Surendra Vikram Singh, were also present along with a huge police force, when the public meeting was being held. Speakers, one after the other, called for defying Section 144 and taking out a procession towards Durg city, and courting arrest. In those days political parties resorted to this conventional way of protest.

The meeting was brought to a close with my strong opposition to any action in contravention to the law. I dispersed the students by 1 pm, after requesting the students to return to their homes peacefully as the purpose of strengthening the agitation had been fulfilled with the holding of the meeting.

As I, along with a few followers, proceeded towards the college, a vehicle driven by the S.P. stopped in front of us. The Collector was also sitting in the front seat. Mr. Singh congratulated me on bringing the meeting to a peaceful end and asked me to get into the vehicle as he wanted to have a chat with me. When I made excuses, the Collector firmed up his voice and authoritatively told me to get inside. With no choice left, I got into the vehicle and was made to sit in between them. The vehicle stopped in front of the Durg police station.

After instructing the T.I. to take care of my comfort till their return, the S.P. and collector left. I prayed and hoped against hope that my boys would not start their scheduled programme till I was released. I waited with bated breath for the S.P. to return.

It was nearly 4 pm and there was no sight of the S.P. or the Collector and the T.I. would not permit me to leave, despite my repeated requests. Ultimately, I resigned myself to whatever was destined to happen. After all, was it not natural justice that I should be the first one to be taken into custody for having planned a series of law breaking acts to be enacted in the city very soon?

And then, telephones started ringing one after another. Vehicles carrying armed police forces rushed out of the station ground in different directions. Later, these vehicles returned carrying two, three or four students who had been arrested. This went on till 9 pm, till the number of arrested students had gone up to over 30.

The students had made my plan a thumping success! They had grouped themselves at crowded junctions and had started shouting slogans. It had been a novel sight for the nearby shopkeepers as well as the onlookers, as they had never witnessed college students shouting slogans in such a manner. They had not taken the promulgation of IPC 144 seriously, which prohibited assembly of more than four persons, or the consequences that would have to be faced for breaking the law. But the main actors had.

The police vehicles had come to a grinding halt on account of the stones being hurled in their direction. The baton wielding police had a field-day beating up the unwary and curious crowd who had remained rooted to their spots, to view this unprecedented occurrence in their city. No one was spared; neither the shop keepers nor the fun watching onlookers. The real culprits received the minimum beatings. Police vehicles had to trace every nook and corner of the city to stop violation of IPC 144. It was the public who faced the brunt of the police attack. But the police knew and were interested only in catching hold of the students. The result of the chase of over two hundred policemen for about four hours, was not very inspiring. Just thirty five students were taken into custody. Our plan had succeeded. The brutalised public had suddenly become aware!

Late that night, in police custody, we were provided with packets of alu-puri ordered from a local vendor. The S.P., Mr. Surendra Vikram Singh, made a round after midnight. He found me sitting wide awake in the crowded lock-up while the others were sleeping. Before leaving, he came close and asked me if I was a Naxalite? I preferred to remain silent and he left with a sporting laugh.

Right from morning, the police station was a bee-hive of activity. Unbelieving relatives came enquiring about their wards. It was difficult for them to swallow the fact that their college-going children had wound up in police lock-up. They looked at me with anger and suspicion. I knew that my brother wouldn't take the trouble of even enquiring about me. Local politicians and reporters loitered about in the hope of tit-bit news from police officers. All hopes of release on personal bonds were dashed when police vans arrived to transport us to Rajanadgoan sub-jail.

While boarding the van, I addressed the small crowd of students who had gathered to see us off and told them to make a great success of the forthcoming 'Durg Bandh' in protest of the brutal lathi-charge on not only students but 'innocent citizens' also.

Rajnandgoan sub-jail was a decayed and dilapidated structure. A barrack in the jail had been reserved exclusively to accommodate us students. But one could not escape the stink of human excreta that pervaded the air. Everyone, from the inmates to the warders, gathered to watch with an element of awe, the entry of the new comers because they had never expected to have college students as jail inmates. I felt a little humiliated when frisked by the guards. When I raised my voice in protest, the jailor told me to take it easy because it was a mandatory regulation and I must cooperate to maintain jail discipline. He promised that if I cooperated with the jail administration, he would also try to make our confinement as comfortable as possible.

Next morning, we read extensive coverage of the lathi charge on students and the public who had tried to break IPC section 144 by shouting slogans and pelting stones on the police. My call for Durg Bandh was also reported prominently.

The first day in jail passed off uneventfully. The only repulsive experience was the toilet. A corner of the jail had been covered with bamboo mats for toilet facilities. It was open and dry with tons of human excreta collected at the bottom and was swarming with flies. I was able to adjust myself to the jail. Not to its stinking toilets.

The news of the sacking of the Vice President, Mr. Rajen Choube, from the services of the Bhilai Steel Plant, appeared in the news papers the next day. I wondered how I had been spared. I waited anxiously for the axe to fall on me too.

On the second day, newspapers were filled with the news of the total Bandh of the Durg city. Not even a pan-thela had opened shop. Students had performed a feat that was the envy of even leading political parties. To my great relief, I found no mention of my termination. In the evening, local leaders of various political parties made a beeline to visit us and said words of encouragement and support for our agitation. CPI leader, Mr. Sarath Kothari, not only treated us with tea and refreshments but also left some money with the jailer to be used for our needs.

As days passed, we started yearning for our homes. Parents of detained students visited at least once. I also had a visitor. The parents of General Secretary, Ashok Gupta, came to visit me. They brought Haluva-Puri, sweets and a lot of other refreshments for me which I shared with others. Their concern for my well-being brought tears to my eyes.

The old couple, Tirathlal and Mohini Gupta, treated me like their own son. I felt a deep knot in my heart, and remained related with them for decades till they breathed their last.

Things had changed while we were in jail. When we were released on bail after 10 days, I found that the principal had been sent on a month's forced leave and though the college had a deserted look, police forces were still camped there.

The Collector sent information for me to meet him at his residence where he asked me to stop the agitation as the principal had been sent on leave. He evaded my questions regarding rustication orders and the police cases pending against us by saying that everything would be taken care of in due course. There was an authoritative note when he asked me to withdraw the strike and allow the classes to start as exams were fast approaching. All the same, he treated me with very sweet words and a few 'Rasagollas' before I left his chamber. I could not help admiring him for dispensing his power, coated with sugar!

The strike could not be withdrawn till Dr. Singh was permanently transferred and the fallouts of the strike set right. Though the strike continued, the number of students coming to the college dwindled drastically, making me feel a little unsettled about the mood of the students as final exams were just around the corner. Even the office bearers were keeping away and showing no interest in the future course of the agitation. So, in consultation with those students who had been in the forefront of the agitation, I decided to call off the strike and announced it through newspapers.

Chapter 6

A Lonely Path

With the withdrawal of the strike next day, there was an enthusiastic response from the students. They returned in large numbers. Professors were eager to restart their classes and the college once again hummed with a studious atmosphere. The students and teachers seemed satisfied with the partial success of 'removing' Dr. Singh.

In the evening, I called a public meeting to spell out future plans. I declared that the classes would continue running but the agitation would not be dropped. It would go on, but in a different form, till our demands were met. We would have to be ready for everything in order to prevent Dr. Singh's return to the college. With his revengeful attitude, he would leave no stone unturned to wreck the lives of the students who had dared to question his mal-administration.

A chain hunger strike at Gandhi Chowk, Durg, was decided upon. A list of student volunteers willing to sit on hunger strike for one day was immediately drawn up. Others were requested to visit the venue of hunger strike to cheer the agitators.

Six of us led the hunger strike. A public meeting was held and enthusiastically attended by students as well as onlookers in the market. Quite a few of the office bearers addressed the gathering. A new batch took our place the next evening. A public meeting was held every evening, just before a fresh batch of students sat for the 24 hour hunger strike.

It was here that I honed my oratory skills. Public demand for my addresses forced me to shed my inhibitions and speak in Hindi, a language over which I had little mastery and no confidence. Though I felt like a fish out of water, I did not avoid speaking. The public in turn, received my high spirited speeches with applause and funny smirks and encouraged me to continue. I used a cocktail of Hindi, English, Sanskrit and Malayalam and seasoned it with a great deal of heat and fire.

The relay hunger strike provided me an opportunity to get to know the local leaders of almost all political parties. Mr. Motilal Vora, leader of the SSP and brother of Mr. Govindlal Vora - editor of Nava Bharat, had high political ambitions and was in search of an opportunity to rise in popularity. I remained in close touch with him throughout the college movement and some time afterwards also because of the newspaper publicity he had provided. In addition, he had been the only reporter who had taken the trouble of meeting me on a few occasions to get news, even while I had been forced to stay underground to evade arrest.

District Congress President, Mr. Udaya Ram Verma, CPI leaders, Rohini Choube and Ganga Choube, Jan Sangh leader, Dr. Patankar, RSS activist and reporter of the Hindi daily, Dharam Yug, Mohanlal Jain, were among the few others I came in close contact with in those days.

And, how could I fail to mention Mr. Dhiresh Kumar Guha Neyogi who had, since a long time, stopped meeting me? I had kept no knowledge about him or his whereabouts post college elections. After forfeiting his Naxalite support base in Bhilai, he had located me, as a last ditch resort, to retain his foothold there, before returning to his hometown, Siligudi in West Bengal. He was disappointed to find in me only a 'careerist,' who was reluctant to be in active politics. But, when the news of my elevation to the presidentship of the college union and the subsequent 'militant student movement' under my leadership reached him, he retraced his steps immediately.

Neyogi accosted me at the venue of the hunger strike – as usual, at midnight. He urged me to prolong the movement indefinitely, to keep the students from appearing in the examinations. He also advised me to identify the militant students so that their energy could be diverted to 'revolutionary' activities. I fervently asked him to keep away from me as well as the students, because I had no intention of having the movement stamped as Naxalite inspired. The movement would come to an end with the removal of Dr. Singh, I reiterated. However, I conceded to his plea to allow him to come in direct contact with a few students who were in the forefront of the movement and a secret meeting was arranged, on the condition that he would never contact me or the agitating students publically.

But Neyogi was not a person to play second fiddle. He could not accept a secondary role, when the limelight was on someone else. His over-confidence, gained from his interaction with a few student leaders, made him throw all commitments and precautions to the wind. He started appearing at the venue of hunger strike publically, when I was not present. Later on, I learned from students that he had been misguiding them by saying that he was my political boss and I was following his instructions

Not long after, while interacting with the press, Neyogi got jittery when Mr. Mohanlal Jain of Dharam Yug, pointedly asked him if he were not the very same Neyogi, who had been dismissed by the BSP management on charges of being a Naxalite? Even with his speedy exit on a rickety bicycle, he was unable to reach Sector 6A market, just 10 kms away, before he was picked up by the police. He reached the Raipur Central Jail, the very next day. Neyogi had no compunction in biting off more than he could chew!

The news of Neyogi's arrest did not disturb me much. I thought that he had invited the trouble on himself and it was better to ignore him altogether.

I was surprised to find my brother seeking me out one evening. He came to inform me that our father had been hospitalised since over a month. That day he had received a telegram informing that our father's condition was critical. He asked me if I could go since he was finding it difficult to leave immediately.

I shared the information with some of my close confidents who persuaded me to leave for Kerala immediately. They not only promised to continue the relay hunger strike during my absence, but also, collected six hundred rupees for my travel expenses.

I was unable to recognise my father when I first saw him in his bed in a private hospital. I remembered him to be of a healthy and hefty physique and a robust frame. Here, I was looking at a deathly pale patient – all skin and bones. The attending doctor answered my queries with a shrug and said that the illness could not be diagnosed. Admitted for over a month and yet not diagnosed! I looked at the skeletal frame lying on the bed and something broke within me. I yelled at the doctor to discharge my father forthwith. I decided to take him to the nearby medical college.

I was left with only three hundred rupees and I needed three thousand rupees to pay the hospital bills before getting my father discharged. I approached my uncle for a loan since I knew that he was loaded with money as his children were posted in lucrative jobs in both India and abroad. And it was he who had got my father admitted in the hospital. But to my shock, I found him seething in hatered and loathing for his own dying brother. Rather than help, he proffered my outstretched hand a long list of my father's sins that had been the cause of his doom. When I protested, he hurled curses at me too. I was provoked to reply that I preferred curses from devils to their blessings. This painful incident has resulted in a deep and long lasting cleavage between me and my ancestral family.

However, with the help of some of my poorer relatives the required amount was managed and I got my father admitted in the medical college the very next day. There, his case was diagnosed as a terminal case of bone cancer. Doctors opined that with or without treatment, he would not survive for more than three months. They advised me to take the patient home and allow him to meet a natural death in the midst of his near and dear. At home, he was administered only pain-killing drugs to alleviate his pain. My father survived just three months

On my return to the college, I found the classes running very smoothly, with Dr. Singh continuing on leave and some leading students carrying on with the relay-hunger strike.

After taking my father back home, I took his final leave. I returned to Bhilai to face my destiny and a life of uncertainties and turmoil. Three months later, father breathed his last, in his home, in the presence of his kith and kin, but not before he had undergone his share of physical and mental pain.

I am thankful for having had the chance to do what I had been able to do for my father.

A few days before Dr. Singh's scheduled return, his supporters formed a ring of students in the college compound, to trap me. Unaware of such a plan, I walked right into it. About twenty of them, led by Mr. Deepak Khanna, started roughing me up and pulling and pushing me around. Khanna kept instigating his henchmen to thrash me. All the while, through their classroom windows, professors and students watched the drama anxiously but no one came to my rescue.

After tolerating the browbeating for about half an hour, I confronted one of them and challenged him to get going and finish the monkey play he was indulging in. I sneered that their leader, Khanna, was a known coward and incapable of touching my skin even when protected by twenty men. He closed in and murmured in my ear that he was the last person to raise his hands against me. I drew courage from his words and forcefully broke open their ring. I didn't stop to look back but moved away as fast as my legs would permit. I took my bi-cycle and made a hurried exit while the humming sound from the classes continued behind me.

I took up the matter very seriously as it made a demoralising impact on our supporters. I told Mr. Choube, and Mr. Gupta, to confront Mr. Khanna and demand an explanation for insulting and intimidating the 'president.' They, however, made very light of the matter.

It was decided that all the CRs and office bearers would abstain from their classes on the day of Dr. Singh's return, to keep a watch and, if necessary, to prevent him from entering his chambers. That fateful day, I, along with over thirty others, had posted ourselves in the college compound, ensuring that the classes continued as usual. At around 11 am, one of my friends and classmate, Sardar Amrik Singh, came running breathlessly to me. Without any explanation, he compelled me to sit on the back of his bicycle and whisked me out of the college compound. We crossed the rail tracks to reach the other side of the college. He dragged me into the compartment of an empty train, parked in the nearby railway yard. From there, a clear view of the college compound was visible.

We silently waited and watched. After about fifteen minutes, we saw a procession of over fifty persons armed with hockey sticks, lathis and swords, moving towards the college, by way of the Station Road, shouting abuses against me and the other student leaders. They pounced upon all those who were in the college compound and started raining blows on them till they were black and blue. Caught unawares, the victims were not in a position to defend themselves. Many of them sustained serious injuries.

When I got up to go to the scene of violence, Amrik stopped me and said that had I been present on the spot, a murder would have taken place. He confided that he had been in the company of the attackers while the conspiracy was being hatched. They were determined to finish me off in a frontal attack, after chasing away my supporters.

At my insistence, Amrik clandestinely visited the college compound after dark and brought back information that those who had sustained minor injuries had ridden off on their own vehicles and those who could not, were carried away in autos and cycle-rickshaws. No one reported the matter to the numerous, ever present police in the campus who had conveniently turned a blind eye towards the violent events and looked the other way. I could not help doubting the role of the district administration in the whole affair.

Chapter 7

Fear Is the Key

A large room in the upper floor of Tirathlal Dau's house in Baniapara, Durg, was our usual meeting place. On reaching this usual 'adda' late that night, to enquire about my wounded colleagues, I found over a dozen, including Choube, Gupta, Kamal Kishore, Subhash Thakur and others sprawled on 'daries' spread out on the floor. The scene had the look of a hospital ward in a battlefield. Some had swellings on their body parts and others had bandages wrapped around their heads, shoulders, legs and hands. A few groaned in pain. They had received first-aid from private doctors, since no one wanted to risk being spotted by the police and arrested.

When they saw me entering the room jauntily, unscathed and looking fresh in clean clothes, their anger knew no bounds. The volume of whining and screaming rose. Some called me a betrayer and others an escapist. I was so deeply grieved by the sight of my wounded colleagues that their angry utterances did not hurt me. Some accused me of gloating over their misery. A few were vehement in decrying that though I had saved myself, I had not bothered to warn them.

Patiently, I pointed out that they themselves had brought on their misery. Had they retaliated firmly after the 'hooligans' had tried to assault, insult and humiliate their president, the other day, no one would have dared to attack them. I reminded them of their visit to Khanna's house to demand an apology, but subsequently returning happily instead, after accepting his sweets. I chided that I was not available to be their president in order to be publically insulted and humiliated by a bunch of hooligans. 'My skin is not that cheap' was the actual phrase that came out of my mouth. I was quite capable of taking care of my own skin and henceforth, they could bother about their own. 'Leading a bunch of spineless fools who could be so easily manipulated, was not my cup of tea' I said.

As I prepared to leave the place in disgust, Choube, who had been silent all along, blocked my path and contritely asked me not to leave. He conceded that the mistake had been their own. He, as well as the others expressed regret for not following the directives of the president. He said that for the success of the agitation, now on, everyone would follow the directives of the president with sincerity and commitment.

It was only long afterwards that I realised that Choube was quitting his position as the real commander and desisting from scheming behind my back, because he had accepted his own limitations to lead the students any further.

I accepted their change of heart. My queries revealed that it had not been Mr. Khanna, but one Mr. Laddan Khan who had commandeered the attack. I told them that the first thing to do was to crush the enemy's high morale. It was essential to create fear in their minds by a far severer counter-attack. It was agreed that from next day onwards, when the principal was to rejoin the college, none of his supporters should be visible in the campus. Anyone identified as the principal's supporter would be beaten up and chased out of the college campus.

The next day was declared 'cleansing day' of all anti-social elements in the college. I told them to select a leader of their own choice, whose orders should be followed without question. They discussed the leadership issue among themselves but no one was willing to accept the leading role. Ultimately, they asked me to lead them in this operation also, as I had had been doing all along.

Yes, I would have to do the dirty job myself.

Our plan was to take immediate action. All those who were not suffering from severe pain accompanied me to search out our supporters in the city. Throughout the night we spread out through narrow lanes and bi-lanes to locate the homes of over a hundred students. They were instructed to reach 'Baniapara' by 8 am, wielding either a hockey stick or a lathi. By the time we had completed our mission, the sun was rising.

On our way back to our 'adda,' we found an open tea shop and decided to have tea after the night's activities. We were dumbfounded to find Laddan Khan, the organiser of the previous day's attack, standing there sipping his tea. I had never seen him before. He was around 30 years old, tall, hefty and muscularly built and had the imposing look of a confident man. At the very sight of the man who had been the cause of the assault and their sad plight, the same victims started whimpering and whining before him. Jovially, he waved away their complaints and ordered tea for everyone. Hot tea was promptly served and accepted by all but me. When a cup was brought to me I pushed it away so angrily that it shattered to the ground. With overriding confidence, Khan confronted me and advised me to cool down because though the college president, I was a man of no consequence. The shattering sound sent such a wave of shock that my collegues put down their half emptied cups.

Khan's misplaced swagger, could not, however, hide his jittery reaction to my action. With a taunting smirk on his face Laddan Khan asked me what I hoped to achieve with a bunch of innocent fools as my followers. I left the place along with my 'innocent followers' after daring Khan to come to the college and see for himself.

At 9 pm, as scheduled, I led about sixty hockey sticks and lathi wielding supporters in a procession from Baniapara to the college campus. When we reached the campus we found hundreds of Arts faculty students loitering about. I held a small meeting and announced that not one of Dr. Singh's supporters was to be allowed within the periphery of the college.

Suddenly, a Singh supporter who must have surely been six feet tall, dared me to remove him from the campus. Something in his words electrified me and I took a step forward and slapped him in his face with all my strength. It was the first act of physical violence in my public life. But it paved the way for my followers to jump upon the man. Beaten black and blue, he had to run to save his life.

This triggered off a chain of physical assaults on Singh supporters by different groups of students. Scores of bicycles belonging to them were set on fire. By around 5.30 pm someone shouted that Laddan Khan himself was coming. I had a heady feeling. I recalled clearly his smirk of the morning and grabbed a hockey stick and ran to meet him. My followers also rushed behind me

Khan raised both his hands to ward off the raised hockey stick - uttering blasphemies. Not a moment did I lose. The stick in my hand fell on his shoulders with blinding force. He lost balance and fell to the ground. I did not a get a second chance to strike because so many others were raining their lathis on him. I saw him falling again and again. He was trying to crawl away. I came to my senses only after I saw a raised lathi falling on his head and heard the sickening sound. My shout stopped all action. Just before leaving the spot, I saw him writhing over the red soil like a wounded python, with his clothes soaked in blood.

By the time our operation ended, it was dark. The police remained aloof and watched from a distance. Students dispersed silently. Expecting arrest, I exchanged my clothes with another student and left the campus as unobtrusively as possible.

Exhausted to my bones, I reached my quarter in Sector 7, Bhilai, but only after taking a round about route to avoid the various police posts situated between Durg and Bhilai. A vigorous bath washed away the sweat and dirt but could not rouse my appetite. The thought of food sickened me so I took a glass of water and fell into a deep slumber. The sleep was fitful and nightmarish.

I had a horrible dream of Laddan Khan hanging upside down from a hook in a butcher shop, side by side of other carcasses of skinned goats. Suddenly, followed by a piercing shriek, Khan's bloody and skinned hands groped towards my throat to strangulate me. Clenching at the bloody hands strangulating me and struggling for breath, I woke up drenched in sweat. My heart was pounding violently and I was scared to go back to sleep. I began recounting the events of the day. But, only the sight of Khan, rolling over the red soil like a wounded python, his clothes soaked in blood, kept appearing before my eyes. My heart tightened in pain. Tears flowed out in torrents but I found no solace. Was it the tears of repentance for the violence I had indulged in? That was the night that convinced me that I was personally not fit to indulge in violence and bloodshed, even for a lofty cause.

Alone, I continued in that state of wretchedness for quite a long time before logic and reason gained the upper hand. By nature I was a timid person and there was no violence in my blood. In my 24 years of personal life, I could not remember to have used violence at any time against any one. For the first time, and that also, for a public cause, I had slapped a man. The very same day I had delivered a fierce blow on another human being. And I had left him to bleed. Why did it have to happen? I searched for justification of violence in me and my colleagues. I tried to console myself with a quote from a Russian novel 'A lot of filth in this world needs to be cleared with sword and fire.'

An ideology, for that matter, the Marxist ideology, to be exact, that justified violence to achieve a 'lofty' end took deep root in me. I wondered whether I would be able tp appreciate even the violence indulged in by the Naxalites to achieve their political ends!

Laddan Khan remained hospitalised for over a month. Police had registered a number of serious criminal cases against us, one for attempted murder.

With the creeping in of violence in the agitation and the police hunt to arrest me and some of my followers, we were forced to stay underground and withdraw the relay hunger strike. A clandestine meeting of the leaders and active students was held at Thithuruti to decide the future course. All the participants advocated total strike till Dr. Singh was removed. They decided to lead the strike themselves without involving me and others who were forced to remain underground. I was specifically ordered to stay back in Bhilai and not come out in the open at all because my arrest would leave them leaderless.

Next morning, I couldn't resist the temptation to sneak into the college to see who it was who was leading the strike in my absence. The morning classes were attended by arts students, who had always been in the forefront of the agitation.

I was stunned when I was confronted with the humming sound of all classes being held peacefully. None of the boastful leaders were to be seen. Going back at this stage was not acceptable. It was then that a Marxian thought. 'Idea when gripped by the masses becomes a physical force, wafted through my mind.

Inspired by the thought, I confronted the students attending classes. My idea became a physical force and soon a crowd of over five hundred students were assembled and sent in a procession for a demonstration at the Collectorate. I stayed back to address the science students who had started arriving. But the procession did not get very far. A transport bus was held up, vacated and set ablaze. Standing in front of the college, some lady students, professors and I were witness to the bus being engulfed in flames leaping sky-high. I watched and wondered who could be the 'bus-burning' expert, a phenomenon common only to Calcutta in those days.

After the bus had been consigned to flames, the participants in the procession ran helter-skelter from the spot, excepting for Mr. Gautam Bhattacharya, a brilliant student of B.A. final year. He stayed back, nonchalantly smoking a Charminar Cigarette. When the police rushed to the spot, Mr. Bhattacharya was the only one they could nab on the spot.

With the arrival of the students of the science faculty, I changed my tactics and directed them to escalate the agitation by 'picketing' on the G.E. Road, in front of the college, and court arrest. Picketing was a word I had picked up while in school, when a liberation movement was conducted by the Congress-led opposition parties, against the first elected Communist Government in Kerala. The idea was to lie down on the road and compel the police to arrest and remove the agitators physically. However, my boys stood rather than lay on the road to block vehicular traffic. With one bus already consigned to flames, the police were battle ready and reached the spot even as I also reached the students to tell them how to picket.

We were all rounded up and beaten up mercilessly. This time, the power of the batons was ten times more than that of the previous occasions because they belonged to the Central Reserved Police Force. Having been caught up in the police dragnet, I too received a few severe, electrifying blows on my legs and bums. I would have been beaten to a pulp by half a dozen Khaki men but for the timely intervention of Mr. Surendra Vikram Singh, the S.P. who shouted that he wanted to handle me personally. Later, I realised that by collaring and dragging me to the nearby Govt. Circuit House, he had actually saved me from being lynched.

In the Circuit House, I found over a score of my colleagues drenched in their own blood. One of the CRPF men, assuming the bespectacled Mr. Shyamal Chowdhary sitting in our midst, to be the leader, bludgeoned him on his forehead, smashing his glasses and splitting open his eyebrow. The fallout was that stray policemen were assaulted or pelted with stones by infuriated students at many places in Durg and Bhilai and the administration was forced to extend imposition of

IPC Section 144 to the Bhilai Township also. It was an occasion that convinced me that violence begets only greater violence.

Over thirty students were rounded up that day and sent to Rajnandgoan Jail the next day. A few students, whose parents were well-connected, were able to save themselves from jail going. This time the stay in jail extended to about two weeks.

In the course of the movement, extending to four months, I and scores of other students were arrested four times; the first time being a let off after a few hours in police lock-up. On subsequent occasions, we had to spend a week or two in the Rajnandgoan Jail - a veritable stinking shit hell, there being no flush latrines. On the last occasion, police did not allow us to forego the honour of being handcuffed while being transported - despite our vehement protest.

Dr. R. N. Singh was appointed Director of PMT and transferred to Bhopal. Rustication orders were withdrawn. Students were promised a stage by stage withdrawal of all criminal cases. Consequently, by the end of February 1970, the strike was called off. The Administration, it seemed, had realised it's limitations to contain the agitation that had received support from students all over Chhattisgarh. Professors, who were happy about the transfer, however, commented derisively, that though Dr. Singh had been given a hard kick in the arse, it had only helped to catapult him to a higher position.

I could not believe that in spite of my long absences from duty and repeated jail goings, the loss of my job, which had all along been my constant source of fear, had not materialised. It was the last straw for survival left to me. Only later did I learn that though I had been creating strong enemies, I had also been creating staunch admirers among the senior officers who could influence the management's decision. Their college going children, especially their daughters, had defended me before their parents and admired my honesty and courage in fighting the corrupt college administration.

I had nothing to do in the college after the withdrawal of the strike. I was the only student disqualified to appear in the exam for want of sufficient attendance. Being the sacrificial goat, I had been singled out for the disqualification. I felt no pain as I was neither interested nor prepared for the examination. Most importantly my aim in life had already shifted. A lecturer's job ceased to be an achieveable dream.

I experienced a slight heart ache whenever I crossed the college, to reach the district courts on my way to attend the hearings of a number of criminal cases pending against me in connection with the students' agitation. While others were attending classes and preparing for the examinations I was left alone to lick my wounds in solitude.

On the court hearing days, Mr. Vora used to invite me for a cup of tea at his Durg Roadways office. I went but was at a loss to make out what he wanted from me. It transpired that he was only interested in knowing whether I had any political aspirations for the future. My reply was in the negative. Not much later, Mr. Vora left the Socialist Party and joined the Congress and was successful in getting the party's ticket and winning his first election from the Durg Constituency.

Is it not an irony of fate that while Mr. Vora became Minister of Higher Education in the Madhya Pradesh Government, Dr. Singh who had come under the purview of his authority, died of a heart attack soon after!

During the next academic session, 1970–71, the newly elected students' union carried on the legacy of the previous year. From day one it raised slogans and staged demonstrations to demand withdrawal of all criminal cases against all the students who had participated in the previous year's strike. My anxiety and exasperation of waiting from morning till evening outside the courts, once or twice a week, to attend my cases, while absenting myself from duty, came to an end after the cases were withdrawn by the M.P. State Government in the first quarter of the year 1971.

And 1971 heralded the beginning of my political life. It began with the 24 hours surveillance by the CID of police. I saw two plain clothes men shadowing me wherever and whenever I went and it bothered me not at all. I moved in my bicycle and they followed suit. They maintained a safe distance and waited patiently for hours, all the while pretending that I did not exist. After about a month, I felt pity and offered them my assistance. They requested me to forewarn them in advance about my schedule for the day and I readily agreed because I really had nothing to hide.

Owing to my day classes in the college, I had worked in night shifts continuously for four years. After the unceremonious end of my education, I had been reverted to the changing three shifts. Perhaps because of the appearance of my name in the news papers during the last four months, as a popular student leader, everyone in Coke Ovens, including officers, were a little wary of me.

Right from the very beginning I had been just an ordinary and unimposing worker in the plant and no one would have imagined that I could rise to the position of a student leader, capable of leading thousands of college students. As always, I went about my work dutifully. And mercifully there were no officers, including my earlier shift in-charge, who were willing or adventurous enough to oppress or suppress me, as they had done in my college days.

Though I stayed in the top floor of my company quarters, all alone, I had a constant stream of visitors; including some politically motivated college students. It was a period when a few left-leaning political leaders, belonging to the communist or socialist parties also visited me. Mr. Robin Dutta was a regular visitor. Mr. Chandulal Chandrakar, Congress leader and the Durg M.P. sent me a message to meet him at his residence where he asked me to join the Congress and work for his election campaign. I told him that I was not interested in Congress politics. To my close friends and associates I revealed that I had no political ambition at all but I would like to put some of my political ideas into experiment, to see if they could really serve the poor and down trodden.

After sacrificing my life's ambition, I had reached such a mental state that I began to think that the only purpose of my continued existence was to work for the toiling masses who suffered poverty and humiliation, as I had suffered.

Chapter 8

A Fertile Soil

I did not reveal to anyone that I was waiting for Neyogi to return from jail in order to draw up a concrete plan to develop an organisation. I could not think of a better person capable or willing to work untiringly, day and night, for a political cause.

My character and personality had undergone a complete change after I had become a student leader. It was for the first time that I had come face to face with the many facets of the administrative system, especially police and jail. I had recognised fear to be the key factor that determined the outcome of any movement. Fear heralded the beginning of defeat. A fearless man could be eliminated but he could never be defeated. I got an insight into the human psyche which could be moulded or manipulated. Interacting with collector, S.P. and even a Chief Minister, I realised that no one was infallible and none need be afraid of anyone else because of his position or authority.

I had come across political leaders wearing various labels lacking conviction in their own ideology and behaving like cowards and manipulators. I learnt that convictions can make a man strong and courageous, even beyond the imagination of the common folk. And my convictions were founded on the Marxist ideology which I considered infallible. Most of the Communists I came across were pseudo-Marxists or hypocrites, who wore Marxism around their necks like a garland.

I was determined to never engage in a public act unless I was first fully convinced of its justification and correctness.

In the 1970s, Bhilai was populated by quite a large section of migrant Keralites who had been forced to seek jobs outside their own state in order to sustain themselves and their families. Traditionally Communist sympathisers, they felt pride in their past association in some way or other with the communist movements that had taken place there. But, in practice, the leftist ideology had been unable to create job opportunities. Greener pastures lay elsewhere.

Outside of Kerala, Keralites found their leftist labels disadvantageous to their careers. Consequently they swept them under the carpet. Their ingrained traits of honesty, loyalty and intelligence earned them the trust and goodwill of employers all over India. Their sympathies for agitational politics, however, were kept dormant in their heart of hearts. It was, therefore, with furtive and longing glances that the Malayalees of Bhilai witnessed one of their own leading a prolonged and militant students' movement in Chhattisgarh.

Post college, I became obsessed with 'Revolution' and to me, the Marxist ideology was the formidable weapon that would bring about that revolution.

However, first thing first. In order to be perfect, I would have to first shape myself into a real Marxist. But then, I lacked experience and knowledge of how to achieve my goal. All I was sanguine about was my abhorance for those who professed an ideology without living up to it. I branded them as intellectually dishonest - not worthy of respect. Though I was unconsciously acquiring all the traits of over-confidence, arrogance, intolerance, anxiety and the impatience of a bigot, I mistook them as the qualities of an honest, selfless and knowledgeable person, willing to sacrifice even his life to save humanity from social and economic exploitation!

On his release from jail, Neyogi wasted no time in locating me. It made me happy that he had come to me on his own. He expressed pleasant surprise at the transformation that had taken place in my character within such a short time. He quickly unfolded his plan to work as a whole timer to organise the peasants and workers of Chhattisgarh, provided I helped and supported him. Else, he would be left with no alternative but to leave Chhattisgarh forever and go back to his native Bengal.

I remained firm regarding my condition that we could join hands only if he disassociated himself with the Naxalites and their leader Charu Mazumdar, who believed in converting revolutionaries into criminals! He confessed that he was also looking for a new path and eager to work it out with me.

The search for contacting a few supporters in Bhilai had begun in order to constitute a committee to oversee our work. Thereafter, Neyogi became my regular visitor. He brought a few of his staunch supporters who had separated themselves from the Naxalite party. They were introduced to me as Dr. Yadu from Raipur, a Marxist ideologue and Neel Ratan Ghoshal, Manab Sengupta, Ahin Chowdhary and Prem Kumar Simon, all BSP employees. It was again through Neyogi that I came to know about a few other members of the (CPI-ML) unit active in Bhilai, namely Jogi Rai, M. L. Chatterjee, Karmakar, Sivraman; all employees of the Bhilai Steel Plant.

By the fag end of 1970, we constituted a committee in Bhilai to bring about 'revolution' in Chhattisgarh. The committee consisted of a few Bengalis, a Malayalee, a Maharashtrian, a Telugu, a Bihari and a U.P. wala. Ironically it had not one Chhatisgarhi, though the only job of the committee was to discuss revolution in Chhattisgarh!

As an outcome of the college agitation, there came about a close association with many Chhattisgarhi students. Even after I had left the college, they showed great attachment and respect for me, expressing their desire to keep in contact. Many requested me to visit their homes in their villages. Since I was also eager to have a taste of village life, I spent my weekly holidays in far off villages in the midst of the families of my former college mates. I tried to make the most of these visits to sow the seeds of my revolutionary thoughts amongst my hosts. At that time, I had no idea of the probable outcome of these interactions.

What took me by surprise was the peace and contentment prevailing among the villagers and the strong family ties discernable even in the midst of utter poverty. Contrary to my experience about the characteristics of Keralites with which I was familiar, those of the natives of Chhattisgarh were highly simplistic. They accepted life as it came and humbly lived without greed and ambition. Though poor in material comforts, they were rich in human relationships!

Our Committee decided to post our whole-timers in rural villages in order to become compatible with the farmers and learn their language, culture and traditions. Once they became as one with them, building up a peasant's organisation would become easier. And the employed comrades were entrusted with the responsibility of organising the workers at their respective work places. We had two whole-timers. Com. Neyogi was one and the other was a Telegu youth, Com. Prabhu Das. While Prabhu Das was sent to the villages through our student connections, Neyogi was first dispatched off to Bengal openly and then brought back clandestinely, to a village near Balod. This was done to shield him from police surveillance. Others busied themselves in organising the workers of their respective departments.

Prabhu Das remained in different villages for around one month and then returned to Bhilai without informing us. He then simply disappeared from our midst, naturally raising suspicion of his being planted as a mole by the police. However, I preferred to think that he was just ashamed of himself and unable to appear before us because of his inability to endure the challenges and hardships of village life.

Neyogi, on the other hand, was determined to stay put in the villages in spite of the many serious obstacles he had to face. Initially, my contacts were keen to receive him but soon got jittery because of the eyebrows that were being raised by neighbours on account of the continued presence of a stranger in their village for no rhyme or reason. Because of his identity as a Naxalite, Neyogi had to lie low and live an underground life to escape detection by the police. The Kotwar system prevailing in villages made it obligatory for the Kotwar to report the presence of any outsider who stayed in the village beyond three days. Therefore, Neyogi was under compulsion to shift from village to village every three days.

One of my duties was to meet Neyogi secretly once in a month while he was in the villages. After my first meeting, I purchased and sent him a second hand bi-cycle and a few hundred rupees' cheap hosiery so that he could move around in the surrounding villages in the guise of a trader. Of course, the fund was raised through contributions. I kept constant touch with Neyogi during his stay in the villages. But after the lapse of three months, he appeared suddenly before me at Bhilai, asking for medical aid to treat his festering skin infections. So, I kept him in hiding in Bhilai while Dr. Yadu treated him.

After his cure, Neyogi refused to return to the villages, citing practical problems of staying there and the suspicious and non-cooperative nature of the farmers that he had to face daily. He relented, though only after tireless persuasion by almost all members of the committee.

From then onwards, till 1971, during my off hours, I utilised my time in visiting scores of labour slums in and around Bhilai to impart lessons in Marxism and Socialism to a selected few. I honestly believed that I was sowing the seeds of a novel kind of revolution. I took it as my bounden duty to educate and enlighten the poor and illiterate workers about their rights and responsibilities – their rights as a worker and responsibility as a vanguard of revolution! There was no way for me to gauge the effectiveness of what I was doing. But, that did not deter me. I carried on headlong even though I had no clear concept about the time or shape of the revolution for which I was paving the way. They say Love can make one blind but can it be so with revolution too?

The 1960s and 70s were witnesses to thousands of educated and rebellious youths, blinded with the urge for revolution, destroying their lives and careers pursuing an unknown path. Naxalism and JP's movement were the two different manifestations of this phenomenon. The JP movement petered out by 1977, after the dethronement of Smt. Indira Gandhi from Prime Ministership, following imposition of Emergency by her. However, Naxalism, which died many a death, got resurrected time and again with the slogan of capturing political power through the barrels of a gun. With the disparities between the rich and the poor widening through the decades, and the still continuing displacement of tribals from the forest land, for development purpose, the Naxalite movement has refused to die down till even today

It was during this period that a graduate student of Arts faculty, Namita Desarkar, came along with her brother to visit me in my quarter. I had seen and interacted with her in the college earlier but never expected her visit at my residence. She was nineteen years old and appeared to be simple, self confident, daring and smart. She wore no ornaments or facial make up, unlike the other college girls. She spoke English fluently with an American accent. I appreciated the fluency but did not like the accent because it belonged to the 'capitalist America,' a country I did not admire in those days. But then, she revealed that she had completed her schooling in Washinton D.C., America, before coming to Bhilai, two years earlier.

My esteem in myself and my ideals, especially before an 'America returned' girl, could not keep me from admiring her command over the English language, a feat aspired for by every English medium student. Yet, I decried her for speaking English with an 'artificial' accent and asked her why she couldn't speak Hindi, the language of the common

Indian. Instead of rebutting my ego, she pleasantly agreed to learn to speak Hindi as early as possible.

In reality I had never been a centre of attraction for girls, though at the fag end of my college days, a few girls had shown interest in seeking my companionship and friendship. Maybe it was because of the fame and glamour attached to me as a student leader. They soon lost interest after I revealed a bit of my ideas and the purpose of my life. But Namita expressed a keen desire to repeat her visits and I was only very eager to welcome her.

My life had already been dedicated to the cause of revolution though I had no definite idea about its culmination. I only knew that revolution demanded sacrifices from me including my own life. Therefore, though I was already twenty five years old, marriage was not on my cards. I even considered it a great hurdle in my life's mission. All the same, I did not grudge the companionship of an intelligent and capable lady, willing to travel along with me.

Namita's repeated visits made me feel that perhaps she also contributed to the same ideals and so was fated to be my life partner.

It was during this period that one Mr. Murali Menon approached me with a request to accommodate him in my two room quarter. He was all pleasantness. His disarming smile and huge round spectacles added to the charm. His famished appearance endeared him to me. I acceded to his request without hesitation because of my trusting nature and a little over-confidence in myself. Moreover, after being continuously surrounded by a crowd of students, their absence made me feel very lonely.

Murali came with bag and baggage - a wooden cot, a few bed sheets, one tea kettle, about a dozen porcelain cups, a bundle of English magazines and a few books. My own household possessions were no less meager since I used to have my meals at my brother's house which was only a walking distance away.

It did not take long for me to realise that Murali was a wanderer without any set rules in life. Except for sleeping in the night, most of the time he stayed away from my home and then also, he sustained himself on innumerable cups of tea and biscuits. He excused his absence by saying that he liked to spend his spare time, after duty in the plant, with his other Malayalee friends. My attempt to cook at home for both of us failed because he was interested neither in extending a helping hand in cooking nor in eating the food I cooked. I was unable to fathom him but resigned myself to life with him.

Chapter 9

Dilemma of Choice

In the aftermath of the college movement, many of my Keralite acquaintances showed apprehension in associating with me. Therefore, Murali's courage and willingness to stay put in my house roused my admiration. Slowly, I got attached to him and treated him with love and compassion and extended all possible help to enable him to tide over many of his personal problems.

Murali was present during many of the political discussions that took place in my home but he never contributed his views. He was friendly and jovial with everyone. My secret association with Neyogi, while he was working clandestinely in some remote villages, was quite well known to Murail. He got very friendly with Namita also and visited her home on a few occasions. She was staying with her elder brother and mother in a BSP quarter at sector 7. It was situated only a few streets away from my own home in Sector 7. They had had to shift to a non-executive, small quarter from their big officers' quarter in sector 4, after her father's transfer to Calcutta. They had stayed back in Bhilai because of Namita and her brother's education. Murali used to egg me on to consider making Namita my life partner. She was also happy to welcome him at her place because of his friendly and pleasing nature.

It was only after a year that I learned from Murali that he was related to a cinema producer in Madras (Chennai), Balaji Productions. Balaji was his maternal uncle. Murali had his schooling in Madras, where his father worked as a Post Master. He also told me that his sister had been classmates and close friends with the daughter of an IG police, who had been posted in Madras on deputation from the M.P. cadre. Their friendship had developed into an intimate relationship between the two families. The IG was later transferred back to M.P. with promotion as ADGP and posted at Bhopal.

After Murali had finished his schooling and was in need of a job, it was this high ranking police officer, who had called him to Bhopal and appointed him as a clerk in the Police Head Quarters at Bhopal where he had worked for a few years.

Then again, in the middle of the 1960s, when recruitments in the Bhilai Steel Plant was at a peak, the then DGP of MP used his good offices, through the Commandant of the CISF in Bhila,i to get Murali a job in the Bhilai Steel Plant. He had also entrusted the local guardianship of Murali, to one Dy. S.P., Mr. Srivastava, at Durg. Murali had revealed to me his compulsion to take lunch every Sunday with the family of the Dy. S.P. only after staying over a year with me. It was intriguing that while he had been staying with me, who was under police surveillance all 24 hours, he had all the time been in close contact with a senior police officer. It had never once occurred to me that Murali might have been a mole, planted by the police, to gather information about me and Neyogi!

About a year after my father's demise, mother came to stay with us in Bhilai. She lived with my brother in his Sector 10 quarter where I went to take my meals. Being the youngest of her five children, I was her most beloved. The news and rumours she had been hearing about my public activities and repeated arrests filled her with anxiety and apprehension. She lived in constant fear of my getting killed by the police and was unable to understand why I was risking my life and jeopardising my job for the sake of others. Her efforts to dissuade me were countered by me with a question as to why her beloved Jesus Christ had allowed himself to be crucified for others' salvation. Still she was not consoled.

Then, one day, on my return from night duty, feeling a little feverish, I sat down quietly after my usual breakfast at my brother's house. Seeing me very much exhausted, mother persuaded me to cover myself with a blanket and lie down and sleep before going out again. Brother had gone to day time duty and his children were at school. The house was empty save for me, my sister-in-law and mother. I lay in a disturbed sleep.

At about noon, my mother came rushing in from outside and shook me awake. Overwrought and anxious, she wanted to send me out through the backdoor as a large posse of policemen were positioned at our front door. When she hurriedly opened the back door, she found a few policemen standing there too. Both she and my sister-in-law stood there, numb with fear. After thinking for a minute, I instructed them to keep their mouths shut and to remain quiet till the end. As I deliberately removed the blanket and was getting out of bed, I saw a police inspector entering through the front door. He held a pistol in his hand and watched me belligerently.

Slowly, I got out of bed and leisurely walked to the front room. Nonchalantly, I sat down on a chair and offered another to the police officer. Though my head was pounding, I kept my cool. My mother and sister-in-law, in the meantime, watched silently with bated breath. My relaxed appearance put the officer also at ease. So he put his pistol down on the table in front of him. He took out a cigarette and lit it. The tension on his face, like the smoke from his nostrils, eased out slowly. His searching eyes told me instantly that he had not recognised me.

"Are you looking for my brother?" I asked.

"Where is he?" was his reponse.

I saw my route for escape. I simply donned the role of my brother and without batting an eye, told him that only my mother and wife were at home and my younger brother came only for his meals.

"Where might he be now?" asked the officer.

I replied with a straight face that he might be either in his own quarter in Sector 7 or out visiting his friends. With an innocent posture, I queried about the new grounds for searching for George Kurian because his college agitation had ended a long time ago and the criminal cases against him had been already withdrawn. Saying that it was for a different reason, the inspector went out hurriedly. I did not go outside, fearing that someone among the policemen or in the crowd that had assembled in front of the house might recognise me. Or worse still, my brother might appear on the scene.

After the police vehicles had left to search for me at another place, I grabbed my bicycle and sped away through the backdoor, telling my mother not to worry about me at all. I cycled on and on, knowing not where to go.

It was during my wandering that I espied one of my acquaintances standing at the gate of his company quarter in Sector 8. Mr. Daniel, worked in the Time Office of my department. Seeing me, he asked who I was looking for. On the spur of the moment, I said that I was looking for him because I needed his help. I wanted him to keep me at his residence for a day. Even though he was surprised at my blunt request, he readily acceded. While we were having tea, he asked me my compulsion to seek shelter with him. I told him that because I had not been able to attend a hearing of a case in the court in connection with my student agitation, an arrest warrant had been issued against me. I wanted to appear in the court the next day on my own, befor getting arrested by the police.

Daniel's wife was not happy with my stay in her home. She had protested in a hushed voice but Daniel had pacified her by saying that it was not a very serious matter. I was determined not to burden Daniel with a prolonged stay even though I had no idea where to go next.

I took dinner with Daniel without much relish, because of my feeling that I was an unwanted guest in the house.

The next morning I woke up in a feverish state and had tiny eruptions in some parts of my body. I realised immediately that I had come down with Chicken Pox. What a relief! It was a God sent providence as it had opened a new and safe haven for my continued hiding from the police! I managed for my medical book to be brought from my home and got myself admitted in the isolation ward of the BSP Sector 9 hospital.

As I had not committed any crime, I was certain that the search for me was to merely detain and question me about Neoygi and my political connections with him. It would certainly stop after some time. So, after fifteen days of hospitalisation in the isolation ward, I sent information to Murali and Namita about my whereabouts. Both of them visited me every day thereafter till my discharge. Meanwhile, I received information from a friend working as personal secretary to a top executive in BSP that my termination orders on grounds of long absence without intimation were ready to be issued. I used the hospital telephone to intimate my shift in-charge, Mr. P. M. Mazumadar, who had all along been my beta-noir, and the Superintendent, Mr. S. C. Chatterjee, who were both over-enthusiastic to initiate my termination process, in spite of caution by the higher management about my hospitalisation. To make it short, management had not issued my termination order and I could rejoin my duties without any further police pursuits.

It was again one late evening, after the lapse of a few months, when darkness was setting in, that a police inspector knocked at my door in Sector 7 and told me that a Dy. S.P. was waiting at a nearby street and wanted to meet me. He took me to the street in front of Namita's home where a uniformed Dy. S.P. was standing with a few plain clothed persons of whom two were ladies. They wanted to search Namita's house and she would not allow them entry without a search warrant. The Dy. S.P. told me that I should persuade Namita not to block their path so that they could do their duty and leave silently without creating a public spectacle. He said that he could get as many warrants as she wanted but wanted to save her family from public disgrace by doing his duty discreetly.

Namita relented after I talked to her and in my presence, the search continued for over two hours. They searched out the ins and outs of every single item in the household; the shelves, boxes, almiarahs, literally everything, while her mother ranted at them for violating the privacy of her home and destroying everything. They had to leave without anything worthwhile falling into their hands. When the Dy. S.P. thanked me for cooperating, I retorted that if he was a gentleman with a family of his own, he would go and express regret for his action before Namita and her mother. Namita accepted his apology but her mother drowned him with a volley of curses.

After around 9 months, I had my periodical meeting with Neyogi – in a village near Danitola Quartz Mines, near Balod. This time also I took some money and new clothes for him. But I was stunned to know of the proposal he had put forward for immediate consideration and approval of the so-called Bhilai Committtee.

Neyogi once again narrated the story of his isolation and the hardships he was facing in the villages and his disillusionment over the possibility of any success of our programme. It was a mere wastage of time and resources and he was thoroughly bored and tired of waiting for a positive response from the farmers despite his untiring efforts to organise them. So, he was of the opinion that the only alternative to pave the way to revolution was to shake up the entire Chhattisgarh and its administration by resorting to the killing of a well known and most hated class enemy of the area, as advocated by Charu Mazumdar!

Neyogi said that he had already arranged two accomplices to carry out the annihilation programme and had even marked out his target. On being questioned, he revealed the name of the 'class enemy,' one

"Manoharlal Jain," alias Manohar Seth, of the village Kusumkasa. I had heard of him being not only a big mines contractor, owning a fleet of trucks that transported iron ore at Dallirajha Mines, but had also seen his mansion at Ksumkasa on the Balod-Rajhara road. Only after Neyogi pointed his finger towards the distance, I noticed two ominous looking, dark skinned, thickly-built, sturdy men watching us from the cover of thick bushes. They were his selection. He elaborated that he, along with his accomplices, would vanish from the area after the operation and it would be on the onus of the Bhilai comrades to plaster walls at Durg and Bhilai with Naxalite slogans, hailing the murder of the class enemy.

I simply got up and started walking away after saying that, "Here and now ends all my connections with you." Neyogi was dumbfounded. He remained speechless for some time. Then he sprang to his feet and ran after me and pleaded with me to not to desert him. He said that he was willing to drop his plan, if I stayed and talked. He asked me to at least discuss the issue with him before taking any final decision. I sat on a rock nearby for a long, long time, silently, before relenting and agreeing to discuss the matter.

Neyogi had solemnly committed to renounce the old Naxalite track that he had been following previously. But, here he was, falling back to his old ways and I felt no compunction in pulling him up severely. His frustration and dejection I could sympathise with but a heinous crime like murder was totally unacceptable to me. How could a criminal be competent to lead the people! I would rather disown the revolution than killing people in cold blood for it. Yet, all the while I could not but help searching for the reasons for the failure of my ideas in the practical plane.

I had not, so far, come across a more suitable person than Neyogi, who might have been able to give our ideas an honest try. If a person like Neyogi had become frustrated and disillusioned, there must have been something intrinsically wrong with our ideas themselves. At this juncture my thoughts were turned to the Marxian postulate, that, when there is a contradiction between theory and practice, one must rely more on practice.

As the sun set, the workers could be seen from a long distance, moving about in the mines. An idea struck me. I asked Neyogi why he could not start his work with labourers first and then reach out to the farmers, through them. Was it not possible for him to change his name to 'Shankar' to cover up his identity and join the workforce at Danitola? It had become essential to review our theory and practice to obliterate the gap between them. We would take a final decision after a review meeting and I promised to call him to Bhilai very soon. First, however, I needed to make secret arrangements for him to come and attend.

I was under police surveillance day and night. When I was at home, two plainclothes men kept watch over my quarter, from under a tree at a distance. They shadowed me to the market and even to my duty place inside the plant. But that did not deter me from attending to my responsibilities, political work, included. I was confident that I was doing nothing illegal and therefore need not bother about the police watch.

It was Murali, who had introduced me to one Mr. K. V. Sahadevan. I was a little amused to see him because of his looks and body language. Intermittently, as and when he tossed his head, up and down went the long curly hair that danced around his nape. He wore fashionably loud and costly dresses and talked with a nasal quiver in his voice and, to me, appeared like a lascivious dance master. I was taken aback to hear him spout out revolutionary jargon, trying to impress me as being a staunch supporter of both the Naxalite ideology and Neyogi, with whom he spoke of having a close association.

I had been in the lookout for a safe hiding place for Neyogi during his stay in Bhilai for our proposed meeting. I supposed that the police would never imagine that Sahadevan, with his comically dandy looks and bearings, would have any revolutionary links. Since all my associates were under police observation, I asked Sahadevan if he could accommodate his old friend, Neyogi, for one or two days in his quarter in the Hospital Sector. He was caught off guard but owing to his false bravado, he could not refuse. However, he was clever enough to put his whole quarter at my disposal, saying that he would make way and stay a few days with his friends at Sector 6. He vacated his quarter at the top floor of a three storied building in the Hospital Sector and handed over a spare key to me.

I had handed over the key and the responsibility of the care of Neyogi to one of our comrades, Damodaran, who lived in Khursipar with his wife and family. The meeting was fixed for the next evening after Neyogi had been secretly lodged in the Hospital Sector quarter. In the afternoon, his caretaker, Damodaran had gone out to collect his salary, leaving Neyogi inside all alone. He locked the door from outside so that no one would doubt the presence of anyone inside.

At about 6 pm, when I was getting ready to attend the meeting, Damodaran came rushing to tell me that on his return he had found the whole building swarming with rifle wielding policemen. He was so scared that he was not even able to speak coherently. I felt sympathy for him and asked him to go straight back home after handing over the key to me and to forget everything.

I rushed to the Hospital Sector to make an on the spot survey of the situation. Taking advantage of the darkness I went up to the roof of the neighbouring building and examined the scene from different angles. The police had covered the entire area: the ground, the intervening floors and even the roof of the building. I overheard from the curious crowd that had assembled to watch the drama, that a Naxalite was hiding inside a locked quarter upstairs and two of his accomplices had already been arrested. There was fear and anxiety in each face. I also gathered that a police jeep had gone to fetch Sahadevan to open his locked quarter.

Realising that Neyogi could not possibly escape and he had no other alternative but to surrender, I rushed to Sector 6, where Sahadevan had taken up temporary quarters with his bachelor friends. I found him engrossed in playing cards with them, though he was supposed to be at his duty place. I called him out and unfolded the situation and told him to return to his work spot forthwith as the police was already on their way to fetch him. I advised him to say that Neyogi, an old friend, was his guest and he had locked the door at Neyogi's own request.

All Hell broke loose. Sahadevan's friends started hollering at me for compromising the innocent life of a 'guileless man.' They advised him to leave for Kerala on the first available train. Then Sahadevan too started blubbering and accusing me. I just handed over his keys to him. He was free to do as he liked. Even so, I reminded him that at that very moment he was on duty and supposed to be in his department, and not at home playing cards with his friends.

Half an hour later, Sahadevan walked into the custody of the policemen waiting at his work spot.

It was already 8 pm. The police and inquisitive onlookers had waited impatiently for the police to return with Sahadevan to bring to an end this spicy melodrama. It ended. It ended abruptly.

Unseen by all, taking advantage of the darkness and his tall and lanky body, Neyogi crept down to the ground with the support of balconies. He had cleverly tied together the ends of bed sheets that he had ripped and had made a makeshift ladder and used it to his advantage. Someone in the crowd noticed and shouted out an alarm. But Neyogi had, by that time, reached the ground. The flabbergasted policemen were taken unawares. They had no orders to shoot. They could only shout at each other impotently and try to catch the runaway fugitive.

Neyogi was hindered by no such confusion. His response was to shout the slogan 'Naxalbari Zindabad.' It had the desired magical effect. All froze in their footsteps. No one was tempted to give the fleeing hide-away a chase. And in the presence of hundreds of spectators and policemen, Neyogi sprinted away from the scene and melted into the darkness.

By the time Sahadevan was brought to his residence, fifteen minutes later, the bird had already flown. The officer-in-charge of the whole operation vented his anger and frustration on Sahadeavan with a few slaps and was able to comfort himself by finding at least some Naxalite literature in the house of this 'innocent' man.

These developments put me on the alert. I decided to stay away from my house for the time being till everything had cooled down. I sent an application for long leave on medical grounds to my department and left for Jagadalpur to stay put with a personal friend, Mr. Jayadevan. I used this opportunity to tour the district extensively and to learn about the culture and traditions of Adivasis of Bastar.

As expected, the police went for me in real earnest. In my stead, they found only Murali. He was unable to provide any information about my location. So, they dragged him to the Sector 6 Kotwali police station and kept him there overnight. Next morning, the Dy. S.P., Mr. Srivastava, came to Kotwali and ordered Murali's release. He advised him not to reside with me any longer, because whenever the police wanted Kurian they would not get him. Murali would become the scapegoat.

Sahadevan, Neelratan Ghoshal and others, who were taken into custody and interrogated for over a week, were let off on bail after they were produced before the court. I returned from my wanderings in Bastar a month later, after things had cooled down.

One day I received a message from Neyogi to meet him at Danitola Mines to discuss our future plans. There I told him once again to come out of hiding and work in the quartzite mines as a labourer under the assumed name. He would have to make an earning to support himself because most of our committee members were so scared that they did not want to be even in contact.

The hard manual labour exhausted Neyogi so much that when the Contractor offered him a Munshi's job, he readily grabbed it. As Munshi, he had often to go to Mines Head Quarters at Dalli Rajhara to submit the contractor's bills. It was on one such occasion that he was identified by the CID and arrested. Since he was known as Shankar in the Danitola Mines, his name was recorded by the police as Shankar Guha Neyogi.

Chapter 10

Naxalite as Mass Leader

Thereafter, Shankar Guha Neyogi came into existence and Dhiresh Kumar Guha Neyogi was forgotten.

I had unobtrusively metamorphosed from the simple village lad that I had been, into a hard and unbending youth. Now, as I look back at the 26 years old Kurian of 1972, I find that my strong bonding with the Marxist ideology had weakened my ties with my family members and my past. It was my ideology that was my mainstay. Everything and everyone had to go through its piercing glare. Over confidence and harshness had become my hallmark

The glamour and popularity that I had acquired as a student leader in the 'foreign' territory of Chhattisgarh, roused the curiosity of a few in my own Keralite community. They sought my acquaintance directly. Other inquisitive Malayalees who wanted to know, regularly received information about my activities through two sources. One was Murali, my roommate and the other was my friend and college mate, Mr. C. Radhakrishnan. People built up an image of the 'authentic' Kurian through the half-baked and shoddily compiled information eagerly doled out by the two. Such Malayalees turned their faces away from that blighted, nonconformist Kurian who was not a follower of any of the generally 'accepted' communist parties that they were in secret communion and attachment with.

The story of the 'Naxalite' Neyogi being hidden by me in 'innocent' Sahadevan's quarter, and his dramatic getaway from the police dragonet, had been a spicy subject for discussion among many Malayalees. They had no problem in equating me with Neyogi and condemning me as a Naxalite villain and were quite vociferous about it. Those few, however, who had a secret admiration for the Naxalite variety of revolution, kept quiet for fear of losing their jobs.

Even so, revolution was the only word that reverberated through my mind and soul day and night. I found only injustice and contradictions everywhere. I had already decided that I was answerable to none, not my parents, my relations or my community for anything that concerned me. A deep conviction in the ideology percolated into my personal life also. Being governed by any law established by society or ordained by God was not for me. I wanted to live my life in my own way and developed contempt for social customs as being meaningless and useless.

The path I had chosen to tread was novel and unfamiliar even to me. My inner conscious and aim in life to liberate mankind was guiding me and acting as a beacon in the darkness. I would not allow even my own life to hinder me from achieving it.

Even after my college life had come to an end, Namita came to my quarter once in a while. Murali was always very happy to receive her and play the host. He was quite liberal in his offering of his handmade tea and famous buiscuits. He was captivated by her fine English diction and even more overwhelmed by the willingness of an 'American-returned young lady' to sweep out all the dirt that had collected in our home over the week. She never showed inhibition in washing up the dozens of tea cups and saucers lying under Murali's cot.

In addition to going to college, Namita used to manage the whole household affairs of her home in the absence of a male support. She never hesitated to seek my assistance whenever she was at a loss and her mother was only too happy and thankful to receive my help. She never lost an opportunity to regale me with her culinary treats. All the same, she preferred Murali's visits because he was not a grouch like me.

He was not rough and unkempt as I was and his endearing smile did the rest. Namita's father, who was posted at Calcutta, and her brother, who was studying in the Raipur Engineering College, also never expressed objection about Namita's association with me.

One day, in the month of February 1972, when Namita came to visit me she looked very much agitated and in a great hurry. Murali was also there. Once Murali's pleasantries were over, she asked me point blank, if we could get married - that also, immediately. Both I and Murali were non-pulsed for a moment. And then, slowly, wonderingly, I nodded to say 'yes.' Murali laughed loud and long. He said that he was very happy and greatly relieved to find that someone, that also, a fine great lady, had offered to take over the contentious burden that he had been carrying on his shoulders for so long.

Oh! What a misconception! And all this time I had been under the delusion that it had been me carrying Murali on my shoulders!

It was Tarun Desarkar, Namita's elder brother, who had roused her indignation and ire when he had repaid her confidence with scorn and derision. Being her only brother, she had confessed to him her feelings for me and her desire to marry me. Tarun retorted and scoffed at the idea. He told her that I was a pauper and attributed ulterior motives to me for courting her. He was sure that my eyes were on the money their father had been saving for her marriage. So infuriated and provoked was she that she decided to find a new abode.

I knew that it was difficult for a normal person to take to me. It was not in me to kowtow to peoples' whims and fancies. I never shied away from taking decisions. When I took a decision that I felt was right, I would stand by it and make no bones about it. Neither did I mince my words nor was I apologetic about them. I was not in the habit of sugarcoating a spade to convert it into a spoon, to please anybody

So, when Namita came in like a whirlwind and asked, I said yes.

But marriage was not so simple. She belonged to a Bengali Hindu family, steeped deep in tradition. I belonged to a Keralite Catholic Christian family equally steeped in tradition. Namita had had her schooling in America over a long period and was of an open and free mind. My mind had outgrown religious and communal bindings and prejudices. But our families had no such liberal attitudes. So our efforts would not draw consents from them. My family seemed to be more aggrieved over the lack of a fat dowry than the girl being a Hindu. She was in the final year of her graduation and needed to finish her post graduation. My education had already come to an unceremonious end and had not benefitted me in any way. It failed to enhance either my salary or my job prospects. Because of political activities, I had never been regular in my duties and had earned only a meager salary which was just enough to make both ends meet for a single person. I had not a penny as savings. My economic freedom was entirely dependent on my job which was always under threat because of my rebellious mind.

I made my situation crystal clear to Namita. She was made aware of the possibility of my even losing my livelihood. I would not keep her under any sort of delusion. She said that as long as I was honest in my commitment, she had the grit and confidence to face any adversity. She promised to never come in the way of my progress towards my own destiny.

I had none to discuss my marriage other than Murali. Though my own brother lived close by I could not approach him. He had written me off as a lost case when I had dared to question his authority and had joined college despite his refusal to grant me permission. My emergence as a popular students' leader further aggravated things. He considered me a blotch on the family's reputation and an enemy of the church, and so needed to be kept at an arm's distance. By denouncing my activities, he, along with the other 'righteous sheep' of the church, tried to cow me down with their 'better-than-thou-attitude.' The confines of his family were limited to his wife and children. When even his parents were off limits, who was I but an intruder?

I wanted my marriage to be a private affair. No rituals. No legal proclamations. Moreover, I had no money to spend on a traditional marriage feast. But Murali was adamant. He wanted this marriage to set an example for other like -minded couples. So I was forced into applying for a CPF loan of 1800 rupees. Rs. 300 was spent to purchase new clothes for my brother and his family. The rest I handed over to Murali to manage the occasion as per his wish. I added a rider that there was no more money to come by.

It was Murali who fixed 22, May 1972, as the date for our marriage and it was he who invited the guests. He distributed a two-line typed invitation letter to about a hundred people, mostly students and professors. Dr. Yadu, a senior friend and renowned communist ideologue, agreed to preside over the ceremony. Namita's brother and my brother along with his wife and children, participated as guests. The Principal and some of the Lecturers and Professors from our college also joined the ceremony. My classmate and friend, Mr. K. J. Mathew, and his wife Sofiamma, escorted Namita from her home to the venue. The ceremony took only a few minutes. We garlanded each other and Dr. Yadu spoke a few words of wisdom and blessings.

Murali had arranged refreshments for about a hundred invitees. But the arrival of hundreds of college fans, to whom it had not been possible to extend invitations, caused a sort of melee at the marriage venue in the Sector 7 Club. I could not help noticing my friends liberally contributing money to a fund raised on the occasion to maintain a continuous supply of refreshments and soft drinks. So no one was left out from the refreshments. The premise looked like a festive college campus.

After the guests had left at about 10 pm, no one was available to accompany the bride and bridegroom to my quarter. I looked around for my room partner Murali, to take him along, but he was not visible anywhere. I thought perhaps he was being discreet and had wanted to sleep in a friend's house so as to leave the entire quarter for the newly wed.

It was a week later that I learned that Murali had resigned his job in the Bhilai Steel Plant and had left Bhilai for good in the middle of the night of the very day of my marriage.

It was now more than a year ago that Murali had first appeared before me. There had been no prior introduction. With his pleasant behaviour and merry disposition, he had endeared himself to me and persuaded me to accept him as my roommate, that too, at a time when I was under constant police surveillance. He became so special that even after coming to learn of his police background, I refused to believe that he could be spying on me for the police. My love for him was so unconditional that I trusted him absolutely. All the same, many a times, I found myself at a loss to understand the cause of his depressions. His nervous and worried looks and behaviour did not go hand in hand with his general joviality. Occasionally I caught him looking at me with deep concern; as if I was in imminent danger. It was the same look that I often saw in my mother's eyes after she had witnessed the police hunting for me.

Even now, in retrospect, I remain clueless as to why Murali joined me in the first place and remained a close companion for over a year, only to disappear without a word. He left his job and even Bhilai without any apparent rhyme or reason. He just vanished from the scene and left no trace. Nor has he ever made any attempt to contact me in the last 42 years. I know him to be a good man, a good friend and a well wisher for everyone who came in contact with him in Bhilai. Yet, he remains an enigma for me.

My wedding was conducted exactly in accordance with my own way of thinking. It was based on my ideology, the strength of my character, my convictions and confidence in my-self. Not once did I feel it necessary to bother about my social situation or material circumstances. It was just a mutual agreement between me and Namita. There was no outside interference from either man or God. We just decided to live together the rest of our lives. We bothered not whether our actions hurt the feelings of our near and dear ones. By reason and logic, there could be nothing wrong in doing so. But then, human life is not just about reason and logic. In hindsight, I feel that our way of marrying was the outcome of my extreme personal confidence coupled with a sort of arrogance, with which I was willing to defy the whole world. It has taken a whole lifetime for me to understand and acknowledge this.

Cut off from my community, scornful of its culture and traditions, I had to find out my own way of marrying. No Church, no temple, no registration, no rituals, no gifts, no flower-bedecked bed or a first night with a glass of milk. Because of the intolerable heat in the month of May in the top floor of my 2B quarter, we spent our first night in the open field nearby under the open sky. I had nothing but an ideology and the commitment to 'liberate humanity' to sustain me. Now, after all these years, all those grandiose sentiments appear to be nothing but foolishness. But at that time, I could not see beyond my political idealism. But even after 42 years of marriage, I fail to understand what led Namita, a lady of intelligence and practical acumen, to stake her life on such a 'foolish and impractical' man.

Then again, that is life and life refuses to conform to man-made rules.

The only change that marriage brought about in me was that I became more regular in my duty. After all, I had to earn enough to make both ends meet in our small and simple life. Money was also required to pay Namita's college fees so that she could finish her Post Graduation. There was hardly any utensil or furniture in our two-room quarter. Some very close friends decided on their own that our 'house' needed some rudimentary furniture and basic utensils. They went about doing what they pleased. The first two years saw us living in the least possible comforts. But it was a price we were both willing to share for our independent living, free from all social and family bindings.

Chapter 11

A New Political Experiment

My marriage was barely two months old when Neyogi was released from jail. He accosted me with a future plan for our political work. He confided that, after his release, the Collector Durg, had summoned him and told him that he would permit Neyogi to go back to Danitola only on the condition that he would confine his activities to the Danitola Mines only. When Neyogi had expressed a desire to make a living by starting a mutton shop and selling goat meat, the collector had expressed eagerness to help him out. The collector had not only persuaded the BSP management to allot a mutton shop to Neyogi in the Sector 4 Market, but had also helped him with a working capital of Rs. 5000. Neyogi planned to purchase goats cheaply from interior villages of Balod and sell them at Bhilai at a higher price. This would enable him to supply goats to his mutton shop also. He also persuaded me to arrange Rs. 5000 for him as working capital. I collected donations from my friends and well wishers.

Neyogi convinced me that it was all a cover up for continuing our political work. Else, the administration would not permit any one of us to re-enter Danitola or Balod. He had found, during his short stay at Danitola, that it would not be difficult to usurp the leadership of the workers there, and through them, to organise the farmers in nearby villages. And the goat business would be an alibi to keep in touch with the political contacts he had developed in many villages during his long stay underground. Though by then I had become skeptical about

Neyogi's character, I had to accept his idea because there was no one else with me to carry on with my experiment on revolution in the rural villages!

I wondered at the ease with which one could transform himself from a hardcore Naxalite - ready to commit a murder, to a petty trader in search of profit!

Neyogi brought to Bhilai a Bengali fellow by the name Das, who claimed to be a hack practicing medicine among the illiterate rural poor, to run his mutton shop. I visited the shop a few times and always found Neyogi unobtrusively keeping a hawk's eye from a nearby corner, over the cutting and weighing of the mutton and the incoming collections.

Business in a competitive market remained dull. Abruptly, Neyogi slashed the price of his commodity and simultaneously distributed a pamphlet claiming, "It is not merely a mutton shop but a mission to fight inflation."

Naturally, the mutton sold like hot cakes. This lasted for nearly a month till Das became an eyesore to all the other mutton sellers. In addition, he incurred Neyogi's wrath also for incurring heavy losses. The story came to its natural end within a few months, after a quarrel, with Das being branded a thief and banished and the mutton shop being shut down. Slowly, Neyogi's goat business also came to an end, leaving him enough time to live and mix up with the Danitola mines workers.

Samyukt Khadan Mazdoor Sangh (SKMS) affiliated to the CPI, was the recognized union for all the captive mines of the Bhilai Steel Plant. The iron-ore mines at Dalli-Rajhara, was its headquarters. In the absence of a local SKMS leader at Danitola, it was not very difficult for Neyogi to emerge as the leader of the 300 Danitola mines laborers. By organising protests, dharnas, rallies and strikes repeatedly, he could soon emerge as their unchallenged leader – thus, becoming a great irritant to the leaders of SKMS and the CPI. He made frequent forays to the

SKMS office at Dalli-Rajhara and confronted its leaders with unrealistic demands on behalf of Danitola workers to exhibit his militancy before the large number of union activists always present there.

After some time, with the help of the Danitola mines workers, he was successful in organising some farmers also. His rallies, now swollen up with the participation of the farmers also, helped him to slowly emerge as a new political entity at Balod. The then Congress MLA, Jhumuklal Bhedia, apprehensive of the expanding communist influence in his constituency, wasted no time in taking the emerging labour leader into his own fold. Neyogi also had no compunction in playing the Congress against the Communists. All the while, his sole aim was to usurp the leadership of the 12,000 iron-ore mines workers of Dalli-Rajhara, by hook or crook. But all his political tactics and opportunistic moves proved to be futile in shaking the strangle hold of the CPI and SKMS on the Dalli-Rajhara mines workers.

Congress under the leadership of Ms. Indira Gandhi as the PM, was firmly in power at the centre and CPI was functioning as her closest ally when a country wide movement under the leadership of Jaya Prakash Narayan forced her to declare Emergency to keep herself in power.

From 1973 till the declaration of Emergency on 26 June 1975, I had been the only one from Bhilai to keep in constant touch with Neyogi. On his invitation, I had participated in some of his rallies and meetings at Balod. But I became disappointed and disillusioned because of his shifting stances and unprincipled collusions. I began slowly distancing myself from him.

I came to the realisation that Neyogi's only motivating factor was his greed and unquenchable political ambition to gain name, fame and power. With his background, he very well knew that the only way for a man of only secondary schooling and mediocre intelligence to grow bigger than everyone else, was politics. He was deeply influenced by the stature of the communist leaders of Bengal and was willing to face any odds to achieve his goal to become a big leader. He was not the person to sacrifice himself for the good of others. Communism, for him, was only a weapon to gain power. While the Naxalites believed in capturing power by the power of the guns, Neyogi wanted to capture power through any and every means.

On the other side, I was only a man of bookish knowledge and badly biten by the Marxist ideology. I considered it a means for serving the down trodden, poor and illiterate masses. I believed in self sacrifice for the emancipation of the 'people' and abhorred the idea of sacrificing others for any cause. Though I had never desired to be a leader, circumstances had forced me to don such role on a few occasions. But I never relished the position of a leader. Rather I hated to be considered or addressed a leader because of the condemnable image of the contemporary leaders in the country.

It was on the persuasion of Dr. Sinha, the principal who had replaced Dr. Singh, that I had appeared for my M.Sc. final year examination as a private student in the year 1972 and passed it with a third division. Namita appeared for her PG final year in summer 1974 with her ripe pregnancy of our first child. Dr. Sinha had been so considerate of her delicate condition that he had asked her to sit in the principal's air conditioned chamber to write her papers. Just after a week after her examinations were over, our only son was born on 8th June 1974.

It was a period when I had been consistently confronted with the problem of deciding my priority in my life, i.e. between my family and my ideological commitments. I had consciously relegated my wife and son to a secondary position in favor of my public work without even a murmur of protest from Namita, leading me to falsely believe that she was an equal partner in my public life. I never thought of the need to express the natural love or affection of a husband or father either to my wife or to my son because of my deeper concern for the millions of the neglected women and children! My son thus had to grow up without the natural love and care of his parents including that of their families. Neither could they associate with the Malayalee nor the Bengali community. That I had to pay a heavy price and suffer irrepressible losses in my famiy life for my impractical idealism is a different story.

I had utilized most of my free time from duty to organise the workers of my own department of Coke Ovens without making much of a head way. Another comrade, Neelratan Ghoshal also had been trying to organise the Blast Furnace workers. The mounting demands and grievances of the BF workers and the lethargic responses of the recognised union INTUC and its pro-management image paved the way for the emergence of an independent BF workers union. In defiance of the INTUC, independent unions had started emerging from the Personnel as well as the fire brigade departments also. All these new unions were not affiliated to any political parties and the management was finding it difficult to control them.

Hemant Deshmukh, the nominated leader of the INTUC union had been turning insensitive to the growing disenchantment of the employees towards him as well as his 'pocket' union. Mr. Chandulal Chandrakar the Congress MP was it's name sake president which left ample room for it's Vice-President, Mr. Sukumaran also to exercise power. As long as Mr. Sukumaran maintained his position in the union, most of the Malayalees, including the communist minded, considered him as their guardian angel.

It was at this period that a young man aspiring for leadership of the union caught the imagination of the INTUC followers. Mr. Ravi Arya appeared to be sensitive to the employees' problems, more democratic, and sometimes even anti-management. In the initial stage, he had no problem in meeting me and Mr. Neel Ratan Ghoshal also to seek the support of our independent unions to put pressure on the management to solve some problems of his own supporters. So while the old leaders were gradually losing their credibility, Mr. Ravi Arya was emerging as a rallying point for the disenchanted union followers. He forged his way to become General Secretary of the INTUC union, replacing Mr. Hemant Deshmukh. It was the elevation of Mr. Arya to the leadership that forced the two senior leaders of the INTUC, Mr. G. P. Sharma and Mr. Bhagavan Das Beri to become rebels.

The BSP management and its recognised union, INTUC, received a real shock when all the works in the Blast Furnace came to a standstill in the second shift one day. In the first shift some workers had gherao-ed their officer for a few hours under the leadership of the secretary of the BF union, Mr. P. S. Nair.

Of course, a complaint was lodged with the police by the BSP management. Mr. Nair was taken into custody by the police when he reached home after duty hours. The news spread like wild fire. The unprecedented outcome was an instant strike in all the Blast Furnaces. The demand was Nair's unconditional release. For the first time in the history of the steel plant, management had to eat humble pie and surrender before the unity of the workers of the BF. Normalcy could be restored only after Nair was released and brought back to the plant to be presented before the striking workers.

We recognised our power to become an alternate to the recognized union. We were elated. Our morals were boosted.

It was bonus time for the steel workers and our independent unions came forward to lead an agitation in support of 20% bonus in place of the minimum 4% paid in the previous years. Our demand was based on the consistent profit making of the Bhilai Steel Plant, as compared to the other SAIL units. An office was opened in Sector 4, at the residence of a senior CPM activist, Mr. S. K. Moitra. It was here that the leaders of the four independent unions and the rebels of the INTUC, Mr. G. P. Sharma and Bhagavan Das Beri assembled together to decide the course of the agitation. The leftist unions CITU and AITUC remained assiduously aloof from this agitation.

The agitation started with slogan shouting at the four gates of the steel plant. The assemblage went on swelling day by day, till one day over 40,000 steel employees of the four shifts went to duty wearing black badges provided by the independent unions.

Finding the ground slipping away fast from under his feet, Mr. Arya also came out with the demand of 20% bonus. In addition, he also threatened to start an indefinite strike if the management failed to concede to the demand within 20 days. He announced a relay-hunger strike for 20 days before resorting to a strike. Though we, the independent union leaders, were certain that Mr. Arya's only intention was to snatch away our support base and to derail our agitation, an overwhelming number of the steel workers thought otherwise. They were enthused and happy that the recognised union had taken up the leadership of the bonus agitation. I felt a little shaken to see our comrades-in-arms, Mr. Sharma and Mr. Beri also sitting in the hunger strike pandal, along with Mr. Arya, on the morning on the first day of the relay- hunger strike. They had been with us only the previous day, till late night, discussing our future strategy.

Mr. Arya's movement turned out to be a grand success, leaving me and my comrades high and dry. Our agitation petered out soon while Arya's 'show' gained momentum. Steel employees of various departments came out in thousands in procession to welcome and garland the INTUC leaders sitting on hunger strike. In twenty days not less than 30000 employees visited the hunger strike pandal at Sector 1 to join hands with Arya.

On the day of conclusion of the hunger strike, a secret strike ballot was held through which 100% of the voters opted for an indefinite strike in support of the 20% bonus!

True to the employees' spirit, Ravi Arya declared the date for the beginning of the strike. And the employees waited with bated breath for the D-day. Administration and police made all arrangements to handle any possible situation. A total strike in the whole steel plant was unbelievable but still possible. The entire steel township of Bhilai was caught up in a tense atmosphere after it had been converted into a vast police camp.

Meanwhile rumors circulated about summons to Arya from New Delhi. It raised expectations about the possibility of getting the demand fulfilled without going for a strike. Arya did not return to Bhilai till the date of the proposed strike had passed and not one of his union supporters was visible anywhere. Subsequently, news was circulated that Arya had agreed to withdraw the strike call with the steel ministry's offer to pay Rs. 100 in addition to the 4% minimum bonus. It was also rumored that Arya had been faced with the option of accepting the Rs. 100 or going to Tihar Jail.

There arose a great deal of resentment over the news. Predictions were made about the angry steel workers lynching Ravi Arya on his return to Bhilai. Nothing of the sort happened. The steel workers silently accepted the minimum bonus, laced with an additional Rs. 100. And Ravi Arya became the unchallenged labour leader of the Bhilai Steel Plant, enjoying a status greater than that of even a Director, SAIL.

The bonus agitation had exposed Ravi Arya's intention of becoming more of a management man and less of an honest and dedicated labour leader. After the bonus movement, both the Management and the INTUC became more apprehensive about the growing influence of the independent unions. It had become imperative to destroy these unions to enable the INTUC to maintain it's monopoly over the employees. A two-pronged strategy was adopted to break the morale of our supporters. Both I and Neelratan Ghoshal were portrayed as Naxalite sympathisers, working in collusion with the well known Naxalite, Shankar Guha Neyogi. Nobody knew that my association with Neyogi was on the condition that Neyogi would renounce the Naxalite path for ever. Our activists were threatened with dismissal from service in case of their continued association with us. On the other hand, they were offered the choice of contesting elections in the INTUC and becoming its leaders. The threat of dismissal on the one side and the allurement of leadership on the other side were good enough for most of our activists to shift their allegiance to the INTUC union. Barring a few hard core supporters, most of our union activists deserted our unions and opted to contest elections as INTUC members. Interestingly every one of them won the elections.

It was a masterly stroke on the part of Ravi Arya as well as the BSP management to accept a democratic process to elect the representatives and office bearers of the recognized Union (INTUC) through secret ballot, an unheard of development in the history of the Congress Unions. The whole credit for forcing INTUC union to go for democratic elections periodically goes to our Independent unions. It paved the way for the end of monopoly of some discredited leaders. Now workers could elect representatives of their own choice. It had been the periodical democratic elections that sustained the Steel Workers Union for decades as the most powerful and 'exemplary' model for labour unions. All jargons mouthed by leftist unions and the revolutionary gimmicks of others have failed to make a dent for quite a long time.

Chapter 12

Emergency

It was after a long separation that on 28th June 1975, Neyogi came to meet me in my Sector 4 quarter. Living there with my wife and a year old son, I had been busy with my trade union activities. Moreover I had stopped supporting Neyogi financially after he had started his goat business and he had also ceased to be dependent on me. He told me that he had come just to warn me about the possibility of my arrest. He said that following the declaration of national emergency he had been arrested under IPC Section 151 and later released on bail from the court. He told me that in the police station, he had heard my name being taken in connection with my detention. I should remain prepared for arrest and make arrangements with someone to stand for my bail.

1975 was the year when the country was undergoing a major political turbulence. People were faced with mounting un-employment, price-rise and rampant corruption. They were angry with the central government, led by the then prime minister, Ms. Indira Gandhi. Though the whole country got excited and agitated after a court verdict was pronounced, disqualifying her from continuing as PM, internal emergency was the last thing expected by anyone.

When the news of imposition of national emergency on 26th June 1975 appeared in the news papers, I could not appreciate its possible implications on my life - till Neyogi came to tell me about the probability of my arrest.

Policemen came looking for me at home, late at night on 4th July, after the Central Government had banned all social and political organisations opposed to the Congress rule. They had to return empty handed because I was in the plant attending night duty. They told my wife to inform me to report to the Sector 6 Kotawali police station by 11 am, next morning. They added that from the police station I would be taken directly to the court from where I could be released on furnishing a personal bond.

When I reached the Kotwali by about 11 am, I was surprised to see around 70 to 80 persons already assembled there. Most of them had been awakened from sleep at around midnight and brought to the police station. A few, like me, had come on their own after receiving the police summons. All of us were supposed to be belonging to one or other banned organisations like Jan Sangh, R.S.S., Socialists, Naxalites, Anand Margis and Jamat-e-Islami. We were in a hurry to finish off the formalities of detention as required by the police and get back home as early as possible because none had commited any crime or expected to go to jail. We spent many hours loitering here and there in the police station premises but no response was forthcoming about what the police had intended to do with us.

The intention was revealed only after the S.P. Durg came to the Kotwali and started a very audible telephonic conversation with the police headquarters at Bhopal. There was no question of booking us under IPC section 151 and then releasing us on personal bonds. We were ordered to be arrested under the Maintenance of Internal Security Act (MISA), which had no provision for bail. The Collector came to face us with an uneasy expression to show his regret for having to arrest us under MISA and sent us to the Raipur Central Jail. He expressed hope that we would be released soon as there were no charges as such against us.

A pal of gloom descended on everyone because no one had expected such a turn of events. Many broke down because they had never been confronted with the threat of going to jail. I had been to jail three times, during my college agitation, and so I could maintain my calm. Still, I could not help feeling the tragicomedy of the situation. I was the last person either to be associated with any of the banned organisations fighting to dethrone Ms. Gandhi or bothered about who donned the prime ministerial chair.

Around 60 to 70 MISA detainees, a majority of whom were BSP employees, were taken to the Raipur Central Jail under police escort in two buses provided by the BSP management. Two newly constructed barracks in the new jail were made vacant to house the MISA detainees. We had not taken any food throughout the day and had to sleep with empty stomachs on the first night. But then, most of us were so depressed and emotionally shaken by the bleak future staring at us and our families that no one seemed to be worrying about food.

Next day I woke up in the early morning to the sweet sounds of the Bhajan and Arathi performed by the Jan Sangh and RSS inmates. The bed I occupied was in the centre of barrack no.1. Mr. K. V. Sahadevan occupied the place on my left side and on the right side was an elderly and respectable looking old man, Mr. Ramakant Deshpande, chairman of the Vanvasi Kalyan Ashram. Mr. Lekhiram Agarwal, Mr. Narahari Sai and Mr. Dinkar Dange also had their beds in the same barrack. Mr. Shivkumar Shastri, Mr. Dev Dutt Joshi, Mr. Mahesh Tiwari, Mr. Madan Tiwari, Mr. Vidhya Bhushan Thakur, Mr. Brijlal Verma, Mr. Gautam Singh Thakur, Mr. Anand Kumar Agarwal, Mr. Mahavir Agarwal, Dr. Ramesh Agarwal, Mr. Kalyan Singh Agarwal are some of the other names, I can still recollect. Madhu Limaye, the top Socialite ideologue, had also been detained in the Raipur Central Jail for the first six months, before he was transferred elsewhere. A very colorful person I can still recall was Baba Behari Das alias Gandhiwala Baba who was alleged to be an exploiter of the tribals of Bastar by pretending as the reincarnation of the late Raja Pravinchand Bhangdev.

A constant flow of detainees were brought into jail next day onwards. While most socio-political workers were booked under MISA, the anti-socials were detained under IPC Section 151. Within a month, the two barracks in the new jail were overflowing with prisoners. Most of the non-politicals were sent to the old jail, where the unhygienic barracks were over-crowded and fetid with little provision for water for bathing and flush latrines.

Initially, barring a very few top leaders, all detainees were treated like common criminals in the matter of facilities. There was no morning tea or breakfast. The first half of the day passed in the hustle and bustle of using the limited toilets and bathrooms. By about noon, food not fit for even animal consumption, was served. The sight of dead maggots and cockroaches in the rice was nauseating. The rotis were half raw and the dal watery. The vegetable was boiled without oil or spices. The sight of the food brought forth a chorus of discontentment from the detainees. Many refused to eat the stuff.

In due course each group got together to nominate its respective leader for a jail committee that would interact with the jail authorities. Since the Naxalites, as per their isolation policy, had boycotted the meeting, the jail committee nominated me to represent all the leftists and left extremists. Subsequently, the protests were channelised to confront the jail administration with the demand for better food and better treatment, befitting to political prisoners. As a mark of protest, hundreds of copper eating-plates were thrown down on the cement floor simultaneously, creating a horrific noise. Such confrontations with the jail administration led to severe lathi-charges on a few occasions, causing injuries to many detainees.

Ironically, it was the life-convicts, working as jail officials, who were more eager to beat up MISA detainees than the jail police themselves. I believe it provided the life convicts an outlet to vent their pent up anger and frustration, accumulated through years of suffering, on someone or the other. And it cannot be denied that at least some of the detainees, on account of their attitude and behaviour, might have deserved a beating once in a while!

In everyday social, religious and political gatherings, we come across many people and think that we understand them very well. Actually, we get to know only very little. What we observe is only a fraction of the truth. To know a person well, one must be closeted with that person for at least a few days. A person's true colours show themselves in the course of his twenty four hours of activities. Every action, right from going to the toilet in the morning, brushing of teeth, bathing, eating meals, interacting with others, till he goes to sleep in the night, highlights various shades of his character. The good as well as the bad, concealed within, are bound to be exposed in the course of the twenty four hours of activities.

My previous jail experiences had been in the company of college students, who were young, energetic, chivalrous, helpful and willing to share everything with colleagues. But here, there were grown up and politically and socially motivated men, fighting tooth and nail to defend their selfish ends. This was visible in front of the toilets, washing and bathing places, in the distribution of food and clothes. Everyone was for himself. Except for a very few, I found most of the political and social leaders and activists - mean to the core.

It was only in jail that I learned that good men are good men and bad men are bad men, irrespective of the society, religion or political party they belong to or the ideology they believe in. Even in the jail, while there were a few gems of human characters in all sections, most were found to be carriers of unrefined minds.

Mr. Ramakant Deshpande, whose bed was adjacent to mine, appeared to me a selfless and enlightened soul, devoted to the welfare of his fellow beings. I wondered how an honest, learned and confirmed Marxist of long standing, Mr. Deshpande, could ultimately turn to

The Bhagavat Geetha and become a confirmed RSS activist. Though our ideologies were diametrically opposed to each other's, as human beings, we got very close to each other by sharing our experiences in life.

As a result of over three months' prolonged agitation within the jail itself, the government did finally accord political status to the MISA detainees. We were put in MISA Class 1 and MISA Class 2, in accordance with our economic and educational status. We thus became entitled to better food, better clothes and other facilities. And, by that time all the anti-socials detained under IPC Section 151, had been released on bail.

Surprisingly, the first three months of jail life saw me cured of many of my 'incurable' and chronic diseases. Prior to my detention, I had been suffering regular bouts of indigestion which led to extreme physical weakness. I had been reduced to skin and bones and even feared imminent death. Allopathic and Ayurvedic treatments for more than a year had failed to give me respite. At the time of my internment in jail, I was not in a position to retain food in my stomach for more than 10 minutes. But, wonderfully, the first three months in jail without my usual medicines, tea, coffee, cigarettes and oily and spicy food did the magic! No trace of indigestion! My digestive system on its own had become quite normal.

All MISA detainees, who were in government or semi-government services, were dismissed from their jobs and their families evicted from their official quarters. Wives and children of the detainees were left to fend for themselves without resources or even a roof over their heads. The fear created by the Emergency was so overpowering that even the closest friends and relations were afraid to visit or extend help to the family of a MISA detainee.

At the time of my detention there was neither savings nor money left at home. However, to provide some succor to my wife and year old child, some of my Malayalee friends managed to get a teaching job for Namita in the KG classes run by the Bhilai Malayala Grandhasala

(BMG). I had never been serious about my own job. But now, Namita thought of fully qualifying herself for a job. So she also joined the B.Ed. classes in the Kalyan College, Sector 7. It was a testing period for her and our son. My in-laws came over from Calcutta to spend some time with their daughter and grandchild.

On receipt of my dismissal orders through the postal service in the jail, I wrote back to the BSP management to make my final payment with as much alacrity as they had shown while dismissing me from service. To be honest, it took not more than a week for some BSP executives to visit me in jail with my final payment checks for about Rs. 1.5 lakhs. BSP also arranged for the SBI officials of Raipur to visit the Central Jail and open an account in my name so that I could deposit my checks. Later, this facility was extended to all other BSP employees who were dismissed while in jail. I had debts of around Rs. 50,000 with a few of my friends. So, I asked my wife to pay them off and keep the rest for herself.

Namita was allowed to visit me once every month. She came to visit me from Bacheli every month with a bundle of books, many a bundles of beedies and cigarettes and many packets of sweets. These I shared with my barrack mates. It was a tiring day for her – travelling, with a big baggage, by bus and tempo up to the jail and then back again. Everything that she brought for me, and I shared with my colleagues, was so precious during our captivity that my colleagues were almost as eager and anxious for her visits. Once her parents accompanied her to visit me in jail but no one from my own family bothered. They thought that my detention was only a befitting punishment for my rebellious life.

In 1976, Namita succeeded in fetching a PG teacher's job in the Kendriya Vidyalaya at Bacheli in Bastar. Thinking that managing a year old child along with a full time job, single-handedly would be too difficult to manage by their daughter, my in-laws took away our two year old son, Dilip, along with them to Calcutta. So, my son at his tender age had to live without the care of his mother and father. Namita continued to work at Bacheli till my release from jail, after 20 months and 20 days of detention.

The constitution had been amended by the Congress government to snatch away even our fundamental rights, denying us the right to seek justice in a court of law. It was an unheard of draconian measure against MISA detainees – a measure not applied even in the case of today's terrorists!

For the first three months, some detainees, including those belonging to RSS, kept themselves busy filing habeas-corpus petitions in courts and sending letters seeking pardon to the government, with expectations of a quick release. Later, it became clear that so long as Ms. Indira Gandhi remained in power, the future of the MISA detainees were bleak and uncertain.

While in jail, I came in contact with some Naxalites also. A few of them were already known to me through my ex-Naxalite colleague, Neyogi. As in the case of Neyogi, the alleged Naxalites were arrested immediately after the declaration of Emergency and then released on bail. However, they all jumped bail and went underground. The only one, who was detained along with me was Mr. Sahadevan. Eventually, Mr. J. B. Singh, Mr. Neel Ratan Ghoshal, Mr. Samarnath Ghoshal, Mr. R. S. Dey, Mr. Sivaraman, Mr. Deepak Bose, Mr. Shankar Guha Neyogi, Mr. Tijau Ram, Mr. Mangal Das and many others were rounded up and brought to jail as alleged Naxalites.

Though I had never embraced the Naxalite ideology of annihilating people, I had a sort of awe and respect for them because of their willingness to make supreme sacrifices to 'liberate' the people from exploitation and oppression. But I was rudely shocked when I saw a few of their specimen from close quarters in the jail. They invariably suffered from verbosity of text book revolutionary jargons; were secretive and dictatorial. They were intolerant of any idea that differed from their own and told blatant lies to prove themselves right. They suffered from a persecution psychology and brimmed over with misplaced ambition, envy, cowardice and hatred.

I recall one Mr. Deepak Bose, a Naxalite who threatened to smash my head on the jail wall on account of my differing views and who appeared to me an embodiment of the said Naxalite 'virtues'! He would dole out false stories about the people's armies, made of peasants and workers, marching from Paton- Selud and Gunderdehi towards Bhilai and Raipur to encircle them and the imminent possibility of capturing them. He carried a body with heavy weight and appeared breathless while talking about his own revolutionary adventures. His blood shot eyes told how passionate and excited he was about the Naxalite path of revolution. Then there was one Mr. Sivaraman, who claimed to be a mentor and guide of the Naxalites. I have yet to come across a person who was so mean and cowardly and capable of telling blatant lies like Mr. Sivaraman.

I have never come across a living Naxalite who was guided by the spirit of love and compassion for the suffering humanity. Their only motive was an unquenching thirst for political power through violence and bloodshed. They had no faith in the people or their mandate. Invariably, each one of them behaved like autocrats and dictators.

After about three months, life in the jail settled down. Many of the leaders preferred to live privately and keep to their own, enjoying the facilities accorded to them. But the majority of us decided to pool the facilities provided by MISA Class 1 and Class 2 and share it with all. To serve that purpose, we started a 'Janatha Mess' in the jail much before the Janatha Party was formed. Jail authorities provided us with convicted prisoners in order to run the mess and do other sundry jobs. The prisoners were more than happy to oblige because of the favours and good treatment they received from us.

Neyogi stayed underground for about six months in villages near Danitola Mines prior to his arrest and internment in Central Jail. Though he was also brought to the same barrack where I was, I assiduously kept a little distance from him. We seldom spoke to each other. He looked on disdainfully at my free interaction with the jail authorities and other inmates and spent most of his time in the company of Bengali comrades. So, when one day he approached me with a request for a talk, I refused. But when he kept on pleading in a painful posture, I relented.

Neyogi took me to an isolated corner and handed over to me a post card he had received from one Mr. Dushyant Tiwari of the SKMS union. He had written that he was writing at the behest of Shia Ram of Danitola Mines as he himself was an illiterate tribal. It was to inform Neyogi that Shia's eldest daughter, Asha Bai, when rigorously grilled about her advanced pregnancy, had held Neyogi responsible for it. Shia Ram, an illiterate manual labourer in the Danitola Mines, had many a times fed and sheltered Neyogi in his home. Shia wanted a reply from Neyogi about what he planned to do with his daughter and her illegal pregnancy.

The contents of the letter left me speechless. But I was more stunned by his silence and furtive glances. After a long pause, he finally opened his mouth to ask me what he should do. From inside I grieved over having wasted so much of my life and resources for creating such an animal who could bite the hand that had fed and sheltered him.

I retorted that it was for him and not me to know what to do.

"How can you spoil the life of an illiterate and innocent tribal girl whose family gave you food and shelter and faced police atrocities to protect you?" I asked.

As an afterthought, I added, "When people come to know they will pelt you with stones and chase you out like a mad dog. This will be the end to all our efforts for revolution in Chhattisgarh. I will neither talk to you nor entertain any contact with you till you have taken steps to make Asha Bai your wife." With that, I went away.

I knew that Neyogi had been hiding in the forests near and around Danitola Mines for about six months because of the police pressure on the nearby villagers to trace him out. He could not have survived so long without the active support of Shia Ram and his family. I guessed that Shia Ram, out of his tribal innocence, might have employed his daughter, Asha to take food to Neyogi and she would have fallen a victim to his carnal passions during her frequent presence all alone with him in the thick forest.

It took him three hours to decide and return to inform me that he was willing to make Asha his wife. He said that it was very difficult for him to take such a decision but with my support he would certainly stand by his commitment. I was willing to give him all support in the matter. I had known Asha and her father since a long time because Neyogi had chosen Danitola as his field of work. Shia had earned my respect due to his innocent, brave and trustworthy character and I was more than happy to be of help to save his daughter from shame and doom.

I managed to contact Shia through my wife and assured him about the future of his daughter. He was told to tell his neighbours about Asha's marriage with Neyogi, while he was living underground. I made monetary arrangements for Shia to take care of her pregnancy as well as delivery. Later, after receiving news of Asha's delivery, I organised a tea party in the new jail in order to cover up the matter from the general public, with cakes and bakeries brought by Namita! When the participants asked about the occasion, I told that my comrade, Neyogi, had been blessed with a daughter. No one embarrassed us by asking when he had married or whom!

The girl child lived without a name till Neyogi was released from jail a year later and had taken Asha for his wife. Later, he christened his daughter, Kranti (Revolution), to symbolize the 'revolution' of owning a tribal woman as his wife! The grip of the Naxalite utopia was so powerful over him that he could not help naming his next two children, Mukti (Liberation) and Jeet (Victory). Perhaps Neyogi, like other Naxalites, lived in delusion and deception and believed in an illusory world where revolution, liberation and victory had already followed one after the other!

I had never come across a more self-centered leader than Neyogi who could declare "I am the leader, I am the ideology and I am the party" All communists appeared to me as self centered and dictatorial and intolerant of others views.

All protests against the Emergency fizzled out within the first six months. Even the image of the socialist leader, George Fernandez, in chains and hand cuffs, had failed to infuse the youth with impulses for continuing the fight. Censorship was total. The media went crawling even when it was asked only to bend. The whole country was in the grip of fear and panic. Ms. Gandhi's younger son, Sanjay Gandhi, became an extra constitutional power-center that dictated the functioning of the government. The arbitrary arrest and detention of thousands of leaders and political workers from all over the country, denial to them their fundamental rights through overnight amendments in the constitution, forcible sterilization of thousands and thousands of unwilling youths and demolition of urban slums for beautification of cities created so much fear and panic that the whole nation fell into a deathly silence, the silence of the grave yard.

But, the MISA detainees within the four walls of their jails did not remain silent. When the whole nation fell into a silent mode, the political detainees felt free to speak out their minds boldly. They spent their days in jail holding daily meetings and making fiery speeches against the Congress, Ms. Indira Gandhi and her dictatorial rule. They also belaboured the communists for supporting Ms. Gandhi and called them the lackeys of the Soviet Union.

We inmates came to know of the news of the massacre of the Bangla Desh Prime Minister, Mr. Mujibur Rehman, and his entire family. Many among us liked to interpret the ghastly event as a warning signal to Ms. Indira Gandhi also. When news reached us that Ms. Lillian Carter, mother of the then American President, Mr. Jimmy Carter, was coming to India with a letter from the President to Mrs. Gandhi, our hopes rose sky high and jubilation knew no bounds. The White House pronounced that future U.S. relations with India would be dependent on the reply to the letter. America, being a staunch supporter of democracy, everyone loved to interpret it as a warning to Ms. Gandhi to bring the Emergency to an end and to conduct elections which were long overdue.

Thanks to the American pressure, parliamentary elections were declared and leaders were ordered to be freed from jail. The grave like silence of the people in the course of Emergency had been interpreted by Ms. Gandhi as the people's consent to her dictatorial rule! The opposition parties also had no idea about the mood of the people but they had to, perforce, come together against the dictatorial government, irrespective of their differences and opposing ideologies.

Mr. Jaya Prakash Narayan, the architect of the total revolution which had led to the declaration of Emergency, was instrumental in cobbling together all the parties opposed to the Congress to form the Janata Party. However, there was not much rush for Janata Party tickets because the political aspirants were neither aware of the peoples' mood nor confident of victory. They were apprehensive of the severe consequences they would face in case of Ms. Gandhi's returning to power. It was only after a great deal of pressure and persuasion that even a humble and junior activist of Jan Sangh like Mr. Mohanlal Jain, could be made to agree to contest from the Durg Parliamentary Constituency. Before leaving jail, to file his nomination papers, he confided to me that in him, his party had found its most suitable sacrificial goat!

The subservient masses spoke at long last. The election results stunned the entire world. The silent voice of the people had thundered out its verdict in definite terms. The Indian people had voted against dictatorship! It meted out a thumping victory to the Janata Party and a most humiliating defeat to Ms. Gandhi and her Congress Party. On 21 March, 1977, orders were out for the immediate release of all MISA detainees. The administration at the Raipur Central Jail had to work overtime and in haste to fulfill the formalities of over two hundred MISA detainees before their release could be affected.

When the jail gates were thrown open there was an ocean of people in front of the jail surging forward to welcome the prisoners with flowers and colours. The whole atmosphere was effervescent with people dancing and singing all around in jubilation. Somehow, I could not bring myself to feel much elation because till then, neither had Ms. Gandhi resigned nor had the Emergency been withdrawn. My foremost thought was that with a pliant President at her command, there was no guarantee that Ms. Gandhi would not try a military takeover to crush her opposition.

Since there was no guarantee that I would not be rounded up before reaching home, I decided to not proceed to Bhilai along with the other detainees but to go to Bacheli in Bastar, to my wife - unobtrusively.

The misgivings that rankled in my mind about the future developments in the country were proved wrong. Ms. Gandhi did resign; Emergency was withdrawn and Mr. Moraji Desai was sworn in as Prime Minister.

I spent a week in Bacheli before returning to my brother's home at Bhilai, thinking that my mother would be there. But she had returned to her own home in Kerala after my internment. That I had gone to see my wife first, rather than to him in Bhilai, aggrieved my brother no end. He had felt ashamed to be associated with me during my stay in jail, and had, therefore, not visited me even once. Yet, he felt highly offended and insulted when he found himself unable to produce me before the hundreds of people who had come to meet me, at his home, on the day of my release.

Bhilai Steel Plant was prompt in reinstating the dismissed employees with half-back wages and offered them accommodations as per their eligibility. I joined duty in my original department, the Coke Ovens, and occupied a new quarter in Sector 10, before going back to Bacheli. Namita resigned her job and together, we went to Calcutta to bring back our son.

The real impact that the Emergency had on my family life was revealed only after I found my son cringing away from both his parents. He was so shy and scared of everyone, including his parents, that he sought refuge in isolation, preferably behind a door or under a cot. We thought that it was a temporary phenomenon, but later years proved that fear had infiltrated his mind and shattered his self confidence. Long isolation at a very tender age, from the love and care of his parents, may have severely distorted his vision about human relationships.

In the post emergency period, I had decided to put an end to my association with Neyogi and concentrate only on Bhilai. MISA detainees, who had been dismissed from the Bhilai Steel Plant, were not satisfied with their reinstatement orders. They wanted full back wages, continued seniority and due promotions, just as if they had not been dismissed at all. So, over a hundred Ex-MISA employees of BSP, belonging to all parties, gathered at my residence in Sector 10 and formed a 'MISA Detainees Association' with me as president and Mr. Narhari Tripathy, an RSS man, as secretary. Our mission was to visit central ministers at Delhi to plead the case of MISA detainees.

I had the good opportunity of watching politicians change colours like chameleons, as per the situation. Many who had been cringing and crying in the jail, had become MPs and ministers. Some central ministers like Mr. Purushotamlal Kaushik, Mr. Brijlal Verma, Mr. Narhari Sai had been our inmates in the jail for 19 months. Biju Patnaik, the Steel Minister, had also been a MISA detainee. Not being a member of any party and hence not being bound by any party discipline, I felt no hesitation in confronting the concerned ministers directly and demanding immediate redressal of our grievances. It did not take more than a month and three visits to Delhi for all our demands to be met. Once free from that responsibility of the MISA detainees, I explored the possibility of building up a 'Janata Union,' as an alternate to INTUC.

I had never got more than Rs. 500 or 600 as salary while on duty because of absenteeism and deductions against loans I had availed. Only after I received Rs. 42,000 as my full back wages for the 21 months that I had been intered in jail, did I come to realise that my monthly salary had been over Rs. 2000! It was the first time in my life that I held such a handsome amount in my hands. What an irony! With a job I had always been in debt, but now, without having done any job, I had got such a handsome amount! So it was my long detention and dismissal from service that ultimately empowered me to purchase a scooter and a fridge for the first time!

I had established a Janta Union for the steel workers of the Bhilai Steel Plant, on the suggestion and support of the Socialist (Janta Party) MP from Rajnandgoan, Mr. Madan Tiwari. Mr. Gautam Singh Thakur (RSS), Mr. Kunjram Sahu (Anand Marg), Mr. Bodhan Singh, Mr. Tribhuvan Nath Pande, Mr. Chinta Mani Mishra (Socialists), Mr. Neel Ratan Ghoshal and Mr. Samarnath Ghoshal (Naxalites) and Mr. Sulaiman Khan(Jamaet-e- Islami) were a few, among others, who had worked actively to build up the Janta Union as a labour front of the Janta Party.

But as time went by, I became disenchanted with the lack of courage and commitment of my co-union workers who wanted to use the union only as another paper union for their personal benefits. It was at this stage that the news of the 2nd Jun, 1977 police firing on the mines workers of Dalli-Rajhara, reached my ears.

My previous week-long trips to the Rajnandgoan jail as a student leader, could be termed as 'picnics' when compared to the 20 months and 20 days long stint in the Raipur Central Jail where there had been no certainty of release or duration of detention. During my college days I had been a bachelor. Now I had a family to take care of. My job had been snatched away. I had no savings to sustain my family.

Mr. S. R. Ramakrishnan, Chief Superintendant of Coke Ovens, who had known me from the age of 16, when I had first joined the Coke Ovens, had thoughtfully sent his emissary to my wife, offering any kind of personal help. She had declined.

As fate would have it, my life as well as my future was completely in the hands of no less a person than Ms. Gandhi, the Prime Minister, whom I had not harmed even in my dreams! She had taken away even my fundamental right to seek justice in a court of law. It was a very depressing and helpless situation. A few among the detainees, including an alleged Naxalite, bemoaned day and night, the tragedy that had befallen them. But, as there was no way out, I chose to put up a brave countenance. Between the option of crying and laughing, I chose the latter. Why not have a good laugh at the irony of the situation and leave the rest to the future to decide?

I utilised my time in jail, participating in the functioning of the Janata Mess in the new jail, where food for about 150 MISA detainees was cooked. Some time I spent playing games as well as taking a daily hour long evening walk. The rest of my time went in reading books that Namita used to keep me abundantly supplied with.

Being a member of the Jail Committee, I had permission to roam around other barracks and visit the jail hospital, situated within the jail compound. The hospital, which was managed single handedly by a physically handicapped doctor, used to cater to the needs of over three thousand prisoners. Of course, the 'para-medical staff' like compounders and nurses were picked from among the long term convicts themselves.

It was the convicts who dressed, injected and sometimes even operated upon the patients!

I recall being an eye-witness to a family planning operation that had been conducted on an under-trial. The patient lay still on a wooden bench placed in a dirty room. The operation in progress was being performed by a convict. It was at the nick of the moment, that the doctor standing nearby, shouted out urgently that the bundle of thin tubes being lifted by the 'doctor' convict to cut into two, were blood transmitting veins and not the ones to be cut! It had been only incidental that the doctor had noticed in time. This was a part of the forced sterilisation programme that had been carried out during Emergency and the doctor was in need of extra hands to fulfill the quota fixed for him!

Almost all barracks in the old jail were filled with the stench of excreta and urine and most of the inmates were infested with lice and bedbugs. They had blistering sores and eruptions on their skins. Most of the inmates belonged to the poorest classes and so were under constant fear of abuses and physical assaults on the flimsiest grounds. Day to day life for them was one of perpetual fear!

The most enriching experience of my life during this time was listening to the thoughts and experiences undergone by the murder convicts before and after they had committed the crime. Patiently and with a great deal of sensitivity, I elicited from them the minutest details of the situations that had led to the crimes and also the bearings they had on the convicts' minds and later lives. For almost a year I spent my time probing the inner recesses of the minds of these unfortunate and unhappy people, who were mostly poor and illiterate or semi-literate. It gave me a great insight into the human folly of playing into the hands of ego, pride and arrogance as well as the fallacy of the all-blinding, ill founded fearlessness of men in hot rage.

For a split second, a murderer has no fear of either God or the police. But once the crime has been committed, he remains under the constant grip of fear. Though while undergoing punishment, a few convicts become more hardened, most start grieving and repenting for their follies and the damage and destruction they have caused to themselves and their families. On a few occasions, I had even witnessed some of them crying like children and shedding hot tears in isolation and loneliness.

Jail life provided me an opportunity to keenly watch the life of the most accursed section of society. My spirit and sense of empathy for the suffering humanity was greatly enriched. I had seen and heard the cursed, the humiliated and the intimidated. Central Jail was the place where I had witnessed it from very close quarters. I had no inkling about what the future lay in store for me and my family, but it was then that I realsied that I would have to dedicate the rest of my life to fight for the poor and the oppressed.

Chapter 13

Post Emergency

News about the turbulences and upheavals that had taken place among the manual mines workers of the nearby Dall-Rajhara Mines, during the last phase of Emergency, reached Neyogi as soon as he reached Danitola, after his release from jail. This was the big opening he had been waiting for. Since over a decade, he had been relentlessly struggling to emerge as a big and famous leader. But all he could achieve so far was the leadership of around 200 contract labourers of Danitola Mines, in addition to the stamp of being a Naxalite.

Over 11,000 manual workers were engaged in the Dalli-Rajhara Mines by labour cooperative societies and transport contractors for raising and transporting iron ore. Most of the labourers were members of the communist union, Samyukta Khadan Mazdoor Sangh (SKMS), which was affiliated to the AITUC and the rest were members of Metal Mines Workers Union (MMWU), affiliated to the INTUC. Thanks to a socialist minded Steel Minister at the centre, Mr. Kumarmangalam and the joint efforts of the two unions, 3300 of these contract workers had been regularised in the year 1972. This had entitled them to better service conditions and the status of Bhilai Steel Plant employees. Both the unions promised to regularise the rest of the miners also, turn by turn.

The nature of job being done by both the contract as well as the regularised workers was exactly same but their wages and facilities were poles apart. This had created a permanent discontentment among the contract labourers. Of late, they had begun to hold their own leaders responsible for the delay in their regularisation.

The simmering anger and discontentment among the contract workers had boiled over by the time their union leaders signed a bonus agreement at the fag end of the Emergency, on 3rd March, 1977. As per the agreement, the contract workers were offered an interim relief of a paltry Rs. 70 while the regularised workers got Rs. 308. Unmindful of the Emergency, the more than 8000 deprived contract workers rebelled against their own unions which had so blatantly cheated them. Mr. Bansilal Sahu, a semi-literate activist of the SKMS union, spearheaded this rebellion.

The contract labourers consisted of illiterate and semiliterate Chhattisgarhis as well as quite a good number of tribals. The trade union leaders, on the other hand, were non-Chattisgarhis. The miners blamed the non-Chhattisgarhi leadership for their brazen exploitation and turned their faces away from the 'outsiders.' They struck work for 21 days in protest of the agreement signed by their erstwhile leaders and signed a new agreement with the management on 23 March 1977, for Rs. 50 only. It was an act of total rejection of their former non-Chhattisgarhi leaders, and celebration of their own freedom that had led them to agree to an even lesser amount!

Destiny of this rebellious group of mines workers appeared to have been already written. Neyogi was also released from jail on this very 23 March 1977. When he reached Rajhara the next day, he found Bansilal Sahu in a meeting with about 400 labour chiefs (Mukhiyas) of his 8000 followers. Neyogi, with his unshaven face and worn out and dirty clothes, remained an unobserved intruder in the assembly for a long time.

His face betrayed him for what he was, a non-Chhattisgarhi, an outsider and the most unwanted of persons in that crowd. However, he skillfully used his appearance as an ordinary labourer and the little

Chhattisgarhi language he could speak to allay the apprehensions of the gathering and its leader, Bansilal Sahu. After all they were all uneducated, inexperienced and lacking in confidence in themselves. Neyogi introduced himself as an independent leader of the Danitola mines workers who had to fight with the earstwhile leaders all along. He narrated the hardships he had undergone, including his imprisonment in jail during emergency for fighting for the cause of the Danitola workers. He blamed the INTUC and AITUC leaders for betraying him to the police. With his oratory skill and knowledge of the union matters, Neyogi could manage to worm into the confidence of Mr. Sahu. And he was armed with a firm determination and an insatiable hunger for leadership. He knew that he coud cerainly bring them into his fold before long and without much difficulty.

In the company of Mr. Bansilal, Neyogi addressed scores of small meetings of miners in all nooks and corners of Dalli and Rajhara. In intelligence, cleverness and inflammatory oration, Bansilal was no match for Neyogi. Initially, though he donned the mantle of Bansilal's right hand man, it took merely 15 days for Neyogi to emerge as the stronger of the two and acquire a greater appeal for the miners. Bansilal, not being cunning himself, was unable to discern that Neyogi was only using him for the time being, as a front before he could usurp the leadership of the miners for his own. Neyogi returned to Danitola only after convincing the rebelling workers of the need to register a new union to fight for their demands and bargain with the management.

Thus was paved the path for the emergence of a 'Mazdoor Messiah!'

8000 mines workers under his very control!

Neyogi could not believe his luck! He was, however intelligent enough to realise that now his destiny was tied up with the soil of Chhattisgarh. He felt my need once again. But, he knew he could not approach me without honouring the promise he had made to me while in jail. He would have to first settle his problem with Shia Ram's daughter. So, after ensuring his hold on the mines workers of Dalli-Rajhara, the first thing he did was to return to Danitola to settle his marriage problem.

Asha, at a very early age, had been married off to one Tika Ram of village Pateli Pacheda on Dalli-Kokan Road. Tika Ram was summoned to Danitola and a settlement was made between him; Asha's parents, Shia Ram and Mantora Bai and Neyogi. Tika Ram was prevailed upon to 'forget' his marriage with Asha and, in lieu, paid a compensation of Rs. 1000. Asha already had a year old daughter by Neyogi and nothing could be done by Tika Ram other than agree.

So, when Neyogi came to meet me at Bhilai after the lifting of the Emergency, he brought with him the news of his two great achievements. One was his extraordinary luck in grabbing the leadership of 8000 mines' workers at Dalli-Rajhara and two, his marriage to Asha. I congratulated him for setting right his personal record but did not show enthusiasm about his emergence as a big leader. I refused to cooperate when he asked me for help in registering a new union. But I promised to get my friend, Mr. K. P. R. Pillai, to help him. Mr. Pillai had been a founder member of the Marxist Union, CITU at Bhilai and was well conversant with the registration procedure. I also phoo-phooed away Neyogi's suggestion that I ought to resign my job in the BSP and join him as a full timer. I told him not to be so cock sure about me as I would have to think deeply before joining hands with him. He appeared to be disillusioned with my coolness and lack of enthusiasm for his great success at Dalli-Rajhara.

After a week, Neyogi came with a dozen mines workers, including Bansilal Sahu, to Mr. Pillai's Sector 6 quarter to prepare the registration papers. Perhaps because of their inner desire to keep all non-Chhatisgarhis out of their union, none of the workers even suggested Neyogi's name to be included in the list of office bearers. Their intention was to avail the service of Neyogi while keeping him out of the union. The list was finalised with Mr. Bansilal as president, Mr. Nathu Ram Bhandari as Vice-president, Mr. Rai Singh Thakur as General Secretary and Mr. Janaklal Thakur as Treasurer and others as Executive Committee Members.

It was with ingenuity and 'far sightedness' that Mr. Pillai had persuaded Mr. Bansilal and others to also include Neyogi's name as the Organising Secretary. He persuaded them to believe that without his name in the office bearer's list, Neyogi would not be able to complete the formalities of the union registration before the Registrar at Indore.

The Chhattisgarh Mines Shramik Sangh (CMSS) came into existence in Dalli-Rajhara on 29 April, 1977. It unfurled its own red and green flag and heralded in a new chapter in the history of labour movement. Within no time, all office bearers of the CMSS, including the president, were maneuvered to backseats and the Organising Secretary, Neyogi, emerged as the sole leader of the Union. He had at his command, a committed and blindly loyal force of 8000 mines workers, seething with discontent and anger against contractors, management officials and former union leaders.

Within a short time, Neyogi groomed over three hundred whole timers to keep a control over his followers; 200 being from among the transport workers and the rest from among the mining workers. They were freed from the grueling, hard and sweating manual jobs and assured full wages. He personally trained and indoctrinated them to always be on guard against enemies trying to influence and manipulate their Mukhyas as they were ignorant and illiterate. He warned them of conspiracies that would be hatched by the contractors and the management to break up the union by using their own Mukhyas. He told them that he had left his landlord family in Bengal and an engineer's job in the Bhilai Steel Plant to serve the poor from exploitation and oppression. He empowered them to severely punish anyone who dared to speak against the union or him because he was the only target of all the enemies of the union.

With a fighting force in order and completely under his control, Neyogi was able to create an atmosphere of violence, tension and fear in the mines as well as the township. He unleashed agitation after agitation in quick succession, for one or the other demand, leading to daily processions, demonstrations and gheraoes of contractors and BSP officials. In the name of gheraoes, Neyogi's trained force abused and threatened the Contractors and BSP officials and made them stand under the scorching sun for hours without even a glass of water. He kept himself aloof in the background. Though a number of criminal cases were registered against Neyogi and other members of his union, based on complaints received from victims, the law and order machinery found it almost impossible to initiate any action against him for fear of severe consequences.

Subsequently, Neyogi called for a total strike in support of fall back wages for the transport workers. Fall back wage was a guaranteed minimum sum that had to be paid to the worker in the event of a breakdown in the transport vehicle which resulted in loss of his wages for no fault of his. Though the demand pertained to only 2000 transport workers, the entire 6000 mining workers of the CMSS also joined hands. The attempt of the management and administration to provide security to enable the 3300 willing regularised workers of the SKMS union opposed to the strike, to enter the mines premises failed utterly. Bansilal had erected a human wall with the striking miners in order to deny passage to the willing miners. When realisation set in that the blockade could not be removed without resorting to police firing, the administration relented and forced the BSP management and the contractors to enter into a dialogue with Neyogi.

The reconciliation meeting was fixed at the Dalli-Rajhara Guest House. After the representatives of BSP management, contractors and the union had entered the Dall-Rajhara Guest House it was surrounded by thousands of striking miners. Even after over 36 hours, the meeting continued and no agreement could be reached. The adamant and slogan shouting furious crowd would not permit anyone other than their own leaders to come out of the guest house, till the agreement had been signed. Perforce, an agreement on fall back wages was signed by the evening of 31 May 1977.

It was the first victory of the CMSS and that also, within a month of its coming into existence. It catapulted Neyogi's image before his suportes to the sky. In the eyes of the labourers, this 'victory' totally justified the violent methods adopted by Neyogi. In addition, it had created fear and panic among those who were opposed to him. This achievement was flouted to declare the power of the union and its leader Neyogi all over the Dalli-Rajhara Township. A victory procession taken out along the township, culminated in the bringing down and tearing out of the red flag fluttering over the SKMS union office.

Forces opposed to Neyogi clamoured for his arrest. The contractors stated that they had been made captive and coerced into signing the fall back wages agreement. As such, they were not bound to honour it. AITUC and INTUC union leaders also joined the chorus of the contractors to demand Neyogi's arrest.

Just at this time, MP state elections were in progress in the midst of a strong anti-Congress wave. Neyogi, as per a secret understanding with the Congress candidate, Mr. Jhumuklal Bhedia, had fielded the union president, Bansilal Sahu, from Balod to cut into the anti-Congress votes. He also fielded Nathuram Bhandari from Dondi-Lohara with the hope of winning the seat with Mr. Bhedia's support. Bansilal was left alone to take care of his poll campaign. With no loss of time, just when the agreement on fall back wages was fresh in peoples' minds, Neyogi began an intensive poll campaign in Dondi-Lohara, with the help of over three hundred of his whole timers.

Chapter 14

Martyrs Galore

It was 2 June 1977, a fateful day that would be etched deeply in the history of Dalli-Rajhara. Neyogi and around 60–70 of his followers returned to the union office at around 11 pm, after a hectic day of election campaigning. Because of the sweltering heat and a nagging fear of arrest, he had chosen to sleep in the midst of his followers in the open ground.

Neyogi was scared of the police. At the same time, the police and administration were in no way less scared of him! Why else, would they have assiduously planned to awaken Neyogi from his deep slumber in the middle of the night to arrest him? Especially, when he had been sleeping in the open ground amongst his ardent supporters?

When a plain cloth man woke up Neyogi and asked for a glass of water he, in half sleep, pointed out to the 'Matkas' kept at a distance. Before Neyogi could regain his normal senses, four sturdy men lifted him bodily and carried him towards the police jeep parked nearby. As soon as the policemen grabbed him, he screamed piercingly, "Bachao! Bachao! Mere Fel-lo!" Before his half-awake followers realised what was happening, Neyogi had been thrust into the waiting jeep and whisked away.

Another group of rifle-wielding policemen had been standing in front of a police van kept ready for follow up action. The mayhem created by the now fully awake miners, awakened the rest of the inmates of the labour camp nearby and thousands of voices joined the cacophony.

Men and women started pouring into the open ground, waving their lathis above their heads, screaming and shouting. The crowd spotted the police van parked at a distance and ran towards it to save Neyogi, believing that he had been kept in it. The furious and uncontrolled crowd racing towards them, so scared the police, that they started firing at the oncoming crowd. When even the firing of many rounds had not made any impact on the maddened crowd, they turned on their heels and sped away in the van. An officer and two constables, who had not been able to reach the van ahead of the crowd, were left behind.

7 dead bodies and a few seriously injured were scattered in the open field. The furiously agitated mob caught hold of the policemen, disrobed them of their uniforms and thrashed them till they lost consciousness. The dead bodies of the miners and the naked bodies of the unconscious policemen were laid down side by side in the middle of the crowd. All injured miners were furtively sent to private hospitals to hide them from the police. It was a miracle that the maddened crowd had not beaten the policemen to death or lynched them.

Within a matter of minutes the entire ground was filled with over 8000 mines workers and their women and children who kept on shouting slogans for the return of Neyogi and the arrest of those who had fired to kill the sleeping miners! Not one from the administration or the police dared to approach the furious crowd for the next 8 hours.

In the morning, at about 8.30 am, police arrived in huge forces, in dozens of vehicles and encircled the ground from all sides. Public announcements were made to order the mob to disperse and hand over the captive policemen. The crowd also had managed a mike to announce their refusal and demand immediate return of Neyogi. Announcements of the administration and counter announcements of the crowd continued for hours, without any change in the inflamed situation.

Meanwhile, the fate of the seriously injured policemen, who had slowly regained consciousness and pleaded for water, was even worse.

Urine was forced down their gullets by the irate men and women. By 12 noon, curfew was clamped on the entire township, including the labour camps. The mob was ordered to disperse forthwith or face police firing. No one budged. Firing started at 12.15 pm. The crowd got scared only after hearing the screams of those who had been hit by bullets and seeing dead bodies falling in their midst. A mad fear for life caught up with the mob, forcing them to run helter-skelter. The field was clear by 12.30 pm, excepting for the dead and the injured. The police rescued the captive policemen and sent them to hospital along with the seriously injured workers, who had been unable to flee.

The 11 dead bodies recovered from the field were cremated en-masse by the police as there were no claimants for them. The fear of the police had seeped in to the extent that the relatives of the dead were not ready to claim the dead bodies of their kin!

All local newspapers carried banner news of the repeated police firings at Dalli Rajhara and imposition of curfew in the township and labour camps. The national media also played it up as a great blot on the Central Janata Government that had come to power fighting against police atrocities during the Emergency. Even the BBC took up the news as a blotch on the new government.

The trepidation and anxiety I felt on reading the news was further heightened at the sight of Shia Ram and his active co-worker, Ankalu Ram, approaching my gate furtively. I realised that they must have come with the news of the Rajhara firings and took them inside and tried to make them relax.

While they were taking tea, two other persons appeared at my gate. They were officers of the police intelligence. To keep them from coming inside, I went out to meet them at the gate, where they asked me if I was aware of the events that had taken place at Rajhara. I told them that I was just reading about it in the newspapers. I, being a leader of the Janata Union, they wanted to know my reaction and whether

I maintained any contact with Neyogi. I told them quite plainly that even though my path differed from that of Neyogi's, I condemned the police firing on the workers for whatever reason it might have been. They tried to probe into my plans for going to Rajhara. When I told them that I had no such plans, they appeared satisfied. Before parting, they opined that it would be best for me to stay away from Dalli-Rajhara.

Shia gave me a detailed narration of the events that had led to the repeated police firings. But whatever he could relate was second hand information as he had gathered it from the Rajhara workers who, out of fear of police atrocities, had fled their own places and sought shelter in the homes of their relations at Danitola. Shia expressed genuine fear that Neyogi would be killed by the police. He asked me to accompany him to Danitola from where he would arrange for my secret passage to Rajhara. He was sure that my presence would help to infuse confidence in the demoralised workers. He had no information about Bansilal Sahu, Janaklal Thakur, Nathuram Bhandari or the other local leaders. All were sure to have fled to nearby villages to protect themselves from the police who were hunting for them.

We reached Danitola on 5 June, late in the night. A few policemen were posted at the mines office. On 6 June, again by late evening, I and Shia found ourselves in one of the labour camps at Rajhara. I had donned Shia's clothes in order to appear like a mines worker and used a bi-cycle to complete the rest of the journey. Curfew was still in force with relaxation for a couple of hours. Rifle wielding policemen were posted in every nook and corner of the labour camps. Shia, however, managed to find ways to evade them and reach his destination. He took me to his distant relation who lived in a mud hut in the middle of one of the labour camps and introduced me as Neyogi's Bhilai comarade and the only one who could guide and lead them in place of Neyogi. He added that I could be fully trusted and depended upon.

The labour camps were heavy with silence, darkness and fear. People moved from one hut to another, silently holding their breaths, for fear of being heard. Slowly, news of the presence of a leader from Bhilai in their midst had spread. Throughout the night, miners came one after the other, to meet me and I spoke to them in a hushed voice. All of them were concerned about Neyogi's safety. I assured them that there was no longer any danger to his life as his arrest had already become public. I tried to embolden them by saying that the situation would soon change for the better and that in due course, their union would emerge stronger. I also waved away their apprehension about there being another police firing for whatever reason. They were uncomfortable when I told them, that had they freed the captive policemen there would not have been a second police firing.

Curfew was lifted two days later. IPC section 144 remained in force, prohibiting assembly of more than four persons. Fear among the workers was so deep that they were not even willing to come out of their houses. When one of the Mukhyas suggested taking out a procession to demand Neyogi's release, everyone opposed it, fearing another brutal attack by the police. After gauging their mental state, I suggested intermittent shouting of slogans only for a few minutes at a time, by five or six men and women from within their homes. I felt that only the united sound of their own voice could free them from their fears. It was accepted by one and all after I agreed to start it myself. At a midnight, I began the slogan shouting with five others, from a hut. It lasted only a few minutes. After a silence of a few anxious minutes, the shouting was repeated from another hut. This went on till the early morning - from hut after hut and camp after camp.

The repeated slogan shouting had a two-pronged effect. Whereas the mines workers were emboldened, policemen were demoralised and subdued. The policemen positioned themselves only at selected points outside the camp and stopped patrolling within. Slogan shouting and non-interference of the police, coupled with daily news in all the news papers about nationwide condemnation and protest against the police firing at Rajhara, bolstered the morale of the workers to the extent that they had started openly taking out small processions and conducting meetings demanding release of their leader. After withdrawal of Section 144, former MISA detainees of Raipur Central Jail, Mr. Purushothamlal Kaushik, now Union Cabinet Minister, Madan Tiwari and Mohanlal Jain, now Janata Party MPs, visited Rajhara and addressed meetings in the township in support of the mines workers.

The non-interference of the police paved the way for the other leaders of the union to come out of hiding and mingle with the workers. It took only about a fortnight for the 8000 strong members of the union to come together again. Daily processions were taken out, demanding Neyogi's release. His bail applications had already been rejected twice. However, in the third attempt on a revision petition by Adv. Kanak Tiwari, Neyogi was ordered to be released on surety of Rs. 20000. It was a CPI leader, Mr. Meghnath Sahu of village Kuthrel, Durg, who stood surety for Neyogi's bail, with his own land records.

In the course of my long stay at Rajhara, I had visited my home only once and attended my duty only for a day. During my stay at Rajhara, I had the entire cooperation and assistance of the leaders of the union. But they, being illiterate, I had to shoulder all matters relating to the union as well as Neyogi's release. After finalising arrangements in consultation with Bansilal, Rai Singh, Nathuram Bhandari and some others regarding the reception to be organised for Neyogi's return from jail, I left to get Neyogi from Raipur. Neyogi was released at around noon on 9 the July 1977 and we boarded a bus to Bhilai. We refreshed ourselves at my home before catching a bus from Durg to reach Dalli-Rajhara. Neyogi insisted that Namita should also accompany us for his reception at Rajhara, because, according to him, she had been silently suffering because of my long stay at Dalli-Rajhara.

By the time the three of us reached the border of Rajhara it was already 5 pm. We had seen a constant stream of people moving towards the township to attend the reception meeting. People in their hundreds from nearby villages of Dalli-Rajhara were gathering to have a glimpse of Neyogi, now a nationally and internationally famous leader arisen from among their midst. It was getting dark and the rush on the road had become so heavy that the bus had come to a halt. We decided to get down and walk to the meeting place along with the surging crowd.

I could see an ocean of people, men, women and children, overflowing the venue of the meeting. It was with great difficulty, after much jostling and pushing, that we ultimately reached the stage. I was so overwhelmed by the emotionally surcharged crowd that I could not believe my eyes. I had never in my imagination thought of Neyogi being loved and admired by such a multitude of poor and innocent people! Surely, the Neyogi, whom I knew personally as a greedy, selfish and immoral person and the Neyogi, now being hailed by thousands of enthusiastic admirers as a messiah of the poor and a great hero, could not be one and the same!

There were only three chairs on the dais. Mr. Bansilal asked Neyogi to sit in the middle and asked me to sit at his left while he himself occupied the third. A beeline of men and women came forward to garland Neyogi and touch his feet. They were all emotionally surcharged. Many cried and whined. Bansilal gave a long speech describing the events that had led to the police firing and the martyrdom of 11 of his brothers and sisters and assured that the fight would continue till all the contractual labourers were regularised.

Impractical and immature in my experience and knowledge of the crowd assembled there, I felt pity for those illiterate and poor people for their blind faith in and hero-worship of their leader, though he was my comrade. So, when I was asked to address the public, I simply hailed the heroic spirit and sacrifice of the workers and said that it would go a long way to help them to achieve their demands. I did not shun from telling the public that it was not the leader who was the real hero, but those who had fought and sacrificed their lives for the cause.

"For the sake of the exploited and the oppressed people, my comrades have shed their blood in the soil of Chhattisgarh. I ask my brothers, sisters and the children only for their blessing. Bless me so that following the path treaded by the martyrs, I will also be able to shed my blood on this very earth"

Neyogi, who was the last to speak, started his address with these emotionally charged words, which proved to be prophetic. It was the only occasion I had witnessed him with wet eyes. And then in the midst of all, crying and whimpering over their near and dear ones who had been killed in the police firing, it was impossible for anyone to remain unaffected.

The meeting was widely covered by the print and electronic media. Thereafter, Neyogi always remained in the lime light of publicity. The educated middle class of Dalli-Rajhara also was curious to have a glimpse of the newly emerged hero in their town. The crowd was estimated to be over fifty thousand, an unheard of assembly in the remote mines of Dalli-Rajhara, over a 100 kms away from Bhilai.

A judicial enquiry into the police firing had been ordered by the central government and Neyogi wanted to present the version of the union before the Commission. At his insistence, I and Namita had to stay put in a labour camp in a mud house, along with Neyogi's wife, Asha and their one year old daughter, Kranti, to record the statements of the workers, who were eye witnesses to the events. I spent hours recording their statements. Shiaram had brought my scooter from Bhilai. On his insistence, I and Namita agreed to stay back one night at Danitola with Shia's family, before proceeding for Bhilai.

Shiaram and his wife Mandora Bai expressed their gratitude to us for persuading Neyogi to accept their daughter as his wife. They were very happy that Asha was married to a great leader like Neyogi. They seemed to have forgiven and forgotten the wrong done by him to their daughter after his emergence as a big leader. They would forever worship Neyogi who, being an 'engineer' by qualification, had left his 'officers job' in the Bhilai Steel Plant only to live for the poor and downtrodden people of Chhattisgarh. They were lucky in the case of Neyogi, when in most such cases the city people impregnated Adivasi girls and then ran away. How could I tell them the truth about Neyogi's qualification and his status in the BSP and why he had been thrown out of his job? No use telling them about his political compulsion to marry their daughter and the honour and reputation he was going to reap from the 'revolutionary' intellectuals all over the country for marrying an illiterate and poor tribal girl.

It was on such occasions that I had to accept that the truth is irrelevant in most occasions and the people are condemned to live in delusions. Perhaps man is destined to live not by truth but by his own perceptions, right or wrong. All the same, I wondered why Neyogi needed to spread falsehood about himself? Did he suffer from an inferiority complex? I knew that he was not in pursuit of truth. He was after success. Perhaps, in the pursuit of success, one needed to sacrifice truth of and on. Could this be the story of all successful people?

It was on our return journey by scooter, on a cool and bright morning that we met with an accident, seven kms. before Gunderdehi, when we were crossing a narrow bridge. A few buffalows were lying in the middle of the bridge, leisurely munching their cud. Just as the scooter had almost cleared them, one lifted its head and brushed it against the scooter. I lost balance and fell on the road along with the scooter. Namita was thrown out of the pillion. Her head hit the concrete floor and she lay there unconscious and bleeding. I ran to her and lifted her head to locate the injury. My hand stopped at a bump at the back of her head. It was the size of my fist. I struggled to lift her when some farmers from the nearby field came running to help. As luck would have it, a truck carrying stone metals arrived on the spot. I begged the driver to help to carry the injured to a doctor at Gunderdehi. He agreed and with the help of some people, Namita was laid on the front seat with her head on my lap. The continued flow of blood through her ears soaked my clothes. At Gunderdehi, she was taken out of the truck and stretched out on a table in the clinic of a private doctor. The doctor refused to even touch her, saying that it was a case of a fatal accident from head injury and she should be immediately taken to Durg District Hospital. I stood stunned for a moment!

In desperation, I came out from the doctor's clinic only to find that the truck had vanished. On a sudden impulse, I ran to the bus stand nearby, where a Durg bound bus was waiting, to leave only after an hour. I recalled that Mr. Motilal Vora was associated with the bus transport business and so requested the conductor to contact Voraji to seek his permission to depart immediately.

Without waiting for his response, I, with the help of others, lay Namita down on an empty seat in the bus. On the one hand, I offered the conductor as much money as he wanted and on the other, I threatened with dire consequences, if the patient died in the bus. A few passengers who had occupied seats joined me in forcing the driver to start the bus before time.

Once he had made up his mind, the driver drove so fast that within 40 minutes we were in Durg. By this time I had also regained some mental balance so that I could think rationally about the medical help available at the Durg District Hospital. I got down from the bus and called a Taxi. I put Namita in the Taxi and took her straight to the BSP Sector 9 Main Hospital. At the porch of the Emergency, I shouted that the patient had suffered a head injury and was bleeding. I saw a stretcher being pushed by two attendants rushing fast towards the porch.

They picked up the unconscious patient, laid her on the stretcher and rolled her away. No strength was left in me to follow.

I was deeply shaken and shattered. My body and clothes were soaked with fresh blood and I had no idea whether she would live or die. Someone from the crowd at the Emergency ward saw me all soaked in blood and the news spread among my friends and co-workers in the Plant. I sat in the porch silently for almost an hour, watched by many curious onlookers, before one among my friends, asked me to get up and go home as my little son was all alone and in the care of my neighbour.

While going home sitting pillion on a motor bike, I felt a sort of peace and tranquility because I thought that I had done whatever was possible and now she was in the hands of the most trustworthy doctors. If it was her destiny to live, she would survive. The rest I left for providence to decide.

Before leaving for Rajhara, we had left our three year old son with Mr. Stephen's family, who was our immediate neighbor. They were all shocked by the news of the accident. While Mr. Stephan and his wife rushed to the hospital, his daughters brought my son, Dilip, to me. I caught hold of him and cried my heart out, while he blinked at me in wonder. Later the girls, Molly, Aney and Lali took him away to their home, leaving me to rest.

After washing out the grime and blood and changing my clothes, I lay down for some time, expecting sleep to come. But for some reason, I got up. I borrowed a scooter from my neighborhood and returned to the hospital, where I found many of my anxious friends waiting for news about Namita. The only information was that she had been admitted in the ICU and continued in an unconscious state and was still bleeding from her left ear. The doctor on duty told me that they would decide about an operation or any other course of treatment only after she regained consciousness, which might take one, two or even three days.

I loitered about in the hospital compound for some time, when all of a sudden I felt a strong desire to revisit the spot of the accident. And without saying a word to any one, I took the scooter and drove about 40 kms, back to the accident spot. While driving, I was almost in a trance. It was late night when I reached the place. I found a few farmers collected at the spot and discussing about the accident. Their conclusion was that the driver of the scooter was safe but the woman might not survive because she was unconscious with a head injury and bleeding to death. No one recognised me. I saw my own scooter, parked by the side of a bush near the road.

Next day, at around 10 am, Neyogi reached the JLN hospital along with a truckload of miners. The news of the accident had reached him only in the early morning. As I was admonishing him for overcrowding the hospital, I caught sight of a procession of five more trucks filled with mine workers, reaching the hospital compound. Within no time, the hospital compound was teeming with over five hundred workers. The unruly crowd in soiled working clothes, covered with the iron ore dust was a sight not witnessed by the hospital before. The miners began talking and shouting, demanding to see the patient forthwith. An untoward melee was created all around. Quickly, a battery of officers from the Industrial Relations and Public Relations Departments arrived to pacify and manage the 'unruly and unsophisticated' mines workers. In the mean, Neyogi engaged himself in excited conversation with the officers and doctors. To my great relief and also others, he left by the evening, taking with him his trucks and followers. What could have been the purpose of bringing such a crowd to the hospital? Just flexing his muscles befor the management perhaps!

On the third day, just before the end of 72 hours, Namita slowly came to. My happiness and relief knew no bounds. There being no blood clot in the head, no operation was needed. Blood due to her internal concussion, had oozed out through the ear. Once her condition had stabilised, she was shifted to the ward. She got the best of medical care and the top management of the Bhilai Steel Plant monitored her condition on a daily basis, not for love of me or her, but for the fear of Neyogi.

Neyogi had metamorphosised himself into a symbol of fear for the contractors, management and the administration. Whereas he had become a source of courage and hope for the toiling masses of not just Madhya Pradesh but all over the country. His fame as an exemplary revolutionary labour leader reached all nooks and corners of the nation, thanks to the media which had found a new messiah in him who was to lead their long expected 'revolution.' Workers who were dissatisfied by their union leaders turned to Neyogi and his union as an alternate.

While Neyogi was serving in jail after the Rajhara firing, a youth by the name of Prakash came to see me. He had come from Hirri mines near Bilaspur. He confided that he had been a Naxalite for some time but now, wanted to renounce Naxalite politics and work for the working class. When he sought permission to work at Rajhara, I advised him to discuss the issue with Mr. Bansilal and other local leaders. Though they were willing to take him into their fold, I intervened and asked Prakash to prove his credentials first by organising the workers of Hirri from where he hailed. The challenge was accepted and he returned to Hirri.

Praksh's return with a dozen Mukhiya workers of Hirri Mines after the lapse of a fortnight, to invite me to the inauguration of our union branch at Hirri, took me by surprise. Over 500 labourers had, as in Rajhara, already renounced the INTUC and AITUC unions and organised themselves under the banner of CMSS. I asked him to wait till Neyogi's release.

By this time, one Durga Bai had emerged as a very active and strong woman leader from among the agitating women workers engaged in raising the iron ore in Rajhara mines. She also accompanied Bansilal, me and Neyogi for the inauguration of the union branch at Hirri after his release from jail. There, I gathered that Prakash had already established himself as a courageous and trustworthy leader among the 1500 workers of the Hirri mines. He had led a few agitations without support from Rajhara and succeeded in winning some of the demands of the workers. The rest of us could not but admire Prakash for his commitment and devotion but Neyogi was not enthusiastic about Prakash's leadership. Still, he had no alternative other than leaving the Hirri Union at the disposal of Prakash as he had still many things to do and many ends to tie in order to tighten his stranglehold on the Rajhara Workers.

Chapter 15

Spider's Web

While returning from Hirri, Bansilal suggested that since our organisation was likely to be expanded, a central committee to coordinate and guide our movements would be required. Though initially reluctant, Neyogi agreed, to such a central committee being formed at Bhilai. The C.C. was constituted of five members namely, he himself and Bansilal Sahu from Rajhara, Com. Praksh from Hirri and Com. Neel Ratan Ghoshal and myself from Bhilai. He recommended the name of Dr. Yadu to be included as an invitee.

It did not take me long to realise that the Central Committee was only a façade used by Neyogi to cover up his personal and secretive political agenda and dictatorial methods. In spite of repeated requests from Com. Prakash from Hirri and Mr. Bansilal Sahu from Rajharah, to discuss imminent problems being faced in their respective areas, Neyogi took no interest to summon a meeting of the Central Committee. His idea was to run the affairs of the union as per his own will and whims by using his blind followers as per convenience. While just anyone from among the workers was randomly picked to accompany him during his negotiations with the administration and BSP Management, the elected office bearers of the unions were studiously ignored. Consequently, he became the only representative of the organization. Agreements were signed in English, a language understood by none else in the union, other than me. My reluctance to attend negotiation meetings served his purpose well because I was the only person among the union leaders who could have had his own view.

Inspired by the success of the workers in Dalli-Rajhara, one comrade Inderjit Singh of the SKMS (AITUC), along with about ten thousand manual mines workers, also started an agitation at Kirandul, Bastar for departmentalisation and other demands. The agitation came to an end in April 1978, with the arrest of Comrade Singh, followed by a police firing - killing many labourers and imposition of curfew in all the labour slums. A repetition of the Dalli-Rajhara incident! Police set fire to hundreds of huts belonging to the miners and drove them away from their homes. The panic and pandemonium created by police atrocities was such that no other Communist leader ventured to visit the place. Neyogi found it a ripe opportunity to usurp the leadership of the Kirandul Workers. But he was also afraid of being arrested. So, after the situation had cooled down, he despatched one of his very confident union workers, Mr. Devnath Sahu, to Kirandul, with a truck load of rice as relief material for the affected workers. Sahu was detained on the way, but later released. Committedly, he stayed among the victimised workers and re-organised them to a great extent.

When after a fortnight, Neyogi reached Kirandul, he was disturbed and disappointed to see the lack of enthusiasm among the workers to receive him as a hero. That Devnath Sahu, who was supposed to be his mere proxy, had been accepted by them as their hero was something that Neyogi could not digest. Aflame with fury, Neyogi returned to Rajhara and later called Devnath Sahu back. There, before a crowd of his worshippers, he accused Devnath Sahu of betraying the union and joining hands with the Management and government.

An honest and courageous activist, illiterate and inexperienced in union matters, Devnath Sahu found himself speechless before the wild allegations made by his iconic leader. At Neyogi's promptings, he was humiliated and shamed by the gathered workers who put a garland of chappals and shoes around his neck and threw him out of the union on the grounds of being a conspirator and betrayer. His right to earn his livelihood in the mines was snatched away and he was forbidden entry in the mines. Only then was Neyogi's fury ausaged.

Thus rolled head No. one.

This development forced me to come to the conclusion that Neyogi had almost turned into a dictator who could not and would not brook the presence of any other leader in the organisation. The irony was that our movement had started in 1970 with the avowed purpose of developing local leadership. But with the budding of just one probable leader exhibiting the qualities required to organise and lead the workers at a time of crisis, Neyogi could not but resort to the age old Communist tactic of eliminating opponents after stamping them enemy agents. When I talked to the union president, Bansilal Sahu about the treatment meted out to Devnath Sahu, he advised me to keep silent because most of the workers are under the spell of the 'Bengali' who was determined to run the union like a dictator. Bansilal confided that Neyogi's next target would be he himself. I talked to Neyogi about the developments in the union but he refused to discuss the matter, saying that it could be discussed at a C.C. meeting at Bhilai.

I called a Central Committee meeting at Bhilai in the residence of Sahadevan, in which I, Neyogi, Bansilal Sahu and Prakash attended. I sought a clarification for Devnath Sahu's expulsion. Neyogi waved the query aside with the reply that discussions related to publically condemned and expelled persona could serve no purpose. Much time and water had flown since the incident. Instead, he turned his attention on Prakash and started belabouring him about his work at Hirri. He was accused of hobnobbing with the management and betraying the union. Though I objected vociferously, Bansilal remained conspicuously silent. He did not even raise the issues that he had been discussing with me. To me he had opened up that Neyogi was nurturing a mafia gang of over 200 whole-time workers who received full payment without working in the mines. Its purpose was to muffle dissenting voices and frighten the members of the 10,000 strong union. Leaders and activists were ignominiously insulted and heckled at Neyogi's beck and call. Since Banasilal did not raise the issue, I also remained silent. The meeting ended inconclusively.

After about two weeks, I received a postal letter from Prakash. He informed me that he was leaving M.P. for good. He had no other option but to leave the Hirri Mines workers to their own fate. In the letter he depicted Neyogi as a dangerous man who would not stop at taking recourse to threats and even committing crimes to meet his ends. He warned me that Neyogi was an over ambitious man who wanted to run his union as his personal fiefdom, like a dictator. Being an unscrupulous man, he would stoop to any level for his personal gains. He had threatened to betray Prakash to the police as a wanted Naxalite, if he continued in the state of M.P. Anyway, that was the last I heard of Prakash.

As soon as Prakash vanished from the scene, Neyogi took up the reins of Hirri Mines into his own hands. He pacified the concerned and anxious workers of Hirri by saying that Prakash had been transferred to another state for expanding the union work. After this incident my association with Neyogi reduced considerably. Once in a while he dropped in at my house and talked about his conciliation talks with the management and the growing demand for his leadership by workers from near and far. Then one day, he invited me to witness the annual election of the representatives and office bearers of his union at Dalli-Rajhara. I had to go because he had sent a jeep to pick me up. By the time I reached Rajhara, elections of the union representatives were over and that of the office bearers was in progress. I was shocked to learn that Bansilal Sahu had been defeated and a new man, namely, Sahadev Sahu, had been elected President.

I was stunned to see the new President, Sahadev Sahu, immediately after his election, insulting his predecessor by openly calling him a traitor and an agent of the management and contractors in the presence of me and Neyogi. Bansilal retorted by saying that one day Sahadev Sahu, who was so proud to be acting as Neyogi's henchman, would realise that he was only a slave of this cunning 'Bengali Traitor.' He would make use of the innocent Chhattisgarhis only for his own name, fame and money. Later, I came to know that Sahadev Sahu, an illiterate truck driver in the mines, had been hand picked by Neyogi to be the President of the union because he was his most ardent loyalist and had had played a leading role in threatening and silencing of any one opposed to him.

Bansilal had been the sole leader who dared to lead the rebellion of the ten thousand contract labourers against the powerful AITUC Union and he was also the founder of the union, CMSS. Labourers in general considered him as one of their own and had great faith in his courage and honesty. But he suffered from a lack of proper education and could not understand the conspiracy hatched by Neyogi to evict him from the union. He could not fathom that Neyogi had directly interfered and manipulated in the union elections. Neyogi was wary of direct confrontation with Banasilal with his false allegations because of the possibility of unfavourable reaction from the workers. So while spreading lies and canards about Bansilal among the workers through his henchman, Neyogi was also planning to oust him through 'elections.'

I gauged the situation and realised that there was pretty little I could do. The margin for interference was negligible. I stood a silent spectator and knew that the removal of Bansilal was the culmination of the process he had started with Devnath Sahu and Prakash. I decided to keep a distance from Neyogi and Dalli-Rajhara in the future. But in just a fortnight, I was forced to return to Rajhara on hearing of the physical assault on Bansilal Sahu.

Though Bansilal had been removed from the post of President, he continued as the president of a labour cooperative society that had over 600 members who had great faith in him. And this was the only society that did not allow Neyogi to have a free hand in it's finances. Neyogi was confident that things would go his way after the removal of Bansilal from presidentship. When he found things to be otherwise, Neyogi dispatched around fifty baton wielding goons to Bansilal's office where he was at the time holding a meeting with his society members. Calling the meeting an attempt to hatch a conspiracy against the union and its only leader, Shankar Guha Neyogi, they disrupted it with vicious shouts and threats. In addition, when Bansilal refused to follow them, to be brought before Neyogi, he was bludgeoned and dragged to Neyogi's presene in the union office. Neyogi's threats could not subdue him. And nothing could deter him from telling Neyogi what he thought of him. The result was that Bansilal was thrashed repeatedly and then dumped on the road.

On hearing of the assault on Bansilal, I lost no time in leaving for Rajhara, along with Sahadevan who had volunteered to accompany me. We could not trace Bansilal. So, we went to Neyogi's house where he was sitting at his doorstep, in the midst of over twenty of his goons. At the very sight of me, he started hollering and abusing me. He accused me of instigating and misleading his cadres. He alleged that because my wife was an executive in the BSP, I was acting as an agent of the management and trying to break his union. In retaliation I called him a cheat, a scoundrel and a curse on the mines workers. I called him a goon with no sense of guilt in fooling and sucking the blood of innocent Chhattisgarhis. I told him that had it not been for the innocence and believing nature of Bansilal, he could never have got entry in the union. It was he, Neyogi, who was the betrayer to the mines workers and it was Bansilal who was the real leader. By supporting him all along, I had been nurturing a poisonous viper, I contended.

"If I can raise you, I can also crush your head," I threatened.

In retaliation to my utterances, his cohorts, yielding lathis, encircled me threateningly but Neyogi stopped them. He said that since I was in his house, he was sparing my life. He threatened me with dire consequences if I was seen in Rajhara again. All my bones would be broken and my body would be thrown in the forest for the animals to feed on, he shouted.

Sahadevan had remained silent all along though he had been very vocal all the way in condemning Neyogi for the assault on Bansilal. While leaving, I asked Sahadevan to come along but he said he would stay back with Neyogi. And he was only one among the many rotten and opportunistic characters who had crossed my life's path posing to be revolutionaries. Close interaction with many of my close associates claiming to be revolutionaries had been a great eye opener for me. I found most of them to be intellectually dishonest, mentally perverted, over ambitious, autocratic and extremely cowardly. They were good only in mouthing revolutionary jargons that were beyond comprehension of anyone, including themselves. They were always found wanting in opposing or fighting injustice, even when it was taking place right in front of their very eyes. And, in addition, they were invariably scared of the police and suffered from a fear psychosys. Other than myself, Neyogi was the only one amongst the Bhilai based 'revolutionaries' who had led a mass movement and confronted the authorities and the police. Even so, Neyogi also had turned out to be a turncoat and betrayer of the faith.

By 1980, I had been in the public field for over a decade, fighting for various causes. I had gone to jail many times, one of which was detention for 20 months and 20 days, under MISA, during Emergency in 1975–77. My only inspiration at that time was my great faith and conviction in revolution born out of the Marxist philosophy and my determination to lead the toiling masses in their fight against injustice. I had conceived of a mass movement that would differ from those practiced by existing leftist parties, including the Naxalites, as a vehicle to help realise my ideas. It was providence that had chosen Neyogi to be my political partner.

The unprecedented college movement at Durg and its successful conclusion had endeared me to thousands of educated youths of Chhattisgarh. Thus it became a fertile ground for our political work in Chhattisgarh. When Neyogi got established among the mines workers of Dalli-Rajhara, I thought that we were on the threshold of the first stage of our movement. But this proved to be only a mirage. As it turned out, he was a man suffering from inferiority complex, aspiring only for wealth and power. Once he got a foothold in Dalli-Rajhara and control over the black money of the contractors and the muscle power of the ignorant and docile miners, Neyogi showed his true colour – that of an autocrat and dictator. There was no room for discussion or democratic functioning. His was the first and last word – in fact, the only word. Dissenting voices, if any, were painted as the enemy's hand and brutally suppressed. Though I was totally disillusioned with him and his stranglehold on the organisation, my faith in myself and my own convictions remained intact.

It was under such circumstances that in 1980, I decided to withdraw my association from all types of organisations and continue in my path as a loner. I was also disillusioned by the political changes that had overtaken the nation. The Janata Party kept splintering due to its own internal contradictions, paving the way for general elections and return of Ms. Gandhi as P.M. Return she did and with what a thumping majority! During the Janata Party rule at the centre in 1977–79, the BSP management had been treating me with kid gloves. My role in fighting and winning all the demands of the MISA detainees who were BSP employees, might have sent a message to the management that I was cheek and jowl with the power at the centre. No one could imagine that the centre of my power was my own convictions and faith in myself.

So, whenever I took up an issue relating to a BSP employee, management heeded and solved the problem without any dilly-dallying. During this period I never raised my voice for the general or departmental problems of the workers of either my department or other BSP employees. This very well suited the management also. Therefore, when I did raise an individual grievance of an employee, management seriously took note and tried to solve it quickly. My shift manager, who had all along been my persecutor, started behaving as if he was my pet dog. Perhaps, top management had cautioned him to keep off me. No one retaliated about my long absences during this period because of my activities at Dalli-Rajhara and other places or tried to check my irascible behaviour with managers. This boosted my faith in myself and my convictions and at the same time enhanced the faith of my fellow workers in me. I pitied the management personnel for their spinelessness and fear of me. My voice was always at a high pitch and reverberated through the surroundings. The listeners looked on in awe. It had reached such an extent that the top management personnel always tried to avoid facing me.

It was during this period that I came in constant contact with the then Chief Personnel Manager, Mr. Kamal Kishore. He often engaged me in discussions on social and political issues, including the activities of Naxals. He could not hide his admiration for the brilliant students who could renounce their education and bright future to become Naxalites to make extreme sacrifices for the cause of the peasants. He taunted me and Neyogi as pseudo-revolutionaries because we were confining our activities to organised and secure sectors of mines and industries. He teased Neyogi for being a 'a revolutionary,' who had fallen in his esteem when he found him to be incapable of hiding his jubilation after purchasing a new jeep for his personal use. He was just like a child with a new toy. Mr. Kishore could not believe that revolutionaries could be so happy with material possession. Thanks to his empathy for the toiling people, I could make use of his authority to help a few employees who had approached me with their genuine grievances that had remained unresolved for many years. As a matter of principles, he submitted his resignation to the SAIL management. Only after this, I accepted his oft repeated invitation to visit him at his Bungalow. I told him that through his resignation on a matter of principles, he had proven himself to be a much more honest and courageous person than I had thought him to be.

I could not say the same for my own self. I had not been able to find enough courage to throw away my job, though I wanted to devote all my time to serve the people.

After resigning from her job as a Post Graduate Teacher in Kendriya Vidyala, Bacheli, at the end of the Emergency, Namita returned to Bhilai to restart our family life. Though she had tried repeatedly for a job as lecturer in BSP schools, she had to satisfy herself with the job of an Asstt. Tteacher in the primary section of the BSP School in Sector 2.

It was in the middle of 1977 that Namita appeared in the exams for SAIL Executives in which out of the lakhs of candidates from all over India appearing in this exam, only a few hundred got selected for interview. In her very first attempt, Namita was selected for the interview which was held at Calcutta. To her surprise the interviewers, mostly SAIL Directors, were less interested in her own personality or capability and more interested to know about her husband's thoughts and activities. She was repeatedly asked questions about me, my political views and the ideals that motivated me to be a militant man and my ultimate political goals, the total revolution led by Jayaprakash Narayan, the Naxalite movement, and so on. She tried to bypass most of the questions by saying that she was not bound to answer questions about her husband to qualify herself for a job in the SAIL.

In the middle of the interview one of the directors unwittingly let out that he would love to give her the job but he could not. Thereupon, it took no time for Namita to stand up and leave the room saying, "If you are pre-determined not to select me, you have no business to interview me." The shocked bunch of interviewers sent a peon after her to ask her to return. Her father, who had accompanied her, tried to persuade her to go back to the interview but she stood her ground and asked the peon to go back and find out if she was going to be considered for the job. If the answer was yes she would go back, she said. The peon did not reappear and she left the place, perhaps deeply resenting the fact that her future career would always be overshadowed by her husband's public life.

In 1978, Namita appeared for the exams for SAIL executives once again and got selected for interview a second time. Before she left for her interview, I discussed Namita's first experience before the interviewing board with Mr. Kamal Kishore, and asked him how the interviewers dared put very personal questions to a lady candidate. He laughed it away by saying that when they find a suitable candidate they try to put them under maximum stress to see the limit of their tolerance and patience. I retorted by asking him what he would say if the lady in question answered her torturers' questions beyond the limit of her tolerance, with a slap. Anyway, he advised me to send Namita for the interview because he knew that she was competent and qualified to be an executive of SAIL. Namita got selected as a SAIL excutive.

Before she could join, she needed to be relieved from her current job as Assistant Teacher. She sent an application to the Education Department for her relieving order but the only reply she received, even after the lapse of a week, was one excuse or the other. And without the relieving order, they would not allow her to join her new situation. At last, I was compelled to accompany her. To my query, Mrs. Arya, the executive dealing with the matter, told me that she thought that it was not possible to issue a relieving order and Namita would have to resign from her existing job. Relieving meant continuity of service and resignation meant break in service. I got angry and raised my voice. I thundered that even after more than a week of submission of the application, she was still thinking! To Hell with what she was thinking.

I demanded a reply to the application in accordance with the rules. She scampered out of her cabin - Namita's application in her hand. She remained closeted in the cabin of her boss, Sr. Personal Officer, Mr. Behl, for about an hour.

We waited patiently for over an hour. My old friend, Mr. Chandra Mohan Das, who was already an executive, remarked, as he was passing by, that for Kurian, an ordinary worker, anger and raising of the voice was pardonable, but for a lady aspiring to be an executive of BSP, such behaviour was uncalled for. Namita remained silent but I could not help telling him to mind his own business.

Mrs. Arya came out with the relieving order in her hand and apologised for the confusion and delay. I thanked her and expressed regret for shouting at her and we parted with smiles.

By this time, Mr. S. R. Ramakrishnan, who had been my boss as a junior executive in the early days of my service in Coke Ovens, when I was between the age of 16 and 20, had replaced Mr. Kamal Kishore as Chief Personal Manager. After Namita joined as an executive trainee, he asked me one day whether she had resigned or had been relieved from her previous job. I told him that it was better to look at the rule books rather than going on thinking about it. He laughed heartily at my reply!

I used to work as a Gantry Crane Operator in the Coal Handling Plant (CHP), a unit of the Coke Ovens and Bye Products Department. It is in CHP where tens of thousands of tons of coking coal with various ash contents, coming from different collieries, is unloaded, blended in its silos and crushed into fine powder in the Hammer Mills. This powder is then charged into the ovens of the Batteries. This is the process of making the coke essential for melting iron ore in the Blast Furnaces.

In the first three years post emergency, mine was the lone voice raised in support of the grievances faced by individual workers of my unit, numbering around 350. Management also promptly attended to the genuine grievances that I voiced. The recognised union, INTUC, with a membership of almost 90% of workers as well as the Communist Union, CITU, which had the membership of the rest, had become almost defunct during Emergency. Emergency had muzzled the voices of trade union leaders. So, for quite some time, I, with my resounding voice and lack of fear of the establishment, emerged as the sole leader in the CHP. Only, I was a leader without a union or membership in any union.

After my estrangement from Neyogi in 1980, I started taking more interest in involving myself in the problems of my co-workers. Up-gradation of a few posts and some promotions, long overdue, were pending. Many directly affected workers requested me to take up such common issues with the management. They said that they had no faith in the leaders of either INTUC or CITU but had full faith in me. I agreed on the condition that they would unite behind me, defying their own leaders.

Subsequently, a memorandum listing all grievances was drawn up and got signed by 90 percent of the workers. While leaders and activists of CITU signed the memorandum, the representatives of INTUC refused. It was then duly submitted to Mr. Seshasayan, the Chief Superintendent, who asked for a month's time to consider the grievances. Mr. Seshasayan's nonchalant attitude and stony face during the intervening month, was clear indication of what was to be expected. I told my fellow workers that their demands were not going to be considered by the management. They would have to demonstrate their strength and unity to fight for their just rights.

The majority advocated a strike, the last and the only weapon in their hands, but I cautioned them. It would be easy to start a strike but next to impossible to end it. Benefits were not that easy to come by. I suggested stoppage of acting and overtime through which the management filled the gaps and the shortage of workmen at different working places. I was not very much in favour of jeopardising the production and the livelihood of the men by calling for a strike. So, I had already formulated and considered another way to make the management take notice of our memorandum seriously. By stopping acting and overtime, the entire pressure of the management would be brought down upon individual workers. This would be a litmus test for everyone to measure his determination to stand united.

The united action of the workers took the Management unawares. Overtime and Acting came to a full stop. Many a machine and work spot were left unmanned, making it impossible to start the Plant.

Acting and overtime were considered to be benefits given to workers. There was no rule to thrust them on unwilling workers. The CHP workers were very well informed about the rules and I could not help smirking at the failed efforts of a battery of officers trying to put pressure on workmen to force them to accept acting and overtime. After failing in their efforts, the officers themselves had to occupy the vacant places in order to start the plant. So, for about a month, scores of officers and management trainees in every shift got the rare chance of tasting real work in the sweltering heat and dust of the CHP. They would never have forgotten this experience of having to work eight long hours on the Silos' Top, the Hammer Crushers, the long Conveyor Belts and the Coal Towers.

During this period, there was neither tension nor loss of production in the Plant. Only gallons of valuable sweat of steel plant executives had to be shed to keep the plant running. It was fun for one or two days but to continue it day after day was not a joke. Perhaps it was the growing discontentment among executives at the junior levels, who were forced to work hard for eight hours in the midst of coal dust and coke oven gas, that compelled management to strike an agreement with me.

For the first time perhaps in the history of the Bhilai Steel Plant, management entered into an agreement with someone other than the leaders of it's recognised union. The Chief Superintendent,

Mr. Seshasayan, on behalf of the management, and I, on behalf of the CHP workers, signed a written agreement for settling the demands raised through the memorandum by mutual consultations.

We celebrated our victory.

Management wanted to end the movement somehow and there was no way other than making an agreement with me. So, Mr. Seshasayan was asked to sign an 'agreement' with me. However, when no call from Mr. Seshasyan had been received for nearly a month, I understood clearly that the agreement had been used only as an alibi to end the movement. Ultimately, a month later, when I confronted him in his office, he said that management was in consultation with the recognised union, INTUC. About the agreement that had been signed, he confessed with an impish smile, "George, you also know as well as I, that the paper we signed has no legal validity."

I acceded that I was aware that the agreement had no legal sanctity but I had trusted his self respect and the word of a gentleman. I was wrong. By using this underhand means, he had deceived the workers of his department. It bothered his conscious not a bit to know that by agreeing to sign an 'illegal' document, he had allowed himself to be used as a scape-goat.

I reminded him that the agreement might have been illegal but he and I were real. It did not matter whether he consulted me or his stooge union, INTUC, so long as the demands of the workers were fulfilled. Else, he should keep himself and his top management prepared for serious consequences. Before leaving, I repeated my pet slogan and said with a smile, "Mr. Seshsayan, you must have known by now that when I kick, I kick very hard."

Chapter 16

Fascist vs. Democrat

My last confrontation with Neyogi, had been about a month before Bansilal came to see me at Bhilai. He narrated the situation at Rajhara. Neyogi had been acting very vengefully against him and the workers still left in the labour cooperative society that Bansilal led. Their livelihood had been forcefully snatched away by Neyogi and his goons. They were not allowed to enter the mines. The Bhilai Steel Plant as well as the police had expressed helplessness in the matter of Neyogi and his criminal gang. Bansilal pleaded with me to return to Rajhara to guide and help him. He also said that Mr. Jhumuklal Bhedia of Balod, a minister of M.P., had been sending out feelers to offer him help against Neyogi. His response to Mr. Bhedia awaited only my approval.

It had been extreme disgust and disappointment that had led me to cut off my relations with Neyogi.

The transformation of a 'poor and helpless revolutionary, ready to sacrifice even his own life for the cause of the poor and exploited people,' to a dangerously scheming and criminally minded autocrat and dictator, who believed only in money and muscle power, and greed for political power, name and fame, shocked my senses. From the very beginning I was totally averse to any dealings with any mainstream political party. But I had a score to settle with Neyogi and great concern for the livelihood of the followers of Bansilal. So, I advised Bansilal to join hands with Mr. Bhedia, wholeheartedly to face and challenge Neyogi. Joining Mr. Bhedia's camp might provide the only solution.

I knew for a fact about the connection of the then Central Minister, Mr. Vidhyacharan Shukla with Neyogi and how he was using the latter for his vote bank politics. Mr. Kanak Tiwari, advocate and a Congress leader, had sometimes acted as a conduit between the two. Consequently, Neyogi had no problem in accepting money from Shukla to field his candidate against Bhedia and withdraw another from contesting against Arvind Netam. Even so, Bhedia, being a confident of Chief Minister, Arjun Singh, was his bête noire, Arvind Netam had been Mr. Shukla's protégée since a long time.

Mr. Shukla, a Central Minister and Mr. Arjun Singh, the Chief Minister of M.P. were political opponents. I calculated that Mr. Bhedia, the Home Minister, would go to any extent to support Bansilal against Neyogi. The outcome turned out to be a modern day Kurukshetra. Mr. Bansilal and around a hundred of his workers were taken for work inside the mines under strong police protection. Neyogi was furious. The next day he, along with his 8000 strong gang of supporters laid a siege on the entire Dalli Rajhara mines. Undeterred, Mr. Bhedia engaged around a thousand policemen in the mines. The high voltage warring scenario turned out to be historic. There were around a hundred miners breaking iron ore stones under the protection and watchful eyes of about a thousand policemen and the protest of over 8000 infuriated miners, under the egging on of Neyogi and Sahadev Sahu, shouting slogans against Bhedia and his 'agent,' Bansilal.

Neyogi's attempt to provoke a third police firing on the irate mob at Dalli-Rajhara was dashed by the good senses of the police and administration. However, the day to day situation remaining volatile and inflammatory, the state government was ultimately compelled to detain Neyogi and Sahadev Sahu under National Security Act. And the work in the mines came to a standstill.

And, the management lay off the mines indefinitely.

Detension under NSA boosted the fame and name of Neyog sky highi. He had, by this time, gained national and international acclaim as a "Messisha" of the toiling masses. Thanks to the support of various Human Rights Organisations, the JNU activists and the PUCL, Neyogi was being projected as a new-found revolutionary leader, devoted to the liberation of the country. Through the influence of the PUCL over the national media and its wide connections in many European countries, legends on Neyogi were being flashed all overtheworld. Right from the time of his release from jail, following the twin police firings at Rajhara in the year 1977, 'revolutionary intellectuals' and 'progressive young journalists,' particularly of the JNU variety, so far unknown to the people of Chhattisgarh, had been descending, one by one, at Dalli-Rajhara.

The first such person to arrive was Dr. Vinayak Sen. On the very day of his arrival, I asked Neyogi to explain his presence. He said that Dr. Sen was a highly qualified doctor who had been honored by the President of India. When I asked him point blank if Dr. Sen was a Naxalite, he shrugged off the question by saying that he did not know whether he was Naxalite or a CIA agent. He said that external forces were trying to penetrate into our organisation and to make use of his name and fame for their own benefit. To my query as to why they oughtn't to be thrown out, Neyogi disclosed that instead of throwing them out, he would make use of them for his own benefit. I advised him to keep away outside interference in our organisation and warned him of the danger of overconfidence about his own smartness. He should be wary of fooling around with such elements. It was like playing with fire.

Dr. Sen stayed glued to Neyogi till the latter's tragic death in 1991. He had been a frequent visitor to my home at Sector 10, along with Neyogi. Later, his wife, Elina Sen, followed by one Dr. Ashish Kundu, also used to come. Not much later, came another comrade, Arvind Gupta, introduced to me as an IIT professional from Kharagpur, who had thrown away his cushy job to serve the poor in our organisation. Dr. Jane also appeared, from where no one knew. Next, Neyogi brought Swamy Agnivesh to my home and introduced him as a liberator of the bonded labourers. Dr. Rajendra Sail, Secretary of the PUCL, also used to accompany Neyogi in some of his visits to my home.

Though there was no clear cut reason, I could not accept all these elements without a pinch of suspicion. But I kept my discomfort and mistrust about these characters under check because of their humble and friendly behaviour coupled with Neyogi's constant pleading on their behalf. They tried to develop a close rapport with me and my wife but Namita never once accepted their gestures as genuine and remained aloof.

Other 'political luminaries' whom I had to host at my home at Bhilai, on Neyogi's insistence and pleading, were Dr. Susheela Neyyar, sister of Jawaharlal Nehru and Mr. Nag Bhushan Patnaik, a well known Naxalite leader, who had been condoned of death sentence and freed from jail unilaterally by the Indira Gandhi's cabinet. Intellectuals of the 'revolutionary' kind of various hues could simply not resist the temptation of attracting lime light and publicity in the company of Neyogi, who urged them to discuss their politics and philosophy with me as he himself was neither interested nor capable of grasping matters of intellect.

Neyogi had kept me and others as well as the then union president, Bansilal Sahu, in the dark about the construction of the 'Shaheed Hospital' at Dalli-Rajhara. It had been the brain child of Dr. Sen and his PUCL comrades. While the then GM Mines, B. Mukherjee facilitated the work, it was the transport contractors, lead by Shantilal Jain, who had financed it. The hospital was projected nationwide, as a symbol of the constructive nature of the revolution led by Neyogi. It was declared to be meant to provide free treatment to the most neglected people in the remotest villages. The hospital was run by a team of 'revolutionary' doctors led by Dr. Sen.

It took me over a decade to learn from very reliable sources at Rajhara that the Shaheed Hospital was only a front for providing clandestine treatment to Naxalites who had fallen seriously ill or had been injured in police encounters in the jungles of Chhattisgarh and its bordering states.

It may be mentioned here that none of these outside revolutionary intellectuals ever uttered a word or expressed an opinion about Neyogi's autocratic and dictatorial behaviour. Such matters did not seem to concern them. Their consciences were not pricked even when Bansilal Sahu was beaten up and dragged along the road by goons at Neyogi's orders. They had specific reasons to be there and nothing else mattered. Only as late as 1980, did it become clear to me that Neyogi, in collaboration with his new found leftist 'intellectuals,' had been pursuing a totally different path from the one I had been brought about to envisage. It was this knowledge that forced me to snap all ties with Neyogi and his organisation.

I decided to go ahead as a loner.

This total disassociation from the masses created a vacuum in my heart and led me to take keen interest in my co-workers in the Coal Handling Plant. Those were the times when 'leader' was a word which was subjected to all kinds of abuses. So, I also abhorred being called a leader. It was perhaps this strong negative connotation of the word 'leader,' which kept me from aspiring to be one. Moreover, I never had a godfather to goad me towards a particular aim or an ambition to become 'somebody.'

But providence cannot be denied. It would thrust 'leadership' on me, once again, in a most unexpected place, the Coke Ovens Department of Bhilai Steel Plant!

Neyogi and Sahadev Sahu's detention under NSA created a big hue and cry throughout the country. Angry voices were raised against the 'draconian' law applied against a labour leaders fighting for the betterment of the tribals and mines workers. Provoked and prompted by the PUCL network, national news papers criticized and condemned the state as well as central Congress Governments for suppressing the voice of the toiling people.

Ms. Indira Gandhi, goaded on by Mr. V. C. Shukla, her cabinet colleague, sent her confidant, the Jharkand leader Mr. Sibu Soren, M.P., to Bhilai to discuss with the BSP management the possibility of a settlement of the problems at Dalli-Rahara. Ms Gandhi often followed a policy of co-opting and supporting leaders emerging through popular movements at different places, for her own political ends. Thanks to Mr. Shukla's closeness to Ms. Gandhi, Mr. Arjun Singh, his arch rival, had to relent and release Neyogi from detention after 35 days on 18 March 1981.

Though his release was celebrated as a land mark victory by the media, the silence of a graveyard continued in Dalli-Rajhara. The ongoing layoff of the mines continued, throwing the workers out of their jobs and pushing them into the mouth of starvation. Never before, did the miners have to live in such disappointment and frustration as at the time of indefinite closure of the mines. Neyogi shuddered at the prospect of the management running the steel plant with iron ore procured permanently from alternate sources. His only ray of hope was the willingness of the central government to consider the issue.

With the support of Mr. V. C. Shukla, the PUCL had been using all its political influence to make the central government prevail upon the BSP management to agree to the reopening of the Dalli-Rajhara mines. PUCL leaders at Delhi were in constant touch with Neyogi and had been making frantic efforts to arrange his meeting with the then Union Steel Minister, Mr. Pranab Kumar Mukherjee.

Neyogi had been preoccupied by the problem of reopening of the Dalli- Rajhara mines. He had discontinued keeping a tag on my activities after our parting company at Rajhara, following his assault on

Bansilal. He had perhaps thought that disgusted with the developments leading to my isolation in my own organisation, I would quit from any sort of working class movement. He was confident that I would never raise my head again. Knowing me very closely, he was sure that after quitting from public life, I would confine myself to my family and my obsession of reading books to pass my time. His calculation would have been right had I not taken interest in the problems of my co-workers.

Months had passed since I had withdrawn the agitation of stopping acting and overtime in the CHP. My adversaries in the INTUC and CITU unions started spreading canards not only about me but also my wife, who was working as an executive in the Ispat Bhavan. They insinuated that the management had made my wife an executive to reward me for working as its agent, a common epithet for any opponent in the trade union circles. Stoppage of acting and overtime without hampering production in any way was a 'management idea' to establish me as a leader. Otherwise, how could I have dared to lead an agitation without the support of a trade union or a political party, they asked?

The daily pocking and insulting comments of these union leaders propelled me to take up my role as a leader seriously. Finding it of no use talking to the head of the department, Mr. Seshasayan, I started making rounds in the Ispat Bhavan to meet the GM(P&A) and other top officials. I wanted to meet the then recently joined Managing Director, Mr. E. R. C. Sekhar also, before resorting to strike. However, the entire management establishment, overshadowed by the INTUC and its General Secretary, Mr. Ravi Arya, would not permit it at any cost. My last meeting with the GM (P&A), Mr. Balakrishnan, was on 10ᵗʰ April 1981 evening. Before leaving his chamber, I told him not to hold me responsible if work in the CHP came to a grinding halt from the next morning. He pooh-poohed my words away and told me not to bother about it at all as the management was quite capable of taking care of any situation.

The management had reasons not to take me seriously. After all, I was only a single person, without a political 'God Father' or a union to support me. And my threat was confined to a small unit of CHP consisting of only 350 workers. For my benefit, supposedly a mere worker not knowledgeable about the integrated nature of steel making, Management might have thought it expedient to underplay the importance of the Coal Handling Plant and the vital importance of each and every section in the chain of steel production.

Moreover, the Bhilai Steel Plant had never had to face a strike in its true nature in any of its departments. The INTUC, the CITU, the AITUC and other national unions had called for strike on a number of occasions, without having made an iota of impact. Rather, attendance of workers on duty was enhanced on such occasions.

Management was also aware of the history of the collapse of our independent unions in Blast Furnace and the Coke Ovens and Bye Products departments in the '70s. It was the result of the master stroke of the recognized union INTUC, to elect its union representatives through secret ballot and its propaganda that we, the builders of the independent unions, were Naxalites. This had propelled the rank and file of our unions to desert us.

So, with the mighty INTUC and its towering leader, Ravi Arya at their beck and call, the all powerful management had no reason to worry about me at all.

I just picked up the telephone and told my co-workers that I had lost all faith in the talks with management. I now felt that a strike had become inevitable. My colleagues were more than ready and only wanted me to tell them when to start. I suggested strike from the next morning in the first shift. The D-day was 11 April, 1981.

When I reached the CHP in the morning shift, I found the entire force of the night shift assembled in front of the shift manager's office. They were all very excited at the prospect of witnessing an unprecedented event

- a total strike. They had heard a lot about strikes but had never witnessed or participated in one. And, they were just on the verge of witnessing one. However, they were going to be only witnesses. The real participants were to be the workers of the morning shift whose morale and courage required boosting. What better way than slogan shouting! So, as per my directives, the morning shift workers, arriving one after another, were received by their slogan shouting colleagues of the night shift.

The scene was beyond the imagination of the shift-in-charge, Mr. P. M. Mazumdar and his subordinate officers. Caught unaware, fear and apprehension were writ large on their faces. Stoically they continued with their duty of assigning the workmen their jobs for the shift. Not one worker heeded. Work in the CHP came to a halt.

Mr. S. D. Sharma and comrade P. K. Mukherjee, leaders of INTUC and CITU unions in the CHP respectively, were present and refrained from either opposing or supporting the strike initially. They were wise enough to not go publically against the mood of the workers.

At around 8 am, Mr. Seshasayan, accompanied by a few senior officers and scores of CISF men, arrived at the 'trouble spot.' He ignored me and ordered the crowd of workers to go to their work spots. When no one responded, he turned to me and asked, "Why are you stopping them from doing their duty?"

"Have you seen me doing so?" I counter questioned. "If you don't know why we were not working, I will tell you."

I raised my voice and said, "Mr. Seshasayan, you have cheated me and all the workers of CHP. And the strike is our answer to you."

My answer seemed to have not only stunned Mr. Seshasayan but also all others who had accompanied him - including the CISF personnel. No one, including, Mr. Seshasayan, had expected that a worker of lower rank like me, would talk back so loudly in public in such a manner, to a top executive. But my words worked like magic in boosting the courage of the workers who started raising slogans at a higher pitch.

They were no longer afraid of the management. Mr. Seshasayan retreated in haste.

From the very beginning till their retirement, workers of the Bhilai Steel Plant had suffered from a fear psychosis. They nurtured a deep rooted fear of losing their jobs, because a job in the steel plant was hard to come by. It guaranteed them a secure job, a relatively good salary, a rented quarter, a peaceful family life and good education for the children. For most, the job was their only life line. Striking work was equivalent to putting their jobs at stake, for petty demands like promotions and upgradations. Yet, all workmen, rebellious as they were, by their very nature, loved to strike work and see their employers in a fix! It gave them a sense of catharsis. If the Steel Plant workers were wary of striking work, the reason was that they were apprehensive of losing much more than what they could expect from the strike. And, they could hardly trust their leaders who had hitherto proved themselves to be only spineless and dishonest turncoats.

By 9 am, the assembly of the striking workers had swelled up with the joining of the general shift workers also. After witnessing me, standing my ground firmly, while confronting the Chief Superintendant, comrade Mukherjee also appeared to have gained some courage. Thereafter, he also started playing a minor role in the strike.

By 10 am, hundreds of CISF men had been posted on the roads and at important installations. An atmosphere of tension and fear was slowly building up and I felt the need to safeguard my followers from falling victims to intimidation. So, I asked them to stand in two files and follow me in a procession. It needed some persuasion to get them ready for the plunge. I started moving ahead, all the while, shouting slogans and was followed by two small lines of workers. As the procession progressed, the lines also went on becoming longer and longer.

When we crossed the road in front of Battery No.1, with a horde of CISF and police men in front and rear, comrade Mukherjee crossed my path breathlessly. He told me not to misguide the workers as it was quite illegal to take out processions within the plant. I smirked at him for showing off his 'revolutionary zeal' and pushed him aside before continuing with the procession. It went up to the end of Battery No.7 before turning back to the CHP. This maneuver was a morale booster that helped to bolster the faith and confidence in the striking workers. We kept up this practice of taking out processions in the beginning of every shift. As for me, I got the chance to lead it only on the first occasion!

Comrade Mukherjee seemed to have gathered courage after the first procession. From the second one onwards, he was always in the forefront to lead it. I was surprised and yet not so surprised and also very happy to see him taking my place to lead all succeeding processions thereafter. Perhaps his guide and mentor, Com. P. K. Moitra, who was hand in gloves with the BSP management, had reminded him of the old adage, 'If you can't beat them, join them.' However, the revolutionary spirit, the rhythm and the tune of the slogans raised in the Bengali style by comrade Mukherjee was music to my ears!

This was not the first strike to have taken place in Coke Ovens or other departments. Workers of one section or the other had sometimes resorted to 'lightning' strikes to try to coerce the management to redress their grievances. Such strikes petered out within an hour or two, or at the most four, before the management summoned their leaders. It resulted in an 'amicable settlement' and end of the strike. The demands of the workmen being met was an altogether different question. At least the strikes had been brought to an end.

I also did not expect that our strike would last for more than four hours. A strike beyond four hours could pose serious threat to production as well as the safety of the Plant. As the hours passed, the depleting stock of coking coal in the coal towers, forcing a slow-down of production in the coke oven batteries, was nagging me at the back of my head. I was now more eager than the management for a quick settlement.

The sight of the G.M. (P&A), Mr. Balakrishnan, accompanied by a few senior officers, arriving at the CHP at around 11 am, brought to my mind a huge sense of relief. Surprisingly however, I found that their intention turned out to be less to settle the problem and more to crush my 'Netagiri' once and for all. Stopping the loss of production and subsequent damage to the plant seemed to be their last priority.

My heart sank at the thought of the possible loss of hundreds of crores of rupees to the plant if the strike continued indefinitely, and that also, for a few paltry demands pertaining to a few promotions and up-gradations. Had I been in the right in resorting to this strike?

I could not say for sure whether it had been my wounded ego or the urgency of the demands of my coworkers that had pushed me into such a terrible situation. The Silos, that stored coking coal for charging into the coke oven batteries, were getting depleted. Charging could be reduced but not stopped altogether. Once the batteries started cooling down, the result could be immense loss to production as well as damage to the Plant. By about 12 o'clock, my shift manager asked me if I had any objection if he posted an officer in the control panel room to start the plant. He was surprised when I retorted that he should have thought about it much earlier.

In this tense atmosphere, when the striking workers were surcharged with emotions and misapprehensions, it was only natural for anyone going against the wind to face violence. It generally occured when the management was forced to start work by using the workers who were willing to work. But our strike was only against the management's attempt at hoodwinking us and not against the plant or production. Consequently, we allowed the plant to be started with officers manned at all the work places. They would be able to keep up a skeleton production till the end of the strike, just barely enough to prevent the batteries from cooling down, without any fear of assault from the striking workers.

I had many rounds of talks with my followers. I told them not to get provoked by management agents and petty union leaders or indulge in any sort of violence or damage to the plant. Real success could be achieved only if no chance was given to the CISF and police to intervene. I would be willing to make any personal sacrifice for them and the successful culmination of the strike but not if they indulged in violence. After the end of the second shift I advised the striking workers to take turns to go home, get freshened up and return to the arena.

First day evening brought me information from reliable sources that I had already been suspended from service. However, to avoid any untoward incident, management had been unwilling to serve it in front of everyone. They were waiting for an opportune moment to serve me with suspension orders. So from then onwards, I took special care not to stray away from the midst of the striking workers.

From the second morning onwards, a number of district administration officials, led by the ADM and SP, visited the CHP and kept watch over the striking workers. By then, Coke Ovens and Bye Product Plant looked like a veritable police camp. From day one, Mr. Balakrishnan, in the command post of the management, was closeted with Ravi Arya and P. K. Moitra of the CITU union at Ispat Bhavan. Together, they were monitoring and directing the course of action to be taken. The Managing Director, Mr. E. R. C. Sekhar, who had just recently taken over charge, perhaps thought it best to give the old hands freedom to manage the crisis.

What the management, advised and guided by Mr. Arya and Mr. P. K. Moitra, could do so far was to suspend me from service with immediate effect and deploy a large posse of police and security personnel to safeguard the officials manning the jobs as also the key installations. Perhaps it was the union leaders who advised the management to use its stooges to telephone my wife to intimidate and threaten her, in vulgar language, with physical assault. The content of the threat calls was that since I was not leaving the plant to attend to my family they were planning to give her company in the night. I had not returned home since the beginning of the strike and on the second day also I had had no intention of visiting my family. So I could surmise that the threat calls had originated from the management side because it wanted me out of the plant to break the strike and serve me with my suspension order. When my wife informed me telephonically about the matter from Ispat Bhavan, where she worked, I directed her to give a written complaint to the management as well as the police.

I was so aggrieved with the dirty tricks resorted to by the management that when I saw Mr. Balakrishnan walking into the midst of the striking workers, on the second day by 2 pm, I could not contain myself. Right in the middle of the crowd of workers and security personnel, I caught hold of his collar and raised my voice to tell the assembly that this big man wanted to break the strike, not by talking to us, but by telephoning my wife and intimidating and threatening her with abusive language. This infuriated the workers and everyone started shouting 'shame, shame.'

When I saw that the crowd had become restless and started pushing and pulling the G.M. around, I took command of him physically. I ordered the crowd to keep off. I pulled him up by the collar and dragged him to the shift manager's room. There I pushed him down into a chair. I sneered at him, "If I have been staying back in the plant you have also been staying back in your a.c. chamber at the Ispat Bhavan. Your wife is also alone. Shall I call her to tell her that my people would give her company in the night?" I lifted the phone off its cradle and held it for a few seconds before putting it back, saying that the problem was that I was not a low down cad like him. Mr. Balakrishnan went on pleading innocence but no one heeded. Everyone was shouting 'shame on you.' It was perhaps this man alone who had to suffer such utter humiliation in the course of the strike.

After Mr. Balakrisnan left I asked the workers of the batteries if it was possible for them also to join the strike immediately because it appeared that without shutting down the batteries, management would not bend. But it was made very clear that the batteries should not be shut down unless it was absolutely necessary. They said they were solidly behind me and would not hesitate to strike work if the management attacked me in any way. They advocated for the continuation of strike in CHP as it was, but maintained a standby.

It is observed that employers in general have a feeling that workmen have no concern for the loss of production and damage to the plant and machinery. The truth is otherwise. Workmen have grave concern for production and safety of the plant. But the instant workers raise any grievance or demand, employers start considering them as enemies and a destructive force. It is the negative perceptions and prejudices of the employer that forces his employees to seek shelter under the umbrellas of unions and self seeking leaders. It is such leaders who instigate workmen to damage plant and production. As may be seen, even in this case, the workers of the batteries desired a settlement, but without jeopardizing the plant.

So at the end of the general shift, I announced before the crowd of the striking workers that I was taking leave of them to go to my family who was under great pressure following threats from management stooges. Staying back in the plant continuously for 36 hours without sleep or a wash, the state of my body and dress, covered with coal dust, made me look like a living ghost. The striking workers who seemed to have had full faith in me, was happy enough to give me a break from the grueling responsibility. I took leave from the CHP in style, on my Yezdi motor bike, from the midst of the striking workers and the security personnel, allowing all the BSP officers present there, to heave a sigh of relief. They had high hopes that in my absence they would face no hurdle in prevailing over the strikers to withdraw from the strike.

When I got out of the Main Gate of the Plant, I saw two ambassador cars waiting at the gate of the Ispat Bhavan. After a while, I could not help noticing through the rear mirror that I was being followed by them. I smiled inwardly because it was I who was offering this opportunity to the management to serve my suspension order. Some four officials from the personnel and industrial relations departments had been given the onus of serving me my suspension order at my home and getting my acknowledgement. They were surprised at my welcoming reception as well as my preparedness to sign the acknowledgement. Yet, all four looked very tense and politely refused my offer of a cup of tea.

After I left the plant, the CITU union, under the leadership of Mukherjee, had been in the forefront of the striking workers. From behind the scene, comrade Moitra staying at a safe distance had been applying his own strategy to usurp the leadership of the striking workers. A coward thriving always under protection of the government and management, Ravi Arya stayed away from the field. The only thing he did was to send some of his union representatives to convince the workers to end the strike.

Three other INTUC leaders, who were reputed to be frequently used by the management to pacify agitating workers and break strikes were Mr. D. Sukumaran, Mr. Bhagavan Das Beri and Mr. G. P. Sharma. Mr. Sukumaran, a Malayalee, indulged only in manipulative politics. Mr. Bhagavan Das and Mr. G.P. Sharma who had had an opportunity earlier, to associate with me in the labour field, and who knew me from close quarters, refused to play spoil sport.

So, the strike continued uninterrupted even during my absence from the plant. On reaching home, I found that my wife had not returned from office and my son was in the company of the children of my neighbour, Mr. Stephen. After a bath I fell into deep sleep till I was woken up in the night by my wife and son. She was surprised to see me sleeping so comfortably at home while a strike threatening the whole Bhilai Steel Plant was continuing under my leadership. I looked quite fresh, relaxed and happy. I told her that I had been relieved of not only my Netagiri but also my service. I took out my suspension order and showed it to her with a smile. She, on the other hand, looked very disturbed. Because of me, she had always been under tremendous pressure from the management. She retorted with irritation that I was showing her my suspension order as if it was a Padma Bhushan. I pacified her and told her not to worry at all because I had not done anything so far, without thinking a hundred times, and without convincing myself that I was not doing anything wrong. She finally acceded that she was relieved to see me safe and at home and it called for a celebration. She treated me and our son to a special dinner. I spent the night at home in the comfort of my family.

Only the next day I contacted by telephone comrade Mukherjee and others in the plant, who were leading the workers in my absence to inform them about my suspension. I instructed them to inform the battery workers about the urgent need of their joining the strike. I also informed them about my proposed meeting that evening with the leading workers of Coke Ovens, Batteries to discuss the future course of action.

The meeting consisting of about 30 leading workers of the Batteries, also attended by an almost equal number of management spies and CISF and police intelligence agencies, took place at around 6 pm in Sector 6 in an open ground. Unanimous decision was taken to shut down work in the Batteries from that very night shift. For the benefit of the spies, I made it a point to express my regret for my absence from the plant because of my suspension. Everyone eagerly assured me that they would make the strike a total success, despite my absence.

The total strike of the night shift workers of coke ovens batteries was beyond the comprehension of the management. And it was an added threat to the safety of the entire plant. No wonder that Coke

Ovens department is known as the mother plant. Credit must be given to some of the active workers, including members of the CITU, for giving on-the-spot leadership to the battery workers and making the strike a total success. The strike posed a potential threat to production and safety of not only the batteries but also the Blast Furnaces, Rolling Mills and other allied departments. Both coke and coke-oven gases were essential for production in all these units. It being an integrated steel plant, eventually, not only was Coke Ovens in a fix, the entire plant was adversely affected.

Chapter 17

Justified Violations

After jeopardising the jobs of thousands of employees who had placed their entire faith in me, and the plant and its production, could it have been possible for me to stay back at my home? I kept telephonic contact throughout the night with some of the workers to find out if the management and its stooge union leaders had been successful in breaking the strike. By about 4 am next morning, I decided to return to the plant because I gathered that the situation as such could not continue indefinitely and it would have to be brought to an end, one way or the other. I did not want to miss the concluding part.

It was a foregone conclusion that security at all the gates of the plant would have been alerted to prevent my entry into the Plant. So I sent my motorbike inside through a morning shift employee - to be parked at a particular spot. I also entered the premises through the Joratharai Gate which was mostly used by contract labourers. Dressed in befitting clothes I made my entry riding on the back of a bicycle, amidst a group of labourers, both men and women.

The stage was set for the climax of an unplanned drama. The BSP officers, district administration officials and CISF and police personnel who had gathered in large numbers, gazed in disbelief as I made my entry in the CHP plant on my motor bike, in style. Seeing eggs on their faces, I congratulated myself for my ability to do a little script writing too. The over a thousand workers assembled in front of the CHP welcomed me with thunderous cheers. Making a change in the venue, I led the demonstration and slogan shouting from CHP to the office of the Chief Superintendant, at the Works Building.

The strike continued through the first shift. Management had to do something or the other to intervene in order to get control over the situation. Summer was at its peak and the whole atmosphere was clouded with coal dust and coke oven gas. The workers, shouting slogans under the scorching sun, were surcharged with anxiety, tension and exasperation. A small provocation could have pushed the hypersensitive workmen to violence and destruction and confrontation with the police forces.

My relief knew no bounds when an officer informed me that Mr. Seshasayan wanted to talk to me in his chamber, in private. It was about 10.30 am. I followed him to find Mr. Nagi, the then DGM, occupying Mr. Seshasayan's chair. He pointed to the ante-room and informed me that Mr. Seshasayan was resting there. Someone opened the door of the anteroom for me and I saw Mr. Seshasayan lying on a bed. He got up and made me sit on the bed by his side before closing the door. He started crying and moaning before me with folded hands, pleading to end the strike. He said that not only had he been insulted and humiliated by the top management, he was also ordered to vacate his chair.

"You are the only person who can help me to save my job. You are a big leader who does not need the support of a job but I am a mere nobody without my job." he kept blabbering. His pathetic appearance aroused my pity, forcing me to pacify him with soothing words.

It was at that moment that I heard loud and insistent knocks at the door. I opened the door and came face to face with Mr. V. K. Das, the Superintendant of Police, the ADM and a few police inspectors. Mr. Das asked me to follow him as I was under arrest. I cautioned him about a thousand infuriated workers waiting for me in front of the building. He said he had enough force to manage the crowd and I need not worry about it.

While descending down the stairs, surrounded by the police, I could not help recollecting the scene of the police firing at Dalli Rajhara, after which Shankar Neyogi had been taken away by the police from the midst of his sleeping supporters in an open ground. And here it was a crowd of about a thousand alert and infuriated workers, waiting anxiously to know the result of my talk with the Chief Superintendent. They would be willing to go to any extent to protect me. I understood that the responsibility of breaking the strike had been handed over to the police. They would go to any extent to fulfill it - even a police firing. Like Neyogi, I could also instigate my supporters by playing the martyr and pleading with them to save me from being carried away by the police. The choice had to be made immediately. Either I could become a big leader by plunging my followers into a path of violence and thus making headlines in the news papers or I could protect them and the Plant from all possible harm.

I made my decision!

A crowd of around a thousand anxious and excited workers surrounded me and the policemen accompanying me. My calm and relaxed mien gave away no clue about the real situation. The workers failed to make out the meaning of the police surrounding me. On scanning the view over the heads of the milling crowd, I discerned a few pickets of baton-wielding riot police, positioned at different points, on the ready to attack the mob at the first signal. In a resounding voice I told the workers to remain silent. Then I lied and told them that I had been called by the MD for talks and I would go only if they permitted me. There a deep silence. Some CITU supporter raised an almost inaudible voice as to why I alone should talk to the MD. Without heeding to that voice, I gestured to the SP and ADM to move ahead. The surging crowd made way for us to reach the waiting jeeps. The SP took the wheels with me seated between him and the ADM.

After moving some distance, I asked them if I was under arrest.

Mr. Das, the SP, said, "No."

"Then what are you planning to do with me?"

The ADM said he did not know.

"What was your briefing when you took me into custody?" I asked once again.

"Mr. Kurian, you have spoiled all our plans but we are happy about it. Be a little patient with us to enable us to find a happy ending to this drama," said the SP.

After I had left the plant, rumors were flying around about the possible threat to my life and the police fooling everyone in the name of a talk with MD. This manoeuvre had taken recourse to in order to take me out of the plant before cracking down on the striking workers. The workers were becoming restless and turning a little violent, forcing the management to seek my help in pacifying them. So, I was taken to the police control room in Sector 6, where the SP and the ADM had me answer over scores of telephone calls of my striking colleagues. I assured them that I had not been arrested and I was waiting for talks with the M.D.

At 12.30 pm, the SP and the ADM took me to the Collector's chamber in Durg, where the collector informed me that the MD of Bhilai Steel Plant wanted to talk to me. I assented. After 5 minutes MD was on the line.

"Mr. George, I am ERC Sekhar, the Managing Director of the Bhilai Steel Plant, speaking to you."

"Yes Sir."

"George, I am extremely sorry for the developments in the Coke Ovens and I don't hold you at all responsible for it. I admit that it has been an utter management failure and now the plant is on the verge of collapse. Please help me to save the plant and I will ensure that all the demands raised by you are fulfilled. And once the work is normalised, I will personally take you back in your job in the CHP."

"Sir, I am touched by your kind words. I am equally concerned about the plant and it's safety but how can I be of any help to you?"

"George, you know that a few telephonic calls from you to your co-workers would be enough to bring about immediate normalcy."

I kept silent for a few moments.

I was caught between the devil and the deep sea. Mr. Sekhar was offering me a golden opportunity for a decent exit from an impossible situation which portended only destruction for everybody. On the other hand, it could be another ruse on the part of the management to save its own skin by misleading me a second time. Believing the 'sweet and endearing' words of Mr. Sekhar could be tantamount to hara-kiri. I decided to go ahead with the hara-kiri.

My silence seemed to have been a bit prolonged. Mr. Sekhar started calling me "George, George, can you hear me?"

"Sir, I am taking your words as a gentleman's promise, knowing very well the pitfalls ahead. I will see to it that the plant starts working normally with immediate effect," I promised.

Mr. Sekhar thanked me profusely many a times before putting down the receiver at his end. It had taken only a few minutes of telephonic assurance from the MD of the Bhilai Steel Plant to end an ongoing four-day strike! What a tragy-comedy! I spent some time in the office of the SP, calling scores of my followers to end the strike since I had reached an agreement with the MD. Some of the CITU activists including Mr. Moitra, were reluctant to end the strike but they did not have the guts to continue or lead it on their own. Work in the Coke Ovens was fully normalised from 2 pm onwards and by 2:30 pm, I had been chaperoned home in a government car by the ADM and a Dy. S.P.

The SP, Mr. Das, gave me long bearhug, before seeing me off from his office, saying that he would never forget that he had been witness to a historical moment when a great impending tragedy had been turned into a musical comedy by the simple touch of two pure souls.

I knew my soul but was not so sure about the purity of the other soul!

Paulo Koelho, in his celebrated book, "The Alchemist," had written that universal forces conspire together to support one in the pursuit of one's destiny. Though at that time I was ignorant about my own destiny, looking back today, I wonder whether it had not been to support the pursuit of my destiny that the then Steel Minister, Mr. Pranab Kumar Mukherjee, had become accessible to Neyogi, only after the Coke Oven workers had struck work. Neyogi had had, with the help of his PUCL connections, made many an effort to get an audience with the Steel Minister, who, after all was a 'Bengali.' He wanted to play this card to help him revive Dalli-Rajhara, which had become a ghost town since over four months.

Neyogi was nonplussed. He could not believe his own ears when the minster welcomed him with the news of the coke ovens strike threatening production and safety of the Bhilai Steel Plant.

"It is your own comrade, Mr. Kurian, who is hell bent on destroying the prestigious Bhilai Steel Plant," Mr. Mukherjee said.

Neyogi could not imagine that I could ever do such a thing as lead a strike in the coke Ovens – and that too, without him.

"Whereas you have been running from pillar to post to get the Dalli-Rajhara mines reopened in order to save the livelihood of over 8000 miners, this very comrade of yours, Kurian, is jeopardizing the whole steel plant in the name some paltry demands of his co-workers," Mr. Mukherjee added.

"I have not been in connection with Kurian since a long time, Sir," murmured Neyogi, coming out of his stupor.

"I know, I know. Still, I am confident that you can prevail upon him to withdraw the strike immediately. What I suggest is that you should catch the first flight to Raipur and get the Bhilai problem settled. And then come back to me and I will surely do something to help you out," assured the minister.

So, thanks to the Steel Minister, on 14 April 1981, Neyogi flew to Raipur, at government expense. It was due to the stronghold of the Bhilai Steel Plant management on the local media that the local news papers had remained totally silent about the four days' strike or its coming to an end. It was therefore quite natural that Neyogi learned about the withdrawal of the strike only after reaching Bhilai. He was distraught for having lost the golden chance of playing a key role in the strike which would have enabled him to get a firm foothold in the steel plant as well. Though cold water had been dashed on his ambitions, he was still eager to explore the possibilities by using me as his bait. Being a leader of the Bhilai Steel Plant workers was a thousand times more prestigious and valuable than being a leader of the workers of it's captive mines.

It was about 4 pm, when I was sitting in the lawn in front of my quarter, along with a few workers, that a tall and lanky person in white Kurta and Pyjama appeared at my garden gate. It took me only a few moments to recognise Neyogi. I diverted my eyes from him to continue my discussion with the assembly sitting around me. Neyogi was a highly publicised leader and his photographs had appeared frequently in the local as well as national newspapers. Consequently, the working class in general considered him to be a militant and courageous leader. The few sitting with me recognised him and told me that Neyogi was waiting for me at the gate. I told them not to worry and wound up the meeting in haste before going back inside my home. All of them dispersed, but only after greeting Neyogi. I told my wife that a blackguard and scoundrel by the name of Neyogi, wanted admission in my house and was waiting for permission to enter. It was more than half an hour before my wife could persuade me to meet him.

"Never turn away a beggar."

I met him at the gate and asked him what business had brought him to me. His appearance was that of a shattered and broken soul, seeking forgiveness and pardon. He begged to be heard and not sent away without a hearing. He appeared to be sobbing, when my wife came out to persuade me to allow him inside and opened the gate herself. With alacrity, he used his long legs to reach our drawing room and accept her hospitality.

Neyogi stayed put at my home throughout the night and the next evening. He used all arguments in his power, trying to convince me of the need to subdue our individual egos, learn from past mistakes and forget and forgive our differences for the sake of the toiling people. He waxed eloquent on making a new start and availing the fresh opportunity opened before us. He was inquisitive about all the details of my movement and in turn, narrated the events that had followed his and Sahadev Sahu's detention under Nationa Security Act (NSA). He pointed out that the media was so powerful that, more than the agitation of the mines workers, it was the media campaign that had compelled the government to release them. He said that by shutting down the mines indefinitely and rendering the miners jobless, the BSP management was trying to finish him off. He pointed out that the basic weakness of my leadership had been the lack of media support. He continued his tirade and told me that I had also been utterly foolish in allowing myself to be taken out of the plant by the police and ending the strike in a hurry. Without standing together and by each other, both of us would be finished off by our 'enemies.' We could win the day if we supported each other. He was certain that by working in unison, we could ultimately capture the 'key' to the Bhilai Steel Plant and make the management dance to our tune! He advised me to forget my suspicions about the media and the PUCL because both were very powerful and could be our strong allies.

Neyogi insisted that it had been suicidal on my part to have ended an ongoing full-fledged strike simply on the basis of a telephonic assurance from the MD. There had not even been the presence of a third party, at least as witness. I conceded that it had been suicidal for me but I reminded him that it had been beneficial for the Plant and the workers who were on strike.

"If I was totally wrong, then why were none of my workers rendered jobless whereas all your eight thousand workers were thrown out of their livelihood in spite of your great leadership, supported by the powerful PUCL and the media?" I questioned him.

I asked him how he could think it possible for me to work with him after what he had done to me and others in the leadership of CMM. How was he going handle the issue of the canards he had been spreading against me and others? For his supporters I was 'an agent of the government and BSP management and a collaborator with contractors.' How was it possible for him to change the perceptions of the mines workers that he himself had created, I asked.

Even as our discussions were in progress on 15th April, I had been nurturing a faint hope that the M.D. Mr. Sekhar, would send a company car to take me back to my job in the CHP, after withdrawing my suspension order. All the same, I also knew that this was only my delusion. It was only an imagination while the reality was that I had been engaged in an unending dialogue with Neyogi, over the last 36 hours. Slowly, I freed myself from my delusions and came to some real hard hitting conclusions that could not be denied.Neyogi, with his insatiable greed for political power, was led by no lofty aims. He had limitless political ambitions for which he could resort to scoop down to any level. I knew that Mr. Sekhar would certainly ditch me and the management would dismiss me from service and do everything possible to keep me away from the plant and the workers. It would stoop to any level to intimidate and victimise my wife in the Ispat Bhavan, to settle scores with me.

Once again, caught between the devil and the deep sea, I was left with no choice other than to join hands with Neyogi. In the meantime, I could simultaneously go on striving to develop alternate local leaders in the organisation as a counter to his autocratic and fascist methods.

It was Rajendra Sail of the PUCL, stationed at Delhi, who had informed Sahadev Sahu, the CMSS president and Janaklal Thakur, the Chhatisgarh Mukti Morcha(CMM) President, at Dalli-Rajhara, about Neyogi's departure from Delhi. But when they reached the airport in the union jeep, Neyogi was not to be traced anywhere. Their search continued for two days. Finally, after having looked at every conceivable nook and corner in Raipur and Bhilai, while they were resting in the HUDCO residence of Sahdevan, Neyogi, accompanied by me, appeared before them. They were overwhelmed in shock and disbelief. Sahadevan knew about the Coke Ovens Strike and was quick enough to deduct the meaning of our appearing together. But the others from Dalli-Rrajhara, made their displeasure quite clear on seeing me along with their celebrated leader. After all, they had been made to believe that I was a potential and dangerous enemy to their union and leader. Seeing their discomfort, I could not help asking if they did not want to ask Neyogi how it was possible for yesterday's enemy to become today's friend. They lowered their eyes shied away, answering that their leader could do no wrong. That was Neyogi's real strength - the wonder, the blind faith and devotion of thousands of illiterate and ignorant followers!

Slowly, Neyogi explained to them the circumstances and urgency that had forced him to return from Delhi and join hands with me. However, about the canards he had spread against me for over a year, he maintained a tight lip.

Ultimately, that night, Neyogi was able to prevail upon me to begin an indefinite Dharna to re-mobilise the steel workers. It was organised at Sector 1 Chowk, where, to begin with, we both sat on a day-long Dharna, along with a few of my supporters. It was intended to publicise our new founded unity. The Dharna went on for about a fortnight, with the participation of different groups of workers from coke ovens, particularly the CHP.

My expectation was that Neyogi, already a famous leader, both nationally and internationally, would draw a large crowd of steel employees to gather at the pandal. But I was wrong. The crowd was always smaller when Neyogi was present. I gathered from this that despite the steel workers' admiration for Neyogi, they were not willing to accept him as their leader or to associate with him for fear of being stamped as Naxalite supporters.

The Dharna prolonged. But it drew no response from the management. Consequently I decided to go on an indefinite hunger strike - alone. Neyogi agreed. I was firmly determined not to end it till the management consented to talk. As the days passed, one by one, I grew progressively weaker, despite the lemon juice I had been consuming. After four days, I became almost bed ridden. Still, the experience provided an unexpected and pleasant reward for being able to interact with many socially active persons, including a few middle-level managers of the Plant, who had hitherto been unknown to me. They met me clandestinely in the night, and expressed their solidarity. Neyogi, their bête-noire, might have been the reason why no CITU leader or supporter ever visited the pandal.

The fifth day saw me totally free from the pangs of hunger. But occasionally, I suffered from hallucinations about strange upheavals in my life, even my impending death! Seeing my deteriorating condition, the CHP workers were becoming more and more restive. Doctors who checked me regularly expressed concern about my failing health. On the eighth day, in the presence of many workers who had come to the pandal before proceeding for their second shift duty, a team of government doctors checked me up and asked the policemen standing by, to shift me to an ambulance waiting nearby. No one objected. I was bodily lifted and carried away by the police and admitted in the government district hospital, Durg. A few bottles of saline were administered. At my insistence, I was discharged that night, but only after the police had registered a case of attempted suicide!

After coming home from the hospital, I learned about the developments that had followed my eviction from the Dharna Pandal. Neyogi had addressed the agitated and confused workers and exhorted them to challenge the management action taken against me in a befitting manner – even if it meant a strike.

One among the audience, Mr. P. D'cruz, who had been close to me for some time and had watched me lead the four days long strike, thought that he could easily lead one himself. On reaching the plant in the second shift, D'cruz called upon the CHP workers to join him to stop the plant. Barring a few, the majority refused to respond to his call and proceeded towards their work places. An infuriated D'cruz, with the support of a handful of his followers, locked up the Control Panel Room and squatted before the door, obstructing entry. The entreaty of plant officers fell on deaf ears and the squatters refused to budge. As a result, they were arrested and forcefully removed by the police. The plant could be started only an hour later. While all were released on bail by the Durg District Court, D'cruz, as the leader of the gang, had to face suspension also. In the mean, with the fizzling out of the dharna, Neyogi thought it prudent to return to Dalli-Rajhara without informing anyone.

I was left behind to wake up the next morning to find D'cruz and his family waiting at my door, accusing me of making him a sacrificial goat for my own 'Netagiri.' They created a sort of ruckus in front of my house. They wanted to know what I was going to do to support them financially for the period of his suspension. They insinuated that my wife being an officer, I had no need to worry about my own suspension. It would be my responsibility to compensate Decruz's monetary losses.

They were not willing to listen to reason that I had not asked Decuz to take up leadership or lock up the control panel room of the CHP.

After the lapse of a few months, my erstwhile colleagues in the CHP informed me that almost all the demands I had raised on their behalf had been fulfilled. I also came to know that another worker, Mr. Tamrakar, an active member of the INTUC, had also, along with me, been served with suspension orders. Ravi Arya was reported to be trying to prevail upon the management to get his suspension order withdrawn.

Had there been any claimant to such a punitive action, after myself, it could have only been comrade P. K. Mukherjee. Surprisingly, no action had been initiated against him but that did not stop him or the supporters of CITU, from calling me an agent of the management behind my back. Ravi Arya appeared to have become rather compassionate towards me and had sent Tamrakar to inform me that along with Tamrakar's, he was willing to take up my case also. I retorted that it had not been at Arya's behest that I had led the strike. "Let him try to help you to get your job back instead of wasting time on me," I told Tamrakar. I knew that it was only a management ploy to bring me down on my knees and break my independant spirit.

Thanks to Arya, Tamrakar was taken back in his job without any harm or much delay. However, a departmental enquiry was conducted before D'cruz was taken back, though in a lower grade, as punishment. Till that time, I had given him monetary support every month in spite of my wife's reservation in helping such an uncouth and self seeking man. I also had been issued a charge sheet before my departmental enquiry was conducted. The Enquiry Officer, Mr. Saran, a Chief Engineer and the fecilitator, Mr. Chatterjee, were apprehensive about possible obstructions that might be created by me. They anticipated daily demonstrations in front of the venue of the enquiry. But nothing of the sort happened and the enquiry progressed smoothly with about half a dozen shift managers of the CHP and the batteries disposing against me.

The charges against me were for striking work, instigating others to strike work, causing loss of production to the tune of hundreds of crores of rupees, causing damage to the plant and machinery, disobedience to superiors etc.etc. To the surprise of the management witnesses, I did not put forth even a single cross question to any one of them. At a pointed question of the fecilitator, whether I had been obstructing others from working, all witnesses replied in the negative. After the turn of the management was over, I was asked to submit the list of witnesses for my defense. I submitted a list consisting of the names of Mr. E. R. C. Sekhar, MD, BSP, Mr. Seshasayan, Chief Superintendent, Coke Ovens, the District Collector, the A.D.M., and the S.P. Durg.

While expressing his inability to summon any of my defense witnesses, the Enquiry Officer asked me how I could have expected that any one of them would have made a statement in my favour. "I don't want them to defend me but to state certain facts truthfully," I retorted. To the question about what I would do if they lied, I grinned that their compulsion to squirm and lie sitting before me was my reward since I was going to be dismissed any way.

None of the witnesses for the defense appeared before the enquiry and I was dismissed from service in due course after almost all charges against me had been declared as proved. Only the charge of instigating others could not be proved. I accepted my dismissal as a small price, paid for my commitment and devotion for my fellow workers.

In due course, as promised by the Steel Minister, the Dalli-Rajhara mines were reopened and Neyogi was back as the undisputed leader of mines workers. And out of service, I felt like a free man. Though circumstances had brought me and Neyogi together once again, we both had our own reservations about each other. It was not possible for me to trust him completely and he had also nurtured doubts about the possibility of my abject submission. I was the only person in whose presence he felt uncomfortable because he knew that I would never succumb before his newly acquired "charisma and power." And I never spared words while calling his bluffs to fool the public. He grudged my knowledge of all his weaknesses from close quarters. All the same, he needed to use me for his benefit and I also wanted to make use of the organisation for my political experiment.

After all, it had been only the Marxist political philosophy that had egged me on to take up the cause of the toiling people. At this stage, I wanted to continue in it till I had delved out the truth about this philosophy which had inspired, in the last two centuries, millions of youths to take to the path of revolution. So, the crusade would have to go on to free the exploited and oppressed and bring about justice, equality and fraternity.

After our success to build a mass base at Dalli-Rajhara in 1977, I had been egging Neyogi to launch a political organisation that would include youths and farmers also in our movement. I had even suggested the name "Chattisgarh Rajya Sangram Parishad" for the outfit. My idea was to unite the workers and peasants as the vanguard of our organisation to lead a people's movement for a separate Chhattisgarh state. "Work for every hand and water for every cultivable land" was to be the key slogan for the party. But Neyogi kept dilly-dallying and procrastinating on this issue with the excuse that many leaders would have to be consulted before such a step could be embarked upon. To convince me, he took me on a tour to meet a few leaders whom he had considered important. We visited Kolkotta, Rourkela, Durgapur and Bokaro and had discussions with many communist and left minded leaders. But, in my presence, nothing concrete took place.

It was during the period of my estrangement with Neyogi in the year 1980 that a political outfit in the name of 'Chhattisgarh Mukti Morcha' (CMM) was formed with symbols of a "red and green" flag and an Adivasi Janaklal Thakur as president. Thakur, an illiterate transport labourer who was a blind follower of Neyogi, had been handpicked by him for the position. CMM must have been the outcome of Neyogi's association with the PUCL, the Bonded labour, Mukti Morcha led by Swamy Agnivesh and Comrade Mr. A. K. Roy, a communist M.P. from Dhanbad who had been once a guide and mentor of the leader of the Jharkand Mukti Morcha, Mr. Sibu Soren. It was at Mr. Roy's suggestion that the name of a legendary tribal leader, Veer Narayan Singh, who had been hanged to death by the British, had been dug out from history with the help of Mr. Kanak Tiwari. The anniversary of his martyrdom was to be commemorated by the CMM with much fanfare. It was a ploy to attract the tribal population as had been done in the case of the JMM, by celebrating the legacy of the martyred tribal leader, Birsha Munda.

Chhattisgarh Mukti Morcha, with Mr. Janaklal Thakur as its namesake president, also remained a pocket organisation of Neyogi. He did not admit any one from among the Chattisgarhi leaders or intellectuals in the organisation for fear of dilution of his authority. Rather he welcomed leaders and intellectuals from outside Chattisgarh to associate with the CMM. He remained surrounded by activists of the PUCL, Bonded Labour Mukti Morcha, JNU activists and NGOs supporting Naxalite movements all over the countery. He refused my proposal to take up the issue of formation of the Chhattisgah state by expanding our political base in Chhattisgarh, outright. So the best the CMM could achieve was to win an assembly seat for Janaklal Thakur from Dondi-Lohara.

It was only long after, that I realised that though Neyogi had agreed before me to renounce the Naxalite path, he had re-established his connections with the movement once again after getting established at Dalli-Rajhara. And through his newly found revolutionary intellectuals, he had been assiduously supporting the Naxalite movement in Bastar with men and resources.

Chapter 18

An Outsider

I had been living in Bhilai since 1961, but came to be noticed by the Malayalee community of Bhilai only after my emergence as a student leader in 1970. Though many employed Malayalees had joined colleges in order to improve their qualifications, none had stepped into student politics. It was undeniably true that they were all enamoured by the militant students' movement I had led, a rare event in Chhattisgarh in those days. They were in awe, but could not accept me as one among them. My constant association with Neyogi and my detention under MISA during Emergency, were enough reasons for them to think of me as a Naxalite sympathiser. As I had refused to join any of the Communist parties and their trade unions, in spite of their attempts, they also liked to brand me as an extremist.

When my activities started pinching the Bhilai Steel Plant management in the years 1980 and 81, the earstwhile leaders of the Malayalee community seemed suddenly to have woken up to the 'threat' I posed for them also. Vice President of the INTUC union, Mr. Sukumaran, and a few active members of the Bhilai Malayala Grandhasala (BMG), who were positioned near the top management as executives, stenographers or personal secretaries, felt it their bounden duty to 'protect' the management from being harmed by me.

So, I was surprised when some BMG activists requested me to accept the post of Vice President in 1980 because, till then, I had not associated myself with the BMG at all. It was again, at their prompting, that I thought of trying my hand at writing a script for a play to be staged by BMG artists. Namita was hospitalised for a tumor operation and I was left alone at home with my son. My mind was deeply distraught over the bloody violence let loose by Naxalites. I was also intrigued by the attraction of educated and talented youth towards the Naxalite movement and their willingness to sacrifice even their lives for the same.

The script of my drama was the result of my attempt to analyse and understand an extremist mind. I was in a trance during the nights and days when I went about frenziedly creating the script. While wading through my imaginations and writing it, I surely underwent almost the same agonies and ecstasies that must have been experienced by all those enlightened souls who had sacrificed their lives for humanity.

When I handed over my script with the title 'A Spark in the Jungle' to the BMG, it unleashed a big controversy. Its acceptance was a point of heated arguments. But the General Secretary, Mr. Joy Erumakkadu, a senior and outspoken member, was determined to stage the play. Still, the controversy continued till its staging in the Nehru House of Culture in Sector 1, on the occasion of Onam festival. As the director of the play, I had the most shocking and painful experience of losing, in most unexpected ways, two very talented artists during the period of reharsals of the drama, namely Mr. Simon and Mr. Srinivasan. Mr. Simon, who was playing the role of the hero, died of an infection caused from a Novalgin injection that had been administered to him as a part of treatment for a common cold! Srinivasan, a master clarinet player, and also the music director of the play, met his sudden end in a bus accident.

The rehearsals, however, continued with replacements. The new 'Hero,' Mr. Padma Rajan happened to be the leader of the CITU union in the HSCL. He had to face a great deal of pressure to not act in the play because "the play was intended to show the Marxist Party and its union in a poor light." In spite of all oppositions, the play was staged in an almost full house at the NHC, with the four rows of front sofas, fully occupied by the elite of the Malayalee community. Most were there out of curiosity for the script writer, rather than the drama!

The curtains rose to a dark stage. Slowly, a human face covered with blood oozing out of the head, appeared at the centre of the stage. A raucous voice boomed out from the background, "Centuries have passed since I have been shedding my blood for the liberation of my fellow beings, yet they continue to remain slaves. When I am dead and gone, they may put up my portraits and statues and garland them with flowers. But now, while this fresh and warm blood is oozing out of me, only for your sake, once again, is there not even one among you, to stand up with me?" This introduction lasted just a few minutes. When the lights came on, for the play to begin, I found all the four front rows of sofa seats empty! The first glimpse of a few moments had been more than enough for the so called revolutionary minded elite of my community to disown me and my play!

The next year, in 1981, I was unanimously elected to the post of president of the BMG. It was, however, beyond the imagination of anyone in the BMG, that I, while being it's president, would lead a real strike in the Coke Ovens. The majority members, being left minded, had always favoured workers' agitations and strikes. Even though the CITU union, in collaboration with other leftist unions, had, on various occasions, called for strikes in the Bhilai Steel Plant, all had petered out unsuccessfully. How then could a mere individual with no union or political backing, lead a strike? They just smirked behind their whiskers and satisfied themselves with branding me either a Naxalite or a management stooge.

My dismissal from service, as punishment for daring to lead the strike, was not enough to satisfy the BSP management. It wanted me to beg and crawl before it for succeeding in my "folly" of taking up cudgels against it. According to the management records, even the now famous Shankar Guha Neyogi had cringed and begged for pardon, hoping to be reinstated, after he had been sacked. They had witnessed many a trade union leaders roaring like lions while in service and crawling like worms after they were sacked. Management wanted the pleasure of seeing me crawl too.

Just parting ways without breaking my 'rebellious' spirit and snuffing out my 'arrogance' was not acceptable. My self-esteem before myself as well as my community must be crushed to such an extent that I would never be able to raise my head again in any form of revolt. The management had spies in the unions as well as all the social and cultural organisations in the township. And the BMG was no an exception. Therefore, in the middle of my term as President, one Mr. G. V. K. Nair, the Vice President, raised the question of the propriety of my continuing as president after my dismissal from service. In an Executive Committee Meeting, he advised me to resign as president because my continuance would put BMG in a negative light before the BSP management.

The web being woven in order to entrap and defame me by some CITU supporters and Personal Secretaries attached to top bosses of the BSP management, was amply clear. I pointed out that there were no rules in the BMG that debarred a dismissed BSP employee from being its president and the strike I led in the Coke Ovens had nothing to do with the BMG. Even so, I was quite willing to resign but as I had been elected by the General Body, I owed it to myself and the General Body to know whether it also would like me to quit. When Mr. Nair expressed difficulty in calling an extraordinary general body for such a purpose, I suggested that even a resolution passed by the Executive Committee, asking for my resignation, would suffice. Consequently, Mr. Nair and Mr. C. V. Vijayan, the then General Secretary, prepared a resolution asking me to resign and put it up for vote before the Executive Committee. The resolution was defeated, with 8 members supporting and 13 opposing it. And, because they had tried to connive against me behind my back, I was determined not to succumb to their pressure so easily.

The instigators needed an excuse to call for an extra-ordinary general body meeting and so, they cooked up one. The General Secretary, who was the custodian of the keys, kept the doors and gates of the BMG locked for three days, without any notice. It paved the way for the children of the KG classes, numbering over three hundred, and their parents, to create a commotion before the locked gates. A canard was spread that I, as the president, had created such a dangerous situation in the BMG that this premier institution, for the first time in its history, had to be locked up for three days!

Consequently, an extra-ordinary General Body meeting had to be called to resolve the crisis. They spared no efforts to depict me as a dangerous villain. Signature campaigning for an extraordinary general body meeting ended up with the Executive Committee, headed by me, calling for such a meeting.

Generally, not more than 80 to 100 members participated in annual general body meetings. But my 'diligent friends' had done so much ground work to mobilise a larger attendance of their supporters, that more than 400 members attended the meeting that day. The venue was jam packed. The meeting was supposed to be presided over by the president, with all office bearers and executive members occupying seats on either side. This time, however, only two or three of the executive committee members came willingly to sit along with me on the dais. Others thought it prudent to sit in the midst of the audience. The crowd was agitated and menacing. Mr. Nair and Mr. Vijayan, the main provocateurs, were conspicuously not to be seen anywhere!

The crowd - belligerent, noisy, and furious as they were, appeared to have come prepared for a fight. I opened the meeting by addressing them and saying that this extra ordinary general body had been called not by me but by the Vice-President, Mr. Nair and the General Secretary Mr. Vijayan. I called upon Mr. Nair and Mr. Vijayan to come to the stage one by one and explain what they wanted from this meeting. It was neither Nair nor Vijayan, but the whole crowd who stood up and started screaming, gesticulating and abusing me. I sat down and watched them for about five minutes before I came to my real-self. I stood up, gave a resounding thump on the table in front of me and roared back at the crowd in a voice the reverberated through the hall. It had an electrifying effect on them. I warned them not to forget that I was still the legally elected president and that I could call off the meeting at any moment and call the police to vacate the premises.

In the pin drop silence that ensued, I commanded all to sit down and they did so. The crowd was now under my control because its instigators, naturally being cowards, were hiding behind the crowd. I allowed the silence to continue for a few minutes. Then I got up and addressed them once again. In a very soft voice I said that I had no intention of continuing as their president and they were free to choose a new one and hence there was no need for them to shout and scream. They could come one by one to the mike and express their views.

It needed a lot of persuasion from me for a senior member to take courage to come to the mike. He condemned the whole governing body for defaming the BMG by locking it up for three days and suggested immediate removal of the entire body. Another senior member, who was considered the custodian of the BMG by most and known as a lackey of the BSP management by a few, now came forward with a 'sane advice' for one and all. According to him it was better not to discuss or blame anyone for the impasse and a new governing body was the answer for the problems being faced by the BMG today. Yes, he was a very 'honourable' man in the eyes of the crowd and they enthusiastically lapped up his advice.

Someone suggested the name of a senior BSP executive, a Mr. Subramanian, for the post of president. Accompanied by boisterous claps from the crowd, the other posts were also filled up as per the plans of the conspirators. I also felt relieved to be rid of a bunch of hypocrites – a motley group pretending to be revolutionary and progressive but in reality, suffering from an attitude of servility and hobnobbing. They took pride in playing second fiddle before 'important people' like politicians, beaurocrats and moneyed contractors and shining in the reflected lime light of such people. I only felt pity for them.

Chapter 19

Leader with Magic Band

After quitting the BMG, it was only natural for me to go back to trade union work.

BSP management had accepted and accommodated Neyogi as a trade union leader of significance and was handling him with kid gloves. It had regular meetings with him to resolve the unending labour problems coming to fore in the Dalli-Rajhara, Hirri and Danitola mines. Many of such meetings were held in the Bhilai Hotel. Deeeply impressed by Neyogi's stature and standing before the BSP management, the hotel employees sought his leadership to pressurise the management to fulfill their long pending demands. Neyogi told them that he could talk to the management only after they demonstrated their unity through a token strike and allegiance to him by joining his 'Red and Green' flag union. He thought that the puny "Kwality" management of the hotel could be prevailed upon, through the BSP management, to agree to have a settlement with him.

Things proved otherwise.

I came to know about the Bhilai Hotel employees' strike only when one among them came seeking my help because they were not being allowed to enter the hotel. He said that the Bhilai Hotel workers had struck work on Neyogi's advice, just for a single day. But they were being stopped by the police and not allowed to join duty. On reaching the gates of the hotel, I found them locked and barricaded by a posse of police men. Hotel employees were being barred entry. The police said that they had orders to not allow anyone inside.

I confronted a senior inspector and challenged his authority to prevent me from entering the hotel since it was a public place. When I tried to force my entry to pave the way for the hotel employees, a group of policemen surrounded me and an officer told me that I was under arrest. I was taken to the Sector 6 Kotwali Police Station, where I was detained for over an hour. By this time all the hotel employees had marched in a procession to the police station, protesting against my arrest and demanding unconditional release. After some hasty telephonic consultations with the ADM and other district officials, the station–in-charge approached me with a sweet smile and informed me that I was free to leave. While parting, he commented that the administration did not want to create another Neyogi in Bhilai.

Kwality management had decided to shut down their services in the Bhilai Hotel rather than run it with a staff infected by Neyogi and his union. In spite of losing their livelihood, the staff was proud to be followers of a celebrity leader and to have become upholders of his flag, the "Red and Green." Even though business had been wounded up, the hotel employees' agitation continued. Daily processions, dharnas and picketing were the order of the day. Possibility of a settlement, however, was nowhere in sight. Neyogi, being an absentee leader from the field of agitation, I remained with the workers in all their movements. In the process, the district administration put me behind bars twice and kept me, along with the hotel workers, for over a week each time.

In the course of this year-old agitation, I frequently visited the servant quarters near the Bhilai Hotel, where the workers' families lived and was witness to the compounding miseries being suffered by them because of the unending 'strike.' In the face of starvation, the workers were willing to forgo all their demands just to get back to their old jobs. Extreme want and starvation of their families were good enough reasons for them to drop their adamancy.

An odd incident of this period remains in my memory even today. Ms. Elina Sen, wife of Dr. Vinayak Sen, in tow with a comrade, Mr. Sitaram of Jharkhand, on her way from Raipur, landed at our house at about 11 pm. Out of politeness I enquired about their dinner. Ms. Sen replied that she had been so busy that she had not been able to manage it at Raipur. Namita, who as usual, had had a busy day with her household work which she managed herself, caring for her primary-school going child and busy schedule at her job in the Ispat Bhavan, woke up from sleep and went silently to the kitchen. Her intention was to furnish a quick and hot meal for the unexpected guests, a job she was quite adept in. Mr. Sitaram sat chatting with me in the drawing room. Ms. Sen followed Namita to the kitchen to advise her how to cook a quick dinner. Namita put an end to her civility and gave a strong retort.

I was caught unaware by Ms. Sen's rushing back to the drawing room, sobbing and crying. She was followed by my wife. While comrade Sitaram kept consoling Ms. Sen, Namita told me the reason for the commotion. Like Neyogi and his numerous revolutionary guests such as Swamy Agnivesh and Rajendra Sail, Dr. Vinayak Sen and Ms. Elina Sen also frequented our home and shared our dining table. They knew about the heavy household burden on Namita. This time, Ms Sen had been deflated by Namita's remark that it was wiser for people who did not know how to even boil an egg, to keep their mouths shut in other peoples' kitchen and also to save their crocodile tears for better times. I did not scold my wife for her behaviour. Instead, I told Ms. Sen that her behaviour was quite unbecoming of a 'revolutionary.'

Anyway, a hot and steaming meal was on the table within half an hour and our guests enjoyed the food thoroughly and went to sleep peacefully. But then, again, at about 2 am, I was awakened by a commotion at my front gate. A tempo laden with three quintals of rice, along with some mines labourers from Hirri, Bilaspur, had arrived with their contribution for the striking hotel workers. There were two men and a woman. Namita also woke up. Though they said that they were not hungry, my wife, knowing well that they could not have eaten during their long train journey, started preparing rice and dal for them. Also woken by the noise, Ms. Sen advised Namita to not bother as they had said that they were not hungry. Namita gave her a scathing look and asked her to mind her own business and remarked that the labourers had shown more sensitivity and decency than an enlightened revolutionary like her. Some character of those arm chair revolutionaries staying in lime light as the spokes persons of the poor and down trodden!

Once in a while, Neyogi, basking in the aura of a great leader, would appear before the striking hotel workers for an hour or so and assure them of ultimate success. Occasionally, he would send a few bags of rice to be distributed among the starving families. He would exhort me to mobilise more monetary help from my friends and well wishers. I remember, my personal friends like Radhakrishnan, Ravi, Mathew and a few others extending a helping hand for the striking hotel employees.

After the lapse of over eight months of futile agitation, the workers were forced, one by one, to desert the union and seek one or the other menial job to sustain their families. Thus came to an end the first movement of the Bhilai Hotel Employees, under the banner of Neyogi and his "Red and Green" flag.

Even though the hotel workers' agitation turned out to be a flop, thanks to the media manipulations, hundreds of other workers, especially contract labourers of the BSP, the HSCL, the Industrial Estate and the BRP, aspired to be led by Neyogi's union to fight against their employers. In many cases, the nature of jobs being done was of a permanent and perennial nature and called for employment of permanent workers. The contractors treated the labourers in an arbitrary manner, hiring and firing at will and underpaying them, in violation to labour laws. This brewing discontent provided a fertile ground for Neyogi's to spread his wings among the contract labourers of Bhilai. Neyogi was also keen on Bhilai and he found me handy for use to prepare his launching ground.

Soon, I found myself in the middle of a mess of agitations started by different sections of contract labourers under Neyogi's influence. They were willing to fight against anyone hindering their agitation; be it their employers or the police. Being always present in their midst, I was forced to lead them from the front. I, in the course of the two year long agitations, had to court arrest a number of times along with scores of contract labourers. The district administration, goaded by the BSP management, was determined to stop me, at any cost, from emerging as a successful labour leader in Bhilai. Even though the agitations were mainly against particular contractors who were violating labour laws, neither the district administration nor the labour commissioner was interested in bringing the warring parties to the discussion table. Even peaceful agitations were brutally suppressed and I was arrested again and again, without rhyme or reason and put behind bars. I had the fortune of spending weeks and weeks in the Durg Central Jail, turn by turn, along with contract laborers of the Slag Dump, the HSCL, the BRP and the Structural Fabrication Yard. My sufferings and repeated incarcerations along with the agitating workers, had helped only to garner more name and fame for Neyogi, who kept at a safe distance from all scenes of action. However, I had received constant support and cooperation from the Bhilai comrades like Neel Ratan Ghoshal, Kunjram Sahu, Gautham Singh Thakur, O. P. Yadav, D. R. Choudhary among many others.

Only at a much later stage did I come to realise the futility of my continuing in my current path which paved the way for the misery of myself and the labourers. The only outcome in each case was closure of work, rendering the workers jobless, conflict with contractors and intervention of the police, resulting in criminal cases against me and the workers. I found that Neyogi had no empathy or feeling for the miseries of his followers. He was less interested in any mutual settlement and more interested in creating a law and order situation and inviting more and more media coverage for himself. Ultimately, I was forced to ask him about the purpose of his leadership which led only to retrenchment of workmen and registration of criminal cases against them.

Silence was his only answer.

It was during this period that I started a publication entitled "Shramik Disha." Mr. J. B. Singh was its editor. Mr. Singh and I had got acquainted in the Central Jail, Raipur, when both of us had been detained under MISA, during Emergency. Some articles appearing in this publication were very critical of Neyogi's autocratic leadership and his clandestine dealings with the PUCL and other outside agencies. After the widening of the rift between us, Neyogi had confronted me with those articles and had accused me of vilifying him and trying to break the organisation. I retorted that I stood by every word I had written and it was for him to change his ways. I challenged him to justify his nefarious activities in collusion with the PUCL and his intentions behind pushing labourers into suicidal agitations. My firm stand made him flare up. He told me to quit his organisation and not use its flag any more. I reminded him that the flag had emerged from the blood and sweat of illiterate and innocent Chhattisgarhis who had been killed in the police firing owing to his own cowardice. The flag had not been brought from West Bengal. I warned him that unless he changed his callous ways, I would expose his true character to the entire public.

When Neyogi perceived that I meant what I had said, he cooled down and tried to cajole me out of my unbending stand. Once again he tried to shy away from resolving the issue by wishing the conversation to be kept confident and the discussions to be continued and resolved at a later stage.

I felt otherwise. I shared the contents of our discussion with Mr. Kunjuram Sahu and entrusted him with the responsibility of discussing the matter with the other leaders of Bhilai as well as Dalli-Rajhara.

At Dalli-Rajhara, Neyogi tried to override Mr. Sahu by saying that it was a personal matter between him and me and not open for public discussion. But the mines union president, Mr. Sahadev Sahu, once a blind devotee of Neyogi, differed. He considered the matter very serious and felt it ought to be discussed in an appropriate forum. But no discussion could take place in any forum because of Neyogi's firm opposition.

While on the one hand I was vexed by Neyogi's behaviour, it was just at this time that I had a few more differences with the BSP management also. After my dismissal, I had been facing acute shortage of money to sustain myself and my family. My wife's salary was our only source of income and it was insufficient to meet our household expenses in addition to the expenses incurred by my union activities. Printing of pamphlets, paying for mikes and pandals, arranging bail for the arrested workers etc., were expenses that had to be met. I was leading the agitations without enrolling workers as union members or taking any contribution from them. Though Neyogi's union at Dalli-Rajhara was very rich in cash, no economic support other than an occasional supply of a few bags of rice for the starving workers, were forthcoming. The only avenue left open to me was to submit an application to the BSP management for release of the final payment of my CPF. I knew very well that there was no legal provision for the management to deny me.

After an interval of about four months, waiting for the management's reply, I personally met the GM (P&A), who told me that he could not help in the matter till I vacated the quarter that had been allotted to me. I told him that management was free to resort to legal methods to get the quarter vacated but there was no legal provision that permitted them to withhold payment of my CPF, like a ransom. He narrated the sob-story of the widow of the Senior Industrial Relations Officer, Mr. Mathur, who had expired. His wife had approached him with a request for release of her husband's CPF prior to vacating the quarter, which she had promised to vacate at the end of the current academic session of her school-going children. He had been unable to help her. I came out from his office, telling him never to expect my wife to approach him with such a request. Subsequently, I met the Chief Financial Officer who also had no answer to my question about the legal authority of the management to stop payment of my CPF. He admitted that, rightly be wrongly, the management had never ever released CPF payment to its ex-employees without getting their quarters vacated first. Then, for about a month, I repeated my visits to the bosses at Ispat Bhavan, saying that I at least deserved a written reply to my application. But all my requests were ignored.

By nature I am peace loving and try to avoid any sort of altercation or unpleasant situation. But if cornered, I throw all gentlemanliness to the wind and fight tooth and nail. A fight generally ends in loss on both sides but if I am forced to take up cudgels, I stake everything for victory. Invariably the other side is forced to back off because of so many considerations to be protected. It was due to its own shortcomings that the BSP Management had to dismiss me from my service and not for any fault of mine. And to cover up those inadequacies they tried to vex me to the limit. Management had no authority to lay hands on my CPF. Even the law of the land would not permit its confiscation. If it titillated their satisfaction, let them not pay but they could not refuse at least a written reply to my application. After all, it was my money!

So, one day I went to the Ispat Bhavan, determined to create a situation which would force the management to either give me a written reply or call the police and hand me over. My intention was to freeze the activities of a very senior officer, other than the MD, to invite intervention from the top management. The GM (P&A) and the CFO. were, unfortunately, not in their chambers so I had to satisfy myself with a Deputy CFO, Mr. Bose. We knew each other because I had met him a few times with the plea of release of my CPF.

Mr. Bose was busy talking to some out station suppliers, and was a little surprised to see me entering his chamber without appointment, at about 1 pm. I occupied the seat that was indicated, and he continued with his conversation with his clients. After five minutes of waiting, I stood up and addressed the suppliers directly and requested them to leave the chamber as the 'boss' had urgent work with me. They felt non-pulsed and one among them, smelling something fishy, raised a rough voice. I shouted back, "shut up and get out." My booming voice prevailed upon them to make a hasty retreat. Mr. Bose stood up as if under a spell, and I told him in a very casual voice, "Please sit down."

After we were seated I began my harangue. I informed him that from then on, he would be totally under my control and should neither move, open his mouth, attend phone calls nor talk to anyone, unless I permitted him to do so. I threatened him with dire consequences and warned him that in the event of his disregarding my instructions, even his wife would not be able to recognise him after I had gotten through with him. My words mesmerised him to such an extent that all he could do was glare at me silently for about an hour.

In the meanwhile, his lady stenographer entered the chamber to discuss some official matter. She kept talking without eliciting any response from her boss. Intrigued by his odd behaviour, she looked at me questioningly and I told her that her boss would do nothing other than attend to my job. Bose maintained his silence and the steno went out, suspecting something to be very fishy. Later the superintendent of the BTI, Mr. Dutta, entered and started talking to Mr. Bose about something very urgent. Mr. Bose's statue like silence intrigued him. Finding me sitting in front of him, calmly smoking a cigarette, roused his suspicion. Guessing some foul play on my part, he pointed an accusing finger at me and growled his irritation. I told him that Mr. Bose had decided not to work so it would be better for him to leave before he was thrown out of the chamber. He beat a hasty retreat.

After the lapse of about two hours, I told Mr. Bose to relax. He was now totally free to act in whichever way he liked, without any hindrance from me. I expressed regret for the inconvenience I had caused him on account of the stand taken by the management which he also represented. I requested him to call the top management and explain to them the situation he had been facing for the last two hours. I even suggested that he might visit the toilet and get refreshed. All I wanted was a written paper from the management, rejecting my application for release of my final CPF.

While I was just contemplating bringing to an end the two hour siege, a posse of CISF security personnel, led by an Asstt. Commandant, marched into the chamber. They encircled my chair and the commandant tried to pacify me by promising to resolve my problem if I agreed to leave peacefully. I told him to mind his own duty and not to meddle in the management's matters. I asked Mr. Bose, "Do you feel any danger to life or property in your chamber?" He replied in the negative. A little unnerved by Mr. Bose's answer, the Commandant, anticipating a physical stoppage, requested him to step out of his chamber along with him. Mr. Bose looked at me questioningly and I promptly told him to please himself, get refreshed and return to his chamber only if he so desired. Bose went out with the commandant with the security in tow, leaving me alone in the chamber.

After a little while, Mr. Bhaskar Rao, another officer of the Finance Department, was sent to me. He brought with him a very thick bounded law book to convince me of management's inability to release my CPF. I told him to tell his MD that it was not law books that I wanted but a piece of paper rejecting my application, as per law in the law book.

Mr. Bose came back after an hour. He ordered tea and snacks and we spent the next hour in pleasant conversation, while prolonged top management consultations were being held somewhere in Ispat Bhavan.

At about 5 pm, I received a letter from the Personnel Department, assigning a date for the payment of my final CPF.

And, as per agreement of that order, I received my CPF payment in full, without vacating my quarter! Perhaps the only instance in the history of the Bhilai Steel Plant!

The incident in Ispat Bhavan gave rise to rumours about 'my forcefully' taking over one of its chambers, along with its occupant officers as hostages and threatening to kill them with the dagger that I had carried along. Management had been so 'terrorised' that, all my demands, without exception, had been met. And as even over a dozen CISF security men had been unable to take me into custody, I had been allowed to go scot free. And who were the people most responsible for spreading this? Stenos and personal secretaries of highly placed officers, most of whom belonged to my own Malayalee community! They drew immense pleasure from vilifying me as a frightful monster! I did not mind their fear because I had learned years ago that fear was the key that drew respect from cowards and spineless people.

Though the management had been forced to release my CPF, the humiliation could not be taken lying down. A quasi-judicial process was initiated against 'illegal' occupation of a company quarter, culminating in an eviction order. No one came to serve the order. However, one sunny day, at about 10 am, a truck occupied by about a dozen labourers of the demolition squad, came to a halt in front of my gate. Some were even armed with lathis and crow bars. Two Estate Officers of the BSP knocked at my front door and informed me that they had orders to get the quarter vacated forcefully, if needed. I had one hour. They were non-pulsed when I told them not to waste a single moment and to do it quickly. They hemmed and hawed and muttered that they wanted to be just. I asked who the hell they were to dispense justice. Had they come to do a duty or dispense justice? They were so unnerved that when I ordered them to get out of my quarter, they scampered out through the front gate and sped away in the truck.

This ungainly incident infuriated me to such an extent that I went straight to the Estate building and confronted the GM (TA). I asked him how he had dared to send armed goons with lathis and iron rods to my house. He expressed ignorance. I retaliated that I held him solely responsible and warned that if it was repeated I would send a hundred lathi-wielding men to his bungalow to give a taste of this action to his family. He promised nothing of the sort would be repeated and my family continued to stay peacefully in my company quarter.

In the mean, Neyogi, being unable to evict me from the union, used his PUCL connections to mar Namita's career in the BSP. His aim was to cripple me financially. The Union Steel Minister was presented with 'proofs' of her alleged political activities which included some of her photographs in the midst of the mines labourers of Dalli-Rajhara. She was projected as the real king-pin behind my activities and her continuation as an executive, a threat to the steel plant.

It is an irony of fate that it was a CBI officer of Bhilai, Mr. Sebastian, recently transferred from Delhi, who informed me about these developments and warned me about the possibility of Namita's termination. He said he had been in the IB at the centre and knew the inside stories of hundreds of political leaders but had never come across a person like me. He confided to me that I was wasting my life over a self-seeking and dangerous man like Neyogi. He also acquainted me with the fact that management had been advised by some quarters to transfer Namita out of Bhilai instead of terminating her services. As Mr. Sebastian was not aware of the internal rift between me and Neyogi, I told him to mind his own business.

I also had an inkling that we were in for some drastic action by the management. Having no savings to sustain ourselves in case of Namita's termination, we decided to avail the benefit of a car loan. Thanks to the sympathy and goodwill of the concerned officer, it was sanctioned forthwith and we had a good amount of money in our hands. We waited for her termination!

The waiting came to an end with Namita's transfer to the Nagpur Resident Office. Mr. K. S. Saini, an outspoken and honest officer, refused to issue the order, stating that it was beneath the dignity of the management to settle scores with a lady officer on account of the activities of her husband. Of course, later, he paid a heavy price for his 'audacity.' Namita received her transfer from the Industrial Engineering Department to Materials Management Department, as well as her relieving order, both in one stroke, from another senior officer. She accepted both with equanimity as she had been prepared by Mr. Saini's request to not give management the satisfaction of being distressed over her transfer and simultaneous relieving order.

My conscience never accepted my dismissal from service as being justified. Many leaders and 'powerful' national trade unions had been active in the Coke Ovens and I was not even a member of any of them. And if the workers found me more worthy of their faith and trust and felt that I would be better suited to take up their problems with the management, how was I to be held responsible? It spoke volumes of the inaptitude of both the unions as well as the management that the strike in the Coke Ovens had to occur. But they needed to cover up their failure and find a scapegoat. So the onus and responsibility was shifted upon me.

Kurian had to be dismissed!

The only avenue left to me was to file a case in the labour court. Repeatedly, Neyogi tried to prevent me from going to court by arguing that the legal process was futile anyway and he was sanguine that he could prevail upon the management to reinstate me. This unwanted advice I waved away with contempt. I filed my case without his knowledge. Adv. Gulab Gupta of the High Court, Jabalpur, drafted the application and

Adv. R. K. Gupta filed it in the Labour Court, Durg. It took over one and a half years for the case to come up for final arguments. On the last day of the proceedings my advocate did not turn up though he had promised to be there at least an hour before time to take a last briefing from me.

When the presiding Judge, Mr. Mehta found that my lawyer was not present at the most crucial stage of the proceedings, he, on his own, told me that I could seek a postponement. I politely declined his offer and said I myself would argue my case. Adv. Balbir Khanuja was representing the BSP. He was cock sure of winning the case for the management.

I had only one point to make before the honorable judge. I had been careful not to discuss this with anyone, not even my lawyers. Neither the mighty top management nor its powerful and arrogant law department had thought about it. The management had 'proved' through a departmental enquiry that I had struck work, caused damage to plant and machinery, incurred loss of hundreds of crores of Rupees to the company etc.etc. But they had forgotten the fact that they had issued the order of suspension against me before the strike had started!

I had been under suspension w.e.f. 13 April, 1981. I had been paid subsistence allowance from that very day. The strike had taken place from 13 to 16 April. They had suspended me before the starting of the strike and then conveniently blamed me for an offense I could not have committed! According to the management's own records, I was under suspension during the entire course of the strike. My only argument was that even if I had wanted to, I could not have struck work because I was already under suspension. Why was it that no action was being taken against any of the workers who were duty-bound to work but had refused, and I, the only one bound by rules not to work, was being singled out for punishment for striking work?

I may be mistaken but I think I could perceive a twinkle in the honourable judge's eyes.

Seeing the ground slipping away from under his feet, Management counsel Adv. Khanuja, made the plea that I had come to know about the suspension only after two days of the strike. The judge asked him what difference it made. The court struck down all charges against me and ordered my reinstatement with full back wages. It was a good slap on the face of the management. Of course, it had the option of going in appeal to the Industrial court, the High Court and lastly to the Supreme court. I would have to wait patiently for a long time before getting justice from the court.

I spent some time in Nagpur to get a rented accommodation and also to admit my son in a good school. Mr. Bhaskar Rao, Resident Manager of the Nagpur Office, received Namita, his junior, with a lot of disdain and displeasure. His anger appeared to be even greater than the one management itself had against her. He treated her as a persona-non-grata by denying her even a decent sitting place, as per her eligibility. At the same time my entire life's work in Bhilai was in doll drums. Leaving my family to manage at Nagpur, I returned to Bhilai to continue my work.

By now I had definite knowledge about the unholy alliance between Neyogi and the truck owners engaged as transport contractors. To justify such an alliance he made things 'progressive' by making a 'Progressive Truck Owners Association.' The Association was merrily minting money with the tacit underhand support of some corrupt mines officials. The Bhilai Steel Plant was being fleeced on account of the claims for payment for transport of iron ore, based on false bills. Just as Neyogi and the contractors shared the loot, the corrupt officials' palms were greased abundantly. It was these very contractors who were a regular source of big money for Neyogi in the form of hundreds of trucks with their tanks filled with diesel in addition to cash to organise big rallies off and on. This practice had been going on for years with the knowledge and connivance of one and all, till Mr. Sangameswaran, M.D., ordered accounting of iron ore stock received from Dalli-Rajhara. Over five lakh tones were untraceable!

Chapter 20

Internal Feud

The intention behind Namita's transfer was self evident. It was expected that I also would shift my residence, along with my family. My absence from Bhilai would suit the purpose of both Neyogi as well as the BSP management. Though I was a little confused about my future stand, I was certainly not going to make a clean break with my past, as yet. I wanted to try my hand at retrieving the organisation for which I had staked so much. Though leadership was not my goal, development of an alternative to Neyogi from within the organisation itself, was. The founder president of the union, Mr. Bansilal Sahu, had earlier stood up courageously against Neyogi and had, to some extent, succeeded in exposing him before the workers. But Bansilal was only one amongst the labourers – illiterate and ignorant. The majority of the miners consequently reposed their blind faith more on Neyogi's capabilities – capabilities which they themselves lacked.

Not very long hereafter, Mr. Sahadev Sahu, the CMSS president, Neyogi's blind supporter of many years, subsequently started questioning him. CMSS was the mainstay of the CMM and its president, Mr. Janaklal Thakur, was a docile and faithful follower of Neyogi. Sahadev Sahu raised pointed questions about Neyogi's autocratic and dictatorial rule, his secret collusion with transport contractors, the clandestine activities of the doctors connected with the Shaheed Hospital which was run by the Morcha and the PUCL activists that swarmed the organisation.

Neyogi's attempt to malign Sahu with allegations of joining hands with the enemies of the union had to be retracted after Sahu dared him to prove the allegations in the presence of the workers.

It was when the rift between me and Neyogi, over the policies being pursued in the organization was at its zenith, that on 14 July 1984, I read in news papers about the brutal lathi-charge on the BNC Mill workers at Rajnandgoan, the outcome of an indefinite gherao of the management. 19 employees had been suspended and the work in the mills had come to a halt. The banner news carried Neyogi's name as the leader. The implications were crystal clear to me. What had occurred in the mills was in a typically Neyogi leadership style. He neither wanted a peaceful dialogue nor settlement of any issues. Building up of conflict and violence between the workers and the management in order to create a law and order situation was his motto. He was determined that the government should force the management to succumb to him and bow to his dictates.

This policy, when new, had partially succeeded at Dalli-Rajhara. The fact that over a dozen labourers had lost their lives and scores of them had got disabled in the police firing or that thousands of them were trapped in unending criminal court cases, was of least concern to Neyogi. His policy in Dalli-Rajhara had given him name, fame, money and muscle power. He was determined to perp.utate that same policy. It was time to move on. His aim was to flex his muscles once again and extend his grip over the entire Madhya Pradesh. Though all his labour movements at different places had been utter failures in terms of benefits for the labourers, he had been successful in hogging limelight for himself in the media

I made up my mind to play a role in the BNC Mill workers' agitation and try to provide them an alternate to Neyogi.

I.P.C. Section 144 was in force when I, along with Mr. Kunjram Sahu, reached the union office in the labour colony at Motipur in Rajnandgaon. When we could trace out Neyogi, he was found addressing a closed door meeting of about 200 leading workers. Some of them raised their hands in gestures of recognition and welcome in their midst while Neyogi, however, ignored us and went on with his speech. Many of them knew me from the time of my students' movement and also because of my visits to them, along with Neyogi, on a few earlier occasions. But for Neyogi, my appearance was quite unexpected and most unwelcome. Yet, at that time, he was in no position to demonstrate it.

I spent the day meeting and conversing with the workers at their homes in different localities. I learned that the Bengal Nagpur Cotton Mills (BNC Mills), founded in the year 1893, was the oldest industry in Madhya Pradesh. Freedom fighter, Thakur Pyarelal Singh, hailing from the nearby Diahan Village, had been the first person to lead a strike in the Mills in 1920, during the British Raj.

Textile Mills, in general, were known as sweat shops and the BNC Mills was no exception. Ninety percent of the workers were local Chhattisgarhis, hailing from nearby villages and the rest had been brought from Bihar and UP, to maintain a check on the traditionally rebellious local workers. The locals considered those workers as *Pardeshias*.

The Chhattisgarhi workers of the mills were 'notorious' for their rebellion against successive managements who, in turn, were also known for their oppressive measures. In 1982, the recognised INTUC union had made an agreement with the management but the benefits accruing had been denied to the workers for more than two years. Then in April 1984, the Management made another agreement with the very same union to introduce a scheme of participatory management. Since the union had no locus standi before the workers, it was vehemently opposed by them. A strike was resorted to.

BNC mills being the only major source of economic activities of the city, every one among the known leaders of Rajnandgoan, Thakur

Darbara Singh, Thakur Vidya Bhushan, Pandit Kishorilal Shukla, Pasha Khushi, Madan Tiwari and Leela Ram Bhojvani had tried their hands in bringing about an end to the strike. But they had failed miserably. The strike continued, even without a leader, forcing the management to ultimately withdraw the participatory management scheme.

The 'success' of the strike gave the workers a new found confidence in themselves and they decided to free themselves from the 'yoke' of all their earlier unions and leaders and form their own independent union. They sought the guidance of the then most popular, revolutionary and charismatic leader of Chhattisgarh, comrade Shankar Guha Neyogi. Neyogi, who was looking for just such a means to expand his organisation beyond Dalli-Rajhara, was only too happy to accept a readymade union with over 3000 members, on a platter. Little did the workers realise, Neyogi's emergence as their leader was like adding oil to the fire.

Rajnandgoan Kapda Mill Mazdoor Sangh, under the guidance and leadership of Neyogi came into existence on 4 July 1984. With a female worker, overcome by the sweltering heat of the mills and falling to the ground, unconscious, Neyogi found cause to pounce on the Management. On 13th July, within just 10 days of his entry, he 'guided' the workers to gherao the management indefinitely without any notice. The natural outcome was a brutal police-lathi-charge, injury to scores of workers, imposition of Section 144 in the mills and the labour colonies and closure of the mills. Nineteen leading members of the new union were dismissed from service. The administration was so alert and sensitive about the implications of Neyogi's entry in Rajnandgoan that it converted the entire city, including the mill premises, into a police camp. The Mill workers thought that they were on an indefinite strike but the reality was that the management had decided to close down the Mills indefinitely. It took a long time for me also to understand it.

I told the mill workers that I would stay put in their midst till the end of their agitation. They were so happy to welcome my decision that they immediately arranged for my food and stay in a room in the home of one Bisahu Ram Thakur, a poor and semi-literate mill worker. When, after a hectic day, I was about to fall asleep, I was intercepted by a worker sent by Neyogi, to come and share his room instead of staying separately. When only the two of us were left in the room, he, in a hushed voice, questioned the purpose of my staying there and threatened to throw me out physically if need arose. I told him that his very behaviour was underscoring the fact that he was only a crook of the first order as well as an extreme coward. I dared him to act out his threat. Instead of responding, he kept mum and pretended to be asleep. I returned to my room.

Next morning the workers informed me that Neyogi had left for Rajhara at dawn to attend a 'meeting' there, as was his habit of proxy leadership.

In about a week's time, the management realised that it would be impossible to run the mills without coming to an agreement with Neyogi first. But they apparently preferred closing down the mills to messing with Neyogi.

Though I had been leading labour movements for quite some time, it was for the first time that I got an opportunity to live amidst the labourers in their small mud and brick houses separated by narrow, zigzagging lanes and to share their lives over an extended period. There were very little civic amenities to be had. Motipur was mostly occupied by the BNC mills workers who led their lives just above the poverty line. Their wages were paltry when compared to the wages earned by the steel workers in the modern Bhilai Steel Plant.

Other bastis like Shankarpur and Tulsipur, located just adjacent to Motipur, were also primarily inhabited by the mill workers. But, the union office being at Motipur, all the mill workers went there every day, swelling up the crowd there. The labour colonies were separated from the Rajandgoan city by the Bombay Howrah rail lines. Since the beginning of the strike, there was heavy police picketing at the railway crossing at Motipur. Meetings were held to discuss day to day events and share information about developments at the mills. Despite the daily attendance of about 600 pardeshia workers at the mill gates, there was no production at all. However, their very presence served the management's purpose.

Later developments unraveled that the Mill Management, administration, police, rival unions and political leadership of the city had jointly concurred to break the workers' confidence in Neyogi and his union. And for this purpose, they found the 600 paradeshias quite handy. No matter what, Neyogi's foothold in Rajnandgoan was to be blocked, even if brutal suppression, combined with aggression, were to be the only means.

In the meanwhile, I held many small meetings locality-wise to embolden the workers and also to garner support from others. In doing so, I could familiarise myself with almost all leading people and localities of the nearby villages and labour colonies. Neyogi, however, preferred Dalli-Rajhara and left me alone to handle the local situation. Before leaving though, he positioned some of his faithfuls to spread legends about him to the gullible mill workers and also to keep him posted about the daily developments.

After Neyogi's subsequent visit to the union office, in the first week of August, the police raided it and ransacked it. 17 workers present in the office were arrested and sent to jail. Subsequently, I.P.C. section 144 was also imposed on the Motipur Basti, banning any open activity. Naturally, Neyogi stopped even his rare visits to Rajnandgoan, citing the possibility of his arrest as an excuse.

As per instructions received from Dalli-Rajhara, a procession composed of only women and children was taken out on 14th August by the local union leaders. The intention was clearly to defy the Section 144. The women in the fore-front of the procession refused to be intimidated by the lathi yielding police and surged forward. This was the alibi awaited by the police to use tear gas shells on the procession and later to resort to lathi-charge. Though more than 50 women were injured not one deserted her position in the procession. The police was compelled to arrest hundreds of them, of course, to be released, while 25 of the more vocal were sent to the Jail at Durg.

Leaders of the rebel unions did not lag behind in adding their mite to break the strike. Under police protection, they took out processions of their handful of supporters through the Labour Bastis and called upon the striking workers to abandon Neyogi and go back to duty. By 22 August, almost all arrested women and leaders had been released and Section 144 was withdrawn.

Yet, local newspapers were against Neyogi and they kept up their publications of the violent incidents unleashed by Neyogi supporters every day. They also ridiculed Neyogi's cowardly stand of keeping away from the scene of action. While the mill workers, men and women faced batons and arrests their leader, Neyogi, was 'wearing bangles and hiding away at Rajhara,' the headlines screamed.

As weeks passed by, the jobless workers' militancy gave way to complaints and murmurs about their helpless condition and the miseries being faced in absence of any income. They came in groups to convince me about their miserable economic situation and the need to conclude the strike and get back to work. I consoled them as best as I could and admitted that though I was as eager to find a way out, I was helpless in the matter and the only way out for them was perseverance. When I sent an emissary to Neyogi at Rajhara to discuss the matter, he sent a truck filled with bags of rice. Local union leaders were very happy to distribute 20 kgs of rice per family. They had also received some cash in bundles of currency notes for distribution among the very needy.

Though one more truck-full of rice reached the hungry workers, Neyogi appeared at Motipur only on 29th August, over a fortnight after the police raid in the union office. It was then more than one and a half months that the mills had been closed down. During this period he had presented himself in the union office only twice or thrice and that also, for a meager few hours, at the most. I, on the other hand, had been constantly present throughout those 45 days, guiding the workers in their day-to-day problems, without claiming to be their leader. It paved the way for them to develop a natural intimacy with me and led them to look up to me for guidance rather than their absentee leader, Neyogi. This might have been the reason that made him politely ask me for a one to one dialogue before he took a decision on the future course of action that he would take in the case of the BNC Mills workers.

Neyogi told me that he could see no signs of a settlement. Even though the mill workers, facing a hand to mouth situation, were desperate to go back to work the management was adamant to continue with the closure. He admitted that all his political resources and connections had failed to persuade the management to have a dialogue with him. They were firm in their decision to deprive him of any alibi to withdraw the strike. The workers had no way of going back to their jobs, even without achieving anything. Added to this, he was desperate that his name, supported by the local media, was being tarnished by his opponents. And with the police running after his blood with an arrest warrant, he felt that he had no alternative other than courting arrest and going to jail. And he wanted a definite opinion from me about his plan to get arrested!

After due deliberation, I congratulated him on the opportunity he had gained to make a great leap in his career as a leader.

"You had been so scared of being arrested that you had screamed and yelled when the police arrested you at Dalli-Rajhara in 1977. But now in 1984, you yourself are offering yourself for arrest. Certainly you may court arrest, but do so with a procession to follow you along with a 'band- baja,'" I commented sarcastically.

"Courting arrest may solve your personal problem but what about the livelihood of the mill workers who have staked their livelihood and full faith in your charisma and leadership?" I asked.

I told him that I totally disagreed with him and considered his action as most irresponsible. Then he queried about my plans after he got arrested. I told him that I was also being chased by the police with arrest warrants. But, I would make myself available for arrest only after the mills were re-opened and the workers had gone back to work.

"I have made a promise to the workers and I will stick by that promise" I reiterated. Are you going to make public your views about my courting arrest, he asked. I said I had no intention of doing so. So, I remained aloof in the meeting of the leading workers hurriedly summoned to make preparations for Neyogi's arrest.

Neyogi seemed to have lost all hopes of a settlement. He had once confided that he repented for having jumped into the boiling cauldron of the mill workers. In this losing proposition, he personally stood to gain nothing from Rajnandgoan. I told him that he should have realised that BNC Mills had been perpetually sick and was running at huge losses and there were no hundreds of crores of rupees in profit in the hands of the management, to be siphoned out by the contractors and union leaders, as was in the case of the Dalli-Rajhara mines. He had led the semi-starving mills as well as its miserable labourers into a suicidal ditch. He sneered that if I was so pessimistic about any gain out of the strike, why had I continued my stay there. I reminded him that the consideration of gain or loss was his and not mine. I also told him that my presence with the labourers did not free him from the responsibility of his leadership.

It was merely my empathy and compassion for these rebellious and unfortunate human beings that forced me to stay put with them. Moreover, I had to learn a lot more about how our ideology, in terms of classes, class struggle, and revolution was going to benefit the working class. I was candid when I told him that I would watch his moves keenly, without coming in his way. He smirked at me and said, "Oh, you are back to your books and ideas which were going to lead you nowhere."

Years later, I have realised how prophetic were his words!

Subsequent to this discussion, for the first time, Neyogi stayed in Motipur for 3 days, till 31st August. He proclaimed a Rajnandgoan Bandh to be held on 31st August and announced that he would lead a procession to break Section 144 and peacefully court arrest. This he did along with 350 mill workers. Whereas Neyogi was sent to Raipur Central Jail, 17 of his supporters were kept in Rajnadgoan and the rest, released. And so came to an end the first part of the BNC mills workers' agitation.

With Neyogi safe in jail, the police began a manhunt for me. Though I had not even been a witness to any of the violent incidents that had occurred, my name had been included along with the other accused.

The day by day escalating conflicts and violence between the rival workers were instigated by the administration, police and B.N.C. Mills management on the one side and some lumpen elements from the side of our union. The newspapers were rife with stories about masked men indulging in robbery and arson in the labour colonies in the darkness of the night. When queried deeply, I found that the stories were correct and one of the kingpins of such operations turned out to be a popular local union leader Mr. Sevaram Yadav, a man supposedly very close to me and Neyogi. On persistent questioning, he admitted that he had been organising such attacks with the help of some criminal and anti-social elements as per instructions and financial support received from Dalli-Rajhara. I gathered that a few others in the union were also in the know of Seva Ram's activities, though they had kept it a secret from me. My shock and disappointment was such that I wanted to leave Rajnandgoan immediately. How could I stay in such a place where not only the leader but his supporters also were dishonest and unreliable? I informed some senior activists about my decision to leave as I was of no use to them. This triggered a hot debate amongst the workers. Later, men and women came to meet me en-masse to express their faith in me. They promised that in future, no one would act without my authority and approval.

The agitated mill workers kept pressing me to take out a procession and rally to protest against the atrocities being unleashed on them. Making one or the other excuse, I delayed taking a decision. I apprehended a vicious attack on the procession. But when I read a news item about the AICC President, Rajiv Gandhi's visit to Durg-Bhilai on 13 Sept.1984, I thought the opportune time had come to take out the procession. I fixed 11 September as the D-day. I calculated that the police and administration would not allow any violence to take place on account of the impending visit of Rajiv Gandhi. And even if the police failed to stop violence, it would only benefit the mill workers because of the presence of the Congress President in the vicinity.

There were over 5000 people assembled in the procession. I was supposed to lead the procession, while avoiding arrest at the same time. There was a large posse of police to escort the 'Juloos.' The procession, which was to return to Motipur after making a round of the city's main roads, got a start off at about 2 pm. It had to pass the rail crossing at Motipur before entering the city. When the procession was returning and it's head had reached Motipur at about 5.30 pm, the tail end was still passing through the road in front of the BNC mills.

That day was written as a day of shame in the annals of Rajnandgaon.

The horrendous situation began with the entry of the procession in Motipur. The peaceful march was broken up by shouts and screams from the rear with people running helter-skelter. People came running from the tail end of the procession, shouting about an attack from the rear. They screamed that paradeshias and the security guards of the mills, armed with spears, batons and iron rods, were mowing down the processionists. They told me of the many mill workers, fallen to the ground, seriously wounded and profusely bleeding. Then, a few men hurried up carrying the body of a worker, Mahtaru Ram, drenched in his own blood. His skull had been split open and there were deep gashes on his back and shoulders.

I got him and a few other injured workers rushed to the district hospital, in whatever transport I could find. Though I had been witness to over a dozen wounded and bleeding workers, I could persuade only two or three severely wounded, to avail treatment at the district hospital. Others preferred to seek treatment from private clinics, for fear of the police.

As night set in, reports started percolating in about the burning of some houses, and also physical assaults and attacks on unsuspecting policemen, by the goons of the rival factions. It was like living in a battle field. No one in the labour colonies, particularly Motipur, would have slept that frightful night. Reports of attacks and counter attacks in different labour colonies kept pouring in.

It was only in the morning of 12th Sept., that I received a report about the frontal attacks on the mill workers in their homes in Tulsipur, near the mills, the previous morning. A horde of armed Paradeshias, along with the mills security men, had attacked the workers and ransacked their homes. Gunshots had also been fired, injuring 8 persons. The situation started worsening further later on in the morning, after a large posse of policemen in riot garments, made an attempt to cross over to Motipur, through the rail crossing. Workers were guarding all the roads and lanes leading to Motipur. They started pelting stones at the police and compelled them to withdraw. The repeated attempts of the police to enter the Basti from other directions were also thwarted by the stone pelting mob. The scene was that of a war field, with the enemy force wanting to capture the Basti, and its inhabitants resisting the attempts with all their might.

There were crowds of men, women and even children at each road leading to Motipur. I found not an iota of anxiety or worry on the faces of these rebellious mobs. And I found no point in meddling with the developing events. The people of the Basti had the right to defend themselves from the repeated onslaughts of the police and the henchmen of the mill management. And the police had no business in entering Motipur forcefully in such a surcharged situation.

Around 11 am, I noticed a goods wagon being stopped to block the rail crossing completely. By 11.30 am, the police, taking cover behind the halted goods wagons, started firing tear gas shells in the direction of the Basti. In retaliation, many young men, covering their faces with wet cloths, were also throwing the smoking tear gas shells right back at the police, across the railway lines.

A blurred announcement came from mikes across the rail lines. Suddenly there was the sound of firing. I shouted at the mob to take cover to save themselves from the bullets. A worker, in an attempt to throw a stone in the direction of the police, toppled over just ten feet away from where I stood. He was bleeding from a wound in his chest. Minutes later, before I could lift him with the help of another worker, sounds of shrill whistles from the police forces raced towards us. We left the bleeding man where he was and ran for shelter. The police were firing indiscriminately, in all directions and beating up one and all in their way. The road was deserted within no time. Every one sped away from the spot and entered whichever house they could find with open doors. Chasing the running crowd, a large posse of armed policemen moved through the lanes, beating up everyone. They broke open the doors of many houses, dragged out men and women and beat them up mercilessly. They pushed and pulled at young women indecently and abused them in vulgar language.

From behind a closed door, I, along with a few others, could hear the sounds of the doors of the houses nearby being broken open and the inmates being dragged out and beaten up. Though the police pounded their lathis repeatedly at our door too and shouted abuses to open it, no one made even a sound. They perhaps did not persist because it was a strong door, embedded in a cement and brick building. Soon I heard the sound of a police march passing through the roads and lanes, announcing the imposition of curfew in the mill premises as well as the labour colonies.

We remained closeted in that small room till about 6 pm in the evening. The front door was opened only after the announcement of a one hour break in the curfew. The scene that I first came across after coming out in the open, was a most unexpected one. I became witness to an exodus of whole families, including children and old people, emerging from their homes onto the roads and lanes and leaving behind Motipur in search of shelter at the homes of their relatives, elsewhere. Quite a large number of families, frantic from police atrocities, were moving out of Shankarpur also. I also left Motipur for Shankarpur. While doing so, I came across many fleeing workers making way through the surrounding paddy fields. Many of them asked me to join them in their search for a safer place. They, as well as I, knew that the police would leave no stone unturned in their door to door search in order to apprehend me.

In Shankarpur I was happily taken in by two very senior and daring mill workers who were on the verge of retirement. Mr. Gendlal Verma and Mr. Bhuttu Sinha, informed me that the police had been frantically searching for me in both Motipur and Shankarpur as well as other nearby labour colonies. But, I was not to worry. They knew how to ensure my safety. On my enquiry, they told me about the deaths of Mehtaru Ram Chowhan in hospital and also Ghana Ram Devangan and Jagat Ram Satnami in the police firing. After a few days, I received information about the death of a 12 year boy, Radhe Tetwar, who had sustained bullet injures during police firing and succumbed in hospital.

The day and night curfew remained in force till 18th Sept. The night curfew continued till 22nd Sept. and I.P.C. Section 144 continued till the 30th. During this period, the management declared the mills open and called on the workers to join their duties. It calculated that by then the striking workers would have lost all hopes of a victory and would return to their duties, fully chastised.

Only 200 workers turned up.

Though the regular police raids and house searches at Shankarpur to apprehend me continued, the vigilant mill workers kept watch over the police and shifted me from house to house as per the need of the situation.

On 1ˢᵗ October, after Section 144 was also lifted, I was informed by Gendlal and Bhuttu that Adv. Ashok Tiwari of Chikli wanted to meet me on a very urgent issue. He had long been taking care of the cases of the mill workers at Rajnandgoan. He was very well known and honoured for his honesty and compassion for the poor and toiling people. I had a close family relation with him and he was also held in high esteem by the mill workers.

On 2ⁿᵈ October, Gandhi Jayanthi, Adv. Tiwari was brought to me in my hideout. He said that the state government seemed to have changed its mind and had decided to intervene in the matter of the BNC mills. He also said that IG Raipur, Mr. S. R. L. Yadav, had requested him to help him to facilitate a meeting between him and myself. He said Mr. Yadav had been asked by the MP Chief Minister, Mr. Arjun Singh, to find a way out to bring the strike in the mills to an end. According to Mr. Yadav, the news of the police firing on the mill workers had caught the attention of Mr. Rajiv Gandhi during his visit to Bhilai-Durg and it was he who had asked Mr. Arjun Singh to resolve the issue. I told my friend that the Rajnandgoan S. P. Mr. Pendharkar, had taken his failure to arrest me as a personal insult and had not yet stopped the house to house search for me, Mr. Tiwari assured me that the IG was aware of it and would ensure my safe journey to Raipur and back. He reminded me that the mill workers had paid a heavy price to compel the government to talk and allayed my misgivings by confirming that he himself had as much faith in Mr. Yadav as I myself had in him. So, I put aside the thought of this being a trap to arrest me.

I decided to take the risk.

Chapter 21

Search for an End

As per plan, Mr. Ashok Tiwari reached Shankarpur at around the midnight on 3rd Oct. He came in an ambassador car fitted with a red beacon light and driven by a police constable, in order to collect me and the union secretary, Mr. Jagdish Sahu. We reached Mr. Yadav's bungalow by 2 am after the midnight. Mr. Yadav was quite pleased to be an arbitrator of peace and welcomed us enthusiastically. At his request, I gave him a truthful narration of the events that had led to the police firing. He asked me if I, along with the office bearers of the union, could not negotiate with the mill management and reach an agreement. I told him that a settlement was possible only if he could assure me that the suspended workers would be reinstated, the false cases against me and others withdrawn and Neyogi released on bail. When he questioned why not without Neyogi, I explained that I had no plans to replace Neyogi as the leader of the CMM. I was assured that all my points would be taken care of barring the withdrawal of cases involving serious crimes.

T my request, Mr. Yadav talked to the jail superintendant and arranged for my meeting with Neyogi in the jail at about 3.30 am. Neyogi was taken aback to know about the developments leading to my meeting with the IG. Disgruntled, he could not help muttering that I should have refused to meet the IG without him. I told him not to worry, because I had paved the way for his release also. Now he could take bail and come back to Rajnandgoan without fear and act as he pleased. I was back in my hide out at Shankarpur by early morning.

Next day I changed my hideout to the house of Bisau Thakur at Motipur. My meeting with the IG rekindled the hope of a settlement among the mill workers. But most of the families, including the office bearers of the union, were away and had not returned to their homes.

Though the situation had returned to normalcy, the S. P. Rajnandgoan, Mr. Pendharkar, was inconsolable about not being able to arrest me. He considered his failure to do so an insult to his status. So, I had to camouflage my identity to mislead the alert police and visit some of the nearby villages to acquaint the mill workers about the possibility of a settlement and the need for their return to their respective homes.

After normalcy had returned, there was a spurt in the PUCL activities at Motipur. In spite of my assurance, Neyogi was apprehensive that he would be omitted and that I would take upon myself the leading role in reaching an agreement with the management. So, he engaged his PUCL connections to arrange an anticipatory bail for me from the MP High Court, with the aim of forcing me out of Rajnandgoan. As per the application the anticipatory bail order was to stop my arrest anywhere except at Rajnandgoan. I refused to receive the order from Mr. Rajendra Sail, the bearer of the order. Later, another PUCL man, a journalist by profession, Mr. N. K. Singh, managed to meet me in my hideout to advise me to come out in the open, since the Rajnadgoan S.P. had assured him that I would not be arrested. Convinced that this was another ruse by Neyogi, I told him to keep his unsolicited advice to himself. Then a Naxalite ideologue, Mr. Arvind Gupta, an IITian, approached me with the desire to work as my assistant. I told him that since Neyogi had repeatedly described him as a CIA agent, he would have to bring a letter from him, approving his stay with me. He was so much offended by my reply that he left Chhattisgarh for good. I surmised that Neyogi's stay in jail was mingled with a constant fear of losing his hold on Rajnandgoan.

On 15 October, Neyogi was released on bail. He, as their hero, was received by the mill workers with a resounding welcome. A rally was organised to honour him and I was also seated on the dais by his side. His first question was why only three people had been killed in the police firing, although people had been pelting stones for over four hours to stop the police from entering Motipur! I did not answer, but wondered at his devilish thoughts. He was disappointed at the fewer number of 'martyrs' produced at Rajnandgoan firing as compared to the one at Dalli Rajhara where over a dozen had been killed. More the martyrs, more name and fame! Dalli Rajhara gave him global publicity but Rajnandgoan had failed to make ripples even at the national level!

Thereafter began a chain of failed negotiations with the district administration and the mill management. I abstained from the negotiations and Neyogi seemed not to be in a hurry to bring the strike to an end. Though the police hunt for my arrest had stopped, I felt it a little odd to continue in hiding any longer when all others were free to move about. So I asked Adv. Ashok Tiwari to arrange for my surrender in the court. There were over a dozen criminal cases registered against me and they were all of a very serious nature. Adv. Tiwari could not arrange immediate bail for all the cases and so I had to go to the Rajnandgoan Jail once again where I had been kept on three earlier occasions, as a student leader, in the year 1969–70. After fourteen years, I found no change in the conditions of the jail. It was the same story - the same bad food, same un-hygienic conditions and the same atmosphere, stinking with human excreta.

I had to stay put there for a week before being released.

Neyogi was sure that he would get the upper hand through his policy of creating continued law and order problems. The state government was thus left with no choice other than to ask the mill management to enter into a dialogue with him. Having won his point, Neyogi now felt free and bold enough to lead the workers from the front. Though I had prepared the ground for a negotiated settlement, I kept aloof from the negotiations. And true to his style, Neyogi refused to agree to any point raised by the management, thus delaying all possibility of a settlement in the near future.

On 31st October, Prime Minister Smt. Indira Gandhi was assassinated by her own body guards who happened to be Sikhs. The incident created nationwide panic and anxiety and resulted in the lynching of thousands of Sikhs in broad daylight. Per force, the mill workers had to suspend their activities indefinitely. While the country was in a state of mourning, her son, Rajiv Gandhi, took over the reins of the nation as the Prime Minister and declared Parliamentary Elections.

Intending to test his support base at Rajnandgoan, Neyogi also fielded his own candidate for the Rajnadgoan parliamentary seat.

Consequently, his PUCL comrades managed a Janta Party ticket for Swamy Agnivesh to contest from Rajnadgoan against the veteran Congress leader, Mr. Kishorilal Shukla. As Agnivesh had no direct connections or support from the local leaders of the Janta Party, he had to dependent largely on Neyogi and the BNC Mills workers. Seeing no end to the strike and the prolonged miseries of the workers, I became disinterested in the elections. When Neyogi brought Agnivesh before me as his candidate, I told them that my only priority was bringing to an end the ongoing strike. It was on account of my objections that they had to open their election office in the city, instead of Motipur. Though I remained aloof, Neyogi staked all his resources - money, men and muscle power behind Swamy Agnivesh. Over 500 CMM volunteers were made to spend their days and nights canvassing for Agnivesh. Eventually, Agnivesh lost even his security deposit. Congress, with Rajiv Gandhi as its leader, and a sympathy wave in his favour, won an unprecedented majority by winning 404 seats.

M.P. state elections followed and Neyogi once again got busy with his election plans for the state, leaving behind the problems of the mill workers who had no voice of their own. With the intention of expanding his political influence beyond Dalli-Rajhara and to enhance his bargaining power for cash from the other contending parties, Neyogi fielded one candidate each from Dondi-Lohara, Balod, Kanker and Rajnandgoan. The result was that the CMM president, Mr. Janaklal Thakur won the Dondi-Lohara seat. His candidate from Kanker was withdrawn in the middle of the campaign, in favour of the Congress candidate Arvind Netam, a protégée of Vidhya Charan Shukla. The candidate fielded from Balod, CMSS president Sahadev Sahu, turned into a vehement critic of Neyogi after he was ordered to drop his candidature in favour of Mr. Jhumuklal Bhedia, the Congress candidate. RKMS president Prem Narayan contested from Rajnandgoan.

The BNC Mills workers remained jobless and wage-less for about 6 more months. Their mainstay was the rice and salt provided occasionally by the Dalli-Rajhara union. They had spent two months in violent agitation and the rest in hopes of success for their candidates in the elections. They thought that victory in elections would compel the management to come to terms with their union. They considered their life of poverty and starvation a small sacrifice before the 'martyrdom' of their co-workers who had laid down their lives, fighting the police and goons.

At long last, when Neyogi finally did pen down an agreement with the management on 5th December 1984, the only relief the mill workers got was the withdrawal of the dismissal orders of their 19 co-workers. For reasons not difficult to fathom, during negotiations, Neyogi ignored my repeated requests to raise the question of withdrawal of the false criminal cases against the mill workers. It would be necessary for the workers to remain trapped in the criminal cases to ensure their perpetual dependence on him. Alone, they were not financially sound enough to engage their own lawyers.

Even so, the mill workers did not fail to take out a victory procession to hail their 'great victory' and hail the powers of their great leader, Shankar Guha Neyogi.

But they had to join their duties like chastised lambs!

To Neyogi's way of thinking I ought to have departed from Rajnandgoan and returned permanently to Nagpur after the conclusion of the strike. But when he came to know that I had decided to stay on indefinitely, he began searching for motives. So, one evening, just before leaving for Rajhara, he came to my room in Bisahu Ram's house to find out my real intentions.

He ranted on and on about my invaluable contribution in the building up as well as the safeguarding of the organization at times of crisis. He acknowledged his obligation for my support and guidance during difficult times in his private as well as public life and also my contribution in the enhancement of his reputation as a labour leader. But that gave me no right to belittle or condemn him for his minor omissions and compromises. Whatever he had done had been for the benefit of the organisation and if I was unable to appreciate the compulsions he had had to face as the leader of a mass movement, it would be better for me to disassociate myself from the organisation. He added that whether I liked it or not, the PUCL had become an integral part of the CMM. He asked me to be guided by him and be a witness to the progress I would make as a leader of the CMM. He commended my knowledge of English and said that if I wished, I could be staying in foreign places like Beijing, Moscow or London to represent the CMM. His advice to me was to take a break for six months, go to Nagpur and contemplate on what he had said. If my answer was in the affirmative, I could come back.

When my silence stretched for a pretty long time, he got up to leave. I then signaled him to wait. I asked him if he could recall how I had sent him from Bhilai to the house of my student comrade in a village at Balod with a bounty of thirty Rupees and an old second-hand bicycle. In exchange, was he thinking of sending me to London? Had he forgotten that it was I who had shaken off his company for good after he had humiliated and assaulted Bansilal Sahu. At that time I had not wanted to continue my association with him. And was it so long ago that he had stood at my gate for over an hour, pleading for permission to enter my home?

He replied that it had been a big mistake.

Thereupon, I told him not to repeat that mistake again. I did not need him. I had no personal stake in my public life and when I quit, it would be as per my own choice. But he was a nobody without his empire and his leadership. It was I who had saved his empire for him at both Rajhara and Rajnandgoan when they were on the verge of collapse.

In a cold voice I told him not to return to me again.

"Even if I am faced with death, I will not come back to you," were his prophetic words.

In the course of the six months agitation, I had used a few occasions to visit my family at Nagpur for a few days. After the end of the strike, I had decided to end my stay at Rajnandgoan. But as weeks went by, I started feeling the pinch of my idleness. I tried to spend time reading books but could not help contemplating on my past political activities. I was not able to decide what it was that I really wanted to achieve. Did my association with Neyogi help to alleviate even in a small way, the sufferings of the toiling people? What I had witnessed so far was the aggravation of the miseries of the poor who had followed our path. Of course, I had great love and empathy for the toiling and exploited people and held the government officials and capitalists responsible for their sufferings. I had an inherent hatred and contempt for all rich people and considered them as sinners and their wealth as unholy. Whenever I had acted on my own, minimum losses were caused to my followers. On the other hand, Neyogi never expressed concern for the losses suffered by his followers. In the name of improving the lot of the workers, he had actually paved the way for their livelihood to be snatched away. Initially, I thought that perhaps his methods were wrong. I wanted to discuss and clarify.

But he behaved like a dictator and refused to discuss.

A few months after I had left for Nagpur, I got a call from Adv. Ashok Tiwari informing me that 600 of our workers in the Rajaram Glucose Factory, at Foripar in Rajnandgoan, had struck work without notice. It was typical of Neyogi to provoke a strike and cripple the industry to bring the management to it's knees before discussing any problem. 15 days had gone by and the raw materials like Maize and Tapioca were rotting and stinking, causing a serious health hazard. The laying off of six seasonal employees for want of work had been the provocation for the strike. Mr. Tiwari had also gathered that Mr. Rajaram Gupta was eager for an immediate settlement with anyone from the union other than Neyogi. Tiwari advised me to take initiative to end the strike, which, was not in the interest of either party.

During the six months' stay at the BNC Mills, I had spent many days with the workers of the Glucose factory also. Influenced by the BNC Mills strike, they had also joined our union. All the workers hailed from villages nearby. Another union had also been registered for them with Mr. Bhimrao Bagde as president.

The story, as I had heard from the workers as well as the elders of the villages, was that Mr. Rajram Gupta, a local Engineer, had been appointed by the state government as administrator of the BNC Mills which had remained closed for years. The mills were sick and recurring huge losses. Rajram Gupta, armed with full powers, had not only turned this loss making venture into a profit making one, but had also restored employment to over three thousand workers. In the process he had not only helped the mills but himself also! He was alleged to have collected the decade old scraps of the Mills, and to have sold it for Rs. 5 lakhs to put away in his own kitty.

Side by side, he was also credited with the purchase of about 500 acres of barren land from farmers in Tedesara and Mohar villages, at rates varying from Rs. 500 to 1000 per acre. He had converted the waste land into an agricultural farm for growing maze and tapioca. Then he built his own glucose factory to produce glucose and its by-products by using the products of his own farm. He was able to provide employment to over 600 Chhattisgarhi youths from the nearby villages. Of course, there was a great deal of heart burning for the farmers who had sold their barren land to Gupta at throw away prices, when they saw the land turning into a lush green farm, generating a huge tax free income. However the villagers consoled themselves by thinking that at least their unemployed children would become factory workers.

As a labour leader, my concern was better wages and work facilities for the workmen. Even so, I could not help developing a great admiration for Mr. Gupta who appeared to be a capitalist quite different from my general perception.

Bhimrao Bagde and other union leaders who were very eager to make a settlement and end the strike, received me with great enthusiasm. They said that they had gone to Dalli-Rajhara a number of times to call Neyogi to Fotipar to settle the problem. But he had refused to come till invited by Mr. Gupta himself. Out of exasperation they had approached Adv. Ashok Tiwari to call me from Nagpur. They were overjoyed that I had reciprocated so quickly.

In a telephonic talk with Mr. Gupta I told him that it was not seemly for a qualified engineer who had risen from rags to riches to be standing on prestige, in resolving a minor dispute over employment of a few illiterate workers. Especially when he had been providing livelihood to hundreds of such workers! I told him that I had come all the way from Nagpur just for a day and I would like to settle the dispute with him and end the strike before I returned. He expressed so much happiness that he told me that he was just leaving for Bombay but was cancelling his programme to meet me at the factory gate in an hour's time.

I used the intervening time to gather all the grievances of the workers from Mr. Bagde and other workers. The laid off co-workers were to be taken back in jobs. Lack of provision of medical care and supply of safety boots and hand gloves etc were others.

Mr. Gupta reached the factory by 5 pm as promised and sent his representative to invite me to the factory. It was the first time that I was entering the factory premises. There was a mild drizzle and the atmosphere was stinking like hell because of the rotting mazes in huge cauldrons. I saw a woman of about 60 standing in the open under an umbrella and supervising soil digging for some civil work. I was pleasantly taken aback when Mr. Gupta introduced her as his wife.

To make the story short, the laid off workers were taken back and kept for other sundry work in the factory. They had been laid off as per usual practice as they were seasonal workers engaged in his agricultural farm. Mr. Gupta agreed to our genuine demands and a written agreement was signed at about 10 pm by Mr. Gupta from the side of the management and by Mr. Bagde and others from the side of the union. I left Fotipar the next morning, only after the morning shift workers had reported for duty and the agreement had come into force.

When Neyogi got information, he rushed to Fotipar the very next day. He was so relieved to know that I had already left for Nagpur. However, he was clever enough to convert the snub he had received from me into an opportunity. So, he organised a victory march with fire crackers and band baja in the evening to celebrate the victory and honor himself as their great leader.

None of the workers missed my absence!

Chapter 22

An 'Enemy' to Blame

Though both Neyogi and I were products of the same ideology, our backgrounds were entirely different. Mine was that of an Orthodox Catholic Christian family which kept itself leagues away from communists. Our family tradition was to stand against communist movements in our native state Kerala. It was the beconing of the Marxist literature that had deviated me from our traditional path. Neyogi, on the other hand, had been born and brought up in the midst of Communist movements of West Bengal. He had been active in such movements from his school days and was attracted by the name, fame, and respect attached to communist leaders in those days. So our perceptions and understanding about Communism were different.

For me, Marxism was a truly scientific ideology that could enlighten the poor masses about their rights and duties and free them from poverty and bondage. It demanded sacrifice and I was more than willing. For Neyogi, like most communists, it was first and foremost a political ideology for capturing political power by organising and arming workers and peasants. For them, no amount of human sacrifice was too much to meet their ends. The toiling and exploited masses were earmarked as cannon fodder in the war against the enemies. Their inner beings were totally filled with hatred for their class enemies. Anyway, it would be the poor who would bear the brunt of the onslaught, mindless of their own lives, while they reaped the benefits that accrued.

Like moths attracted to light, a considerable number of educated youths were drawn to the ranks of the Naxalites. Along with them, criminal minded, overreaching ambitious elements suffering from loneliness, conflict and hatred were also sucked into the vortex. Neyogi also suffered from an unbridled passion to become famous and powerful. His climb from a non-entity of a sem-skilled worker in the Coke Ovens of the Bhilai Steel Plant, to a nationally acclaimed labour leader, had blinded him to the extent that he believed, in reality, that he was destined to capture power at Delhi and unfurl the CMM flag at the Red Fort. The PUCL, conjoined with the ongoing Naxalite movement, used to provide just the right thrust to fan his ambitions. Forgotten were all his commitments to severe his connections with Naxalism. And the PUCL was more than eager to act as a conduit between him and the Naxalite movement.

It could have been nothing save the acme of an inferiority complex that led Neyogi to project himself as a scion of a landlord family and a chemical engineer working in the Bhilai Steel Plant. He vowed that he had renounced his luxurious life for the sake of revolution. And the vulnerable and illiterate Chhattisgarhis, gullible as they were, believed him. They were made to believe, as perhaps, he himself did, that he was the Mao-Tse-Tung of India. The PUCL and the leftist intellectuals of JNU, who had surrounded him since 1977, ensured that he remained misled.

I was the only stumbling block.

The role I had played in settling the 'dispute' in the Glucose Factory, without the 'approval' of Neyogi, rankled him no ends. He realised that I occupied a very strong presence in the minds of the workers everywhere and, if necessary, they could rely on me without waiting for him. His dilemma was that while on the one hand, I could be used as a great asset because all I did and suffered went into his account without his having to share name, fame or money with me, and on the other hand, it was PUCL who had projected him all over the world as a messiah of the labourers. And I was diametrically opposed to the PUCL.

The choice he had to make was tricky indeed.

Even in my absence, during my stay at Nagpur, most of the time in the year 1985, my ghost haunted him. The local leaders of Bhilai, Rajnandgoan and Dalli-Rajhara had been challenging many of Neyogi's decisions, including his repeated attempts to stamp me as an agent of the BSP management and influential contractors. The workers refused to expel me from the organisation despite his oft repeated orders. Though he was unable to paint me as a betrayer and an enemy to his followers at Bhilai and Rajnandgoan, he could succeded, to some extent, with his blind and simple-minded followers at Dalli-Rajhara.

However, at the end of one of his failed strikes involving all the 8000 miners, dissenting murmurs did start surfacing. Neyogi had pushed them into a very prolonged strike in protest of transfer of about a 1000 workers to Maha Maya Mines, just a few kms away, even though the BSP management had offered to provide residence and other facilities. Once again, the mines remained closed for over six months. Consequently, the BSP management was forced to procure iron ore from alternate sources. The CMSS president, Mr. Shadev Sahu, who had been suffering insults and humiliation at the hands of Neyogi, gathered nerves to take up the voices of the dissenting miners and openly challenged Neyogi's decision to strike.

It was only the fear of losing his dominion that forced Neyogi to withdraw the strike. But he would not forget.

My sojourn in Nagpur with my family this time was over a longer period. Away from the active field of action, I was able to mull over in a detached manner, the events and situations that I had been going through. My views about 'the exploited and the downtrodden' had undergone a sea change. Direct involvement in their problems gave rise to questions regarding the basic tenets of Marxism such as equality, working class, exploitation, class struggle, revolution etc. The very foundation of my faith was tottering. But I had to search for an answer.

Even so, my emotional attachment for the mill workers of Rajnandgoan refused to die down. I thought of visiting them once again to take their final leave. But I found a total turn about in attitude, particularly in their leaders. They were found tense, secretive and without many words to speak. I found a strong presence of Neyogi's ghost in their midst.

I felt deeply hurt by the cold reception I received when I reached the union office on 6 Jan 1985. Everyone remained tight lipped till the union president, Mr. Prem Narain Verma, a known blind devotee of Neyogi, informed me that the union had taken a decision to separate me for the next one year. Naturally, I asked for a reason. But, silence was his only reply. Others present kept their heads down and avoided eye contact.. Though I knew that it was Neyogi who was speaking through Prem Narain, I could not believe my ears.

These were the very same people who had had me in their midst, day and night, and with whom, for over six months, I had shared the worst of their times. The police firing, the curfew and repeated police assaults, their abandoning of their own dwellings, Nyeogi's cohorts running away to safety at Rajhara... It had been me who had stayed back; me who had instilled courage in each one of them and brought them back from their hiding places. It was for their sake that I had not visited my family for more than six months.

Now, they were expelling me from their midst for no reason they could cite.

Chapter 23

The Final Reckoning

With a grief striken heart and tears in my eyes, I returnd to Durg. I went to the Durg Government Arts and Science College, wishing to meet my good friend, mentor and guide, Professor S. B. K. Murthy.

Prof. Murthy, with whom I used to share my public experiences and thoughts, had been a keen observer of my public life, since my college days and used to give me sane advice from time to time. I lay bare my wounded heart before him. He listened with empathy and advised me to return to Nagpur forthwith, as my life was in extreme danger there. When I told him of my intention of meeting some of the ordinary mill workers who had shown love and concern for me, he expressed great concern for my safety and insisted that I was behaving like an emotional fool.

I did not follow Prof. Murthy's advice. I went to Bhilai to spend a night with my friend, Mr. Radhakrishnan. Next morning, Sahadev Sahu came searching for me to discuss the developments in Rajhara and the witch hunt unleashed by Neyogi. He wanted me to accompany him to Rajhara but when I told him of my intention to go to Rajnandgoan first, he decided to accompany me.

We spent the evening and the night of 7 Dec. at Adv. Ashok Tiwari's home in Chikkli, Rajnadgoan. His aged mother, a freedom fighter and a woman of great dignity and wisdom, had always happily welcomed me in her home. She considered her advocate son to be in extreme love with me and cracked jokes about it. Coming to know about our presence there, scores of the mill workers from nearby Shankarpur and Motipur came to meet us. None of them seemed to be aware of the 'decision' of their union to banish me from Rajnandgoan.

At around 9 next morning, just as we were preparing to leave for Rajhara, one Mr. Bhagoli Ram Verma came in a jeep, driven by a truck driver of Dalli-Rajhara Mines, to meet me. He was one of my most trusted men from the mills and had been constantly associating with me all through my stay at Motipur. He told me that Neyogi had arranged a meeting of all top leaders of the CMM at Motipur where almost everyone, including Neyogi, had turned up excepting for me and Sahadev Sahu. Sahadev could not be contacted earlier as he was absent from Rajhara. I had detected a momentary element of fear and anxiety in Bhagoli Ram's shifting eyes. So I asked Sahadev if what Bhagoli Ram said could be true. He replied that Neyogi had been labeling everyone opposed to his views as enemies of the union and demanding their expulsion. But many leaders at Rajhara, Rajnandgoan, Bhilai and other places had demanded an open meeting to discuss and resolve the differences. Neyogi, who had all along been in opposition, might have now relented, he observed. "Better late than never" was his conclusion. Though it was a hope against hope, I decided to take a chance.

When we reached Motipur we were taken to the terrace of a building. Bhagoli Ram vanished, leaving us in the midst of some workers from Rajhara. When I queried about the venue of the meeting they replied that they were unaware. After the lapse of about half an hour someone came to announce that the venue of the meeting had been shifted to Dalli-Rajhara. All leaders, but us two, had already assembled there. We were also to reach the venue as quickly as possible.

Suddenly, there appeared a rush of people trying to hurry us up to sit in two separate jeeps. Not a single mill worker was to be seen anywhere. A small crowd of Rajhara mines workers engulfed us to take us to the two waiting jeeps where we were instructed to sit separately. While being separated from me, Sahadev, with a tremor in his voice, opined that it might be a trap laid by Neyogi. The anger and venom in the eyes of our escorts told us that we were already in their trap. But for what purpose, I could not make out.

The jeeps moved at breakneck speed. When the driver ignored my repeated pleas to moderate the speed, I knew that my fate had already been sealed.

By the time our jeeps reached Dalli-Rajhara at about 12 noon, a crowd of over a thousand mines workers had already assembled in the open ground in front of the union office. We were taken to the rear side of the union building where we were told to sit on two chairs. We sat silently, waiting for the story to unfold. My mind and senses were keenly alert. A mike was blaring out speeches recounting the struggles and sacrifices and martyrdom of their comrades. The hidden enemies within their ranks, trying to break their union and destroy their leader were being lambasted. The assembly was swelling fast with thousands of miners in soiled and tattered clothes and mining tools, rushing in, leaving their workspots. They appeared to be in a hurry to reach the union ground, as ordered by Neyogi.

Some of the workers in the know slithered to the back of the union office to have a glimpse of the two 'criminals.' After the end of about half an hour, Chabbilal Sahu, one of Neyogi's close confidants, appeared before us and started shouting abuses and accusations on Sahadev who continued to sit silently. Turning to me in utter loathing, he yelled that it was I who was the cause of the downfall of their President, their own, Sahdaev Sahu. A small crowd had begun gathering around us when Neyogi appeared. Seething with fury, he began yelling in a shrill voice. In the mean, he pushed me violently out of the chair and snatched it away. This he did with Sahu also. He demanded to know who had offered chairs to the 'bloody betrayers.' We were ordered to be put up before the assembled crowd in front of the union office.

"Let the people have a good look at the hated enemy agents," he shouted.

Thereafter, we were jostled and pushed and made to stand in the middle of the crowd that hooted and howled like wild animals. We stood in the middle of the jeering crowd, a little away from the mike. All around me I saw eyes spewing fire and hatred. While Neyogi sat in the first row, facing us, the crowd sat in a ring around us. My 'trecherous deeds' in collaboration with the BSP management, big contractors and the government officials, to destroy Neyogi and the union were being fed to the crowd, one by one by Neyogi's henchmen. I was accused of trading the rightful claims of the workers of Bhilai and Rajnandgoan for personal monetary gains and to make my wife an officer in the Bhilai Steel Plant. Added to this, they shouted that while they had been starving, I had been gobbling chicken and drinking Scotch whisky. They gloated that at the time of our capture in Adv. Tiwari's house, we had been found gulping down foreign liquor and pulling at enormous legs of murgas. They portrayed Sahadev Sahu as an idiot who had been swayed to the wrong path by me. They recited the list of names of other leaders of the union who had also been misled by me since the very beginning. Though their leader Neyogi ji, had pardoned me again and again, I had refused to stop my nefarious game.

Slowly, it dawned on me that a 'Kangaroo Court' was in progress. It would be the same as the 'Jan Adalat' of the Naxalites, where 'enemies of the people' were put on public trial before their brutal killings. It was because of this realisation that I accepted my inevitable fate of dyeing ingloriously, in the middle of a mad crowd, under the deceptive spell of their leader. I stoically, resigned myself to my fate, but not before getting an insight into the extreme contradiction between the truth and public perceptions.

I ruminated on how I had exchanged a comfortable life, a promising career and the happiness of my family to serve the cause of these very unfortunate souls. I had spent over fifteen years fighting for them and suffering incarceration repeatedly. I had been labeled a Naxalite for my fearless fight against their 'enemies.' I had even staked my life for their cause and now they were condemning me as their enemy no.1 and a man without character. I envisaged the history of the communist revolutions all over the world, through closed eyes, in my mind, as if rolling on a television screen.

Slowly my mind started drifting away from the maddening noise of the wild ocean of 'toiling masses.' I withdrew within myself and felt quiet alone and at peace. I had had such experiences earlier also. On a few occasions, prior to this, when I had been confronted with impossible situations, I had withdrawn my mind within and felt peace and tranquilty. At one point of time, along the way, while contemplating on human life and it's follies, including my own, I might have inadvertently brought a smirk on my face. I was shocked back to reality with Neyogi taking a long jump to reach me and screaming through the mike, "Look, how shameless he is. He is smirking at me. Oughtn't his eyes to be gauged out?"

Electrified by his scream, a dozen miners instantly stood up, pointing their lathis at my open eyes. Just at that moment, a thought flashed through my mind. Of what use were my eyes anyway in the face of certain and imminent death! Neyogi stopped the lathis in midway and returned to his place to glare at me. I also stared back at him, long, and my eyes told him that I could see through him and that he was only a cheat and a despicable coward. He tried to avoid my stare by looking away. But he lost his balance once again. He was desperate to see me break down. So, he stood up and ordered for two garlands made of shoes and sandals. They reached him in no time, as if just waiting for his beck and call. Our necks were forthwith adorned by the garlands. I received mine with bent head. A proper reward indeed for my belief and life mission!

We stood, for many long hours, with shoe-garlands around our necks and were forced to listen to the unending hate speeches. When the speakers tired, someone pushed the mike towards me and asked me to speak, if I had anything to say. Before I could think, Neyogi pounced on the mike and snatched it way. He shouted that enemy agents and betrayers were not to be allowed to speak. Even though I had known since a long time that Neyogi was basically a coward, I was taken aback by the sight of him shivering with fright, regardless of the fact that he was surrounded by over ten thousand of his own blind supporters.

It had been over five long hours that, weighed down with the garland of shoes around our necks, we were kept standing in the open under the piercing rays of the winter sun. Our ears were enundated with varied accusations and abuses. In reality, I had expected Sahadev to break down and beg pardon as many of the speakers had exhorted him to do. Each had depicted me as the real culprit, beyond redemption. Finally, in the twilight, just before the sun set, a small bunch of men pounced before us and started hitting us in our faces and heads. The violent attack almost blinded me and I started reeling. Even as I fell, in my semi-conscious state, my mind wondered whether this was the inglorious reward to be meted out to me for all the sacrifices that I had made for these same men and women. The punching and kicking continued unabated, till I lost consciousness. Taking me for dead, they might have stopped.

I started coming to when I felt buckets of cold water being poured over my body. I lay in a dirty pool within a closed room. Hours seemed to have passed before consciousness started returning to me. The swelling in my face and tightly shut eyes kept me from opening my eyes. However, I was slowly able to discern a little bit of light that filtered in through a small aperture between my eyelids. I tried to change the angle of my head to see if Sahadev also was there. I was not able to see him. Though I could not see, I could feel the presence of people around me.

Then someone was probing with gentle fingers to force open my eyelids. The person parted my eyes and shone a torch light into them. I saw the face and heard his voice and instantly recognised Dr. Vinayak Sen. He ordered Neyogi to be called as both of us had regained consciousness. In a few minutes, Neyogi rushed in and sat on a chair in front of us. We were roughly pulled up and positioned against the wall in order to face Neyogi. Now I could see Sahadev, pulled up by my side. Compared to mine, the swelling in his face and bloodstains on his dress were in a lesser degree. Then I heard Dr. Sen telling Neyogi that he could start his talk with us because we had regained our mental faculties.

Neyogi began his tirade with Sahadev. He told him that the people had already pronounced their verdict against us and it was for him to execute it. We were to be cut into pieces, filled in sacks and thrown as feed to wild animals in the forest. But, as he had been one amongst them, he was willing to give Sahadev a last chance to repent, confess his guilt and beg pardon. Sahadev should confess before the people that he had been misled by Kurian to go against the union and Neyogi. About Kurian, there was neither redemption nor a way to escape punishment. Kurian's story would be finished off in the jungles of Dalli-Rajhara.

In the face of Neyogi's horrendous threat, I was sure that it would be too much for a semi-literate man like Sahadev Sahu, to brave it out. Once again I was expecting him to fall at Neyogi's feet to beg pardon. When it did not happen, I felt great peace and happiness watching the spirit of courage and self dignity embracing my Chhattisgarhi comrade, Sahadev Sahu. The lack of response from Sahadev to his repeated offers of redemption and pardon exasperated Neyogi so much that he turned towards me to tell me that even death was too little a punishment for me.

Just at that moment, I heard the telephone ring in an adjacent room. Someone spoke into the phone and began addressing the caller, "Sir, sir." Moments later, he stormed into the room to ask Neyogi to attend the call urgently. Neyogi rushed out and I heard him also repeating "Sir, sir, sir ………."

Neyogi, ran in – a totally different person. He appeared excited and agitated. He ranted and shouted "Where is the jeep?" "Where is the bloody driver?" "Call the driver, start the jeep, quick, quick" he went on shouting and running around, flaying his arms over his head, like a scared cock. His henchmen rushed helter-skelter to carry out his orders. Within minutes, a jeep appeared at the back side of the office.

"Hurry up, lift both of them and put them in the jeep."

His orders were obeyed with alacrity. We were bodily lifted by half a dozen men and carried to the jeep. The driver was told to dump us in front of the Gurudwara, on the Main Road.

One of Neyogi's overzealous goons, infuriated at the sight of his 'class enemies,' aimed at my head and swung his lathi with such force that my skull might have been shattered. But, Providence had other things in mind for me and played a role to guide the baton onto the steel frame of the jeep, instead. The lathi broke in two and the jeep sped through the thronging, infuriated mob.

The cool, refreshing air, sweeping through my blood-soaked body, dripping wet with muddy water, revived my spirits and energised my body to such an extent that I was able to get down from the jeep, after ten minutes, without help.

Sahdev had escaped with minor injuries. The police arrived on the spot to pick us up. After registering a criminal case against Neyogi, Dr. Sen and others for conspiracy, abduction and attempt to murder, they took us to the Government District Hospital, Durg. I remained in the hospital, under police protection, for a week. There I was treated for crippling injuries on my left ear and three lower vertebrae. The Safety Boots that used to protect the workmen, were responsible for leaving an indelible scar on my back as a reminder of the reward I had been honoured with by the 'working class' whom I had loved the most.

Sahadev was allowed to go home after primary treatment.

The news of the "Jan Adalat" being conducted in front of the union office, against its enemies, captured from Rajnandgoan, spread like wild fire in the labour camps of Dalli-Rajhara. Along with hundreds of other curious women from the labour camps, Draupadi Bai, Sahadev Sahu's wife also rushed to the union office compound to have a glimpse. She was horrified to see that it was her own husband who was on trial. She was shaken out of her stupor when she saw us being assaulted. Without losing a second, she ran and ran and ran over three Kms. to the Dalli-Rajhara Police Station to inform about the possibility of her husband getting murdered by the mob led by Neyogi.

The police and administration acted fast.

The 'sir, sir' that Neyogi had poured into the telephone had been addressed to none other than the Superintendant of Police, Durg. A threat of his possible liquidation in a police encounter in the vicinity of his own union office, was conveyed, if the captives were not released within five minutes. It had the effect of shooting Neyogi into maddening fear! The irony of fate was that it had been the police, against whom I had been fighting all through the prolonged period of my 'class struggle,' who had rescued me from certain death, at the hands of my comrades!

At Nagpur, Namita and my school going son, Dipu, had no inkling about the happenings at Dalli-Rajhara. One day, they were taken aback to see a few rifle wielding policemen guarding their residence when they returned home in the evening. Next day, a police officer visited Namita to enquire about any possible threat from anyone to her family.

Three days after the incident, the MD of the Bhilai Steel Plant, Mr. S. Sangameswaran, met Namita at her Nagpur Resident Office. She had no idea why the MD was asking her about her husband's well being. She was clueless as to why he assured her that her husband was quite safe and she need not have any worry on his account. He upbraided the Resident Manager, Mr. Bhaskar Rao, for not providing her a room befitting her status in the office. He also requested Namita to give company to Mrs. Sangameswaran to enjoy the movie, Mr. India, in a local cinema theatre. Namita could not comprehend the reason why all of a sudden, all such honours were being accorded to her by the management.

Till I returned to my family in Nagpur.

Chapter 24

The Inevitable

After my 'spiritual death' at the hands of the toilers of Dalli-Rajhara, I lived like a living ghost for a few years at Nagpur. My soul burned in self condemnation. My mind remained restless with a desire for revenge. Revenge against Neyogi. I hated myself for having acted as a pitiable idiot and wasting not only my own life, but also the lives of my near and dear ones. I had foolishly run headlong into an idiotic mission of setting right the world. Out of disappointment and frustration, I had contemplated even suicide. But revenge got the upper hand and I made a vow to first expose and destroy Neyogi. I believed that I, who had created this 'Frankenstein,' also had the power to destroy him. I considered him to be a great potential threat to the people, particularly the illiterate and the ignorant toiling masses.

It was at Namita's prompting that I thought of studying journalism in the Nagpur University College. She said that I was good for no other job and no one would dare employ me. It would be better than wasting the rest of my life in simply brooding. It was later, when I was working as a journalist in Bhilai, that Neyogi made his attempt to foray into Bhilai. I was trying to forget him and had decided to do so, as long as he was confined to the mines, away from Bhilai. But in no way, could I allow him to capture and misguide the labour- field of Bhilai. I knew his success would spell the doom of the Bhilai Steel Plant - for which I always had deep concern.

With this conviction in mind, I joined hands with Neyogi's so called enemies, like the Managing Director of the BSP, Mr. E. R. C. Sekhar, the S.P. Durg, Mr. Surendra Singh, and some key industrialists of Bhilai. I was determined to bring to naught all his attempts to get a stranglehold over the workforce here.

Stopped he was. And Bhilai proved to be his waterloo.

In spite of causing damage to the labourers as well as the industries, through repeated strikes and violences, Neyogi failed to get a foothold in the industries of Bhilai. His agitations caused more damage to the labourers, especially his blind followers. Many of them lost their jobs, hundreds went to jail and thousands had to face unending criminal cases. The administration, now grown much wiser through their experiences of Dalli-Rajhara and Rajandgoan, desisted from resorting to police firing in spite of serious provocations.

S.P. Mr. Surendra Singh, had come to understand that, giving a free play to the police and their batons, would be good enough to create the fear of God in the minds of the unruly labourers. Neyogi's strategy of creating a serious law and order situation, by provoking a major ploice firing, to create national and international pressure in his favour, had miseralbly failed at Bhilai. He became a living example of the futility of misusing working class agitations to promote class war. Neyogi would have been condemned to live the rest of his life as a pathetic example of the end of 'militant trade unionism.' But it was not destined to be so.

Some frustrated industrialists of Bhilai, with the active support of some of Neyogi's trusted 'revolutionary intellectuals,' hatched a conspiracy to eliminate him. Industrilaists needed to remove a perennial threat to their industries and the 'revolutionaries' needed another martyr to rebuild their lost ground.

Neyogi was shot dead in the early morning of 28th September 1991.

I felt cheated by the way he had been 'martyred.' How could such a selfish, ambitious, cruel and insensitive man, who had toyed with the lives of thousands of toiling and innocent people, to fulfill his own lust for power, be called a legend or martyr? I felt duty bound to bring out before the public, the truth that I knew.

Through my close association with Neyogi, I came to understand how communist leaders, after capturing power, turn out to be despots, dictators or arbitrators of the people's lives under their rule; like Stalin, Pol-Pot and Kim-il-Sung.

Epilogue

After having lost faith in God at the young age of 16, I used to feel very lonely and small. There was a void in my heart. I wanted to be different from all others. I could not accept the fact that life was meant only for just toiling, eating and drinking, getting married, producing children and dieing, without leaving any trace. In the absence of faith, life itself appeared to be an absurdity. I needed something more purposeful to live and die for. I yearned for knowledge and wisdom. My frantic search for an alternate to God, brought me to the path of Communism. I found another God in Karl Marx. He appeared more relevent and meaningful. I earnestly and truly believed that Marxism-Leninism-Maoism was the only path to equality, justice and peace. I believed that the pursuit of the Communist ideology would lead to the liberation of mankind from all kinds of enslavements and I spent my whole life in that pursuit.

Fifteen years of honest, fearless and relentless fight for the cause of the "exploited classes," my intimate interaction with them that allowed me to observe their lives and thoughts keenly, have forced me to rethink about the basic tenets of the very ideology I had been following.

Ultimately, I realised that ideas about classes, exploitation, class struggle, revolution, equality and justice were all delusions, created by the human minds and did not exist in reality, even as the ideas about caste, religion, God and national identities. All are delusions created by man and hence the root cause of hatred, conflict and bloodshed. Divisions in the world on the basis of such delusions, benefit only those with vested interests, while the common man only suffers. The name and fame of a person like Karl Marx, a Pope or a Godman do not necessarily make their ideas unquestionable.

Life has taught me that the real contradiction in human life is the contradiction between the individual and the universe. One has to manage one's contradictions with spouse, parents, family, community, religion and the society at large, through one's own mind and heart. No one else can resolve them for one. It is the management and resolution of such individual contradictions that create heaven or hell for one and all.

A crowd of any nature is susceptible to manipulation because a crowd has no brain. Cunningly, the individual creator of the crowd manipulates it to serve his purpose. Crowds can never contribute anything positive to humanity. It is the individual, who, through his solitary and lifelong toil, achieves anything worth achieving.

My past has transformed me from an advocate of sacrificing an individual's freedom for the collective, to an advocate of upholding individual freedom, at any cost. In my youth I used to love the Soviet Union and hate America. Soviet Union has disappeared and America continues to flourish as a symbol of the human spirit.

By the end of my public life, I thought that I had wasted my life over a futile idea. Now I know that it has not been so, because it could transform me from a hard-core Marxist to a hard-core anti-Marxist. It taught me to seek knowledge and wisdom from Nature, rather than only from books. And my life remains a living proof of the fallacy of Communism in all its shades.

In hind sight, I feel sorry for the millons of youths who have unknowingly thrown away their precious lives in pursuit of utopian ideologies that have helped only crooks to capture power to lord over the people and perpetuate their own reign of exploitation and oppression.

My close association with Nature, since the last ten years, has amply paved the way to my transformation. I have learned to separate reality from delusion. I needed a spiritual Guru and I got one in Swamy Bhumandji. He has helped me to grasp the essence of the Bhagavat Geeta, the fountainhead of human wisdom. It has helped me to search for God and seek Him out in my own heart. It has widened my perspective, enabling me to embrace the whole universe and to feel one with it.

The End

www.ingramcontent.com/pod-product-compliance
Lightning Source LLC
Chambersburg PA
CBHW050726180626
46814CB00002B/623